THE ROSE AND THE WHIP

The Rose and the Whip is a work of historical fiction. The author has endeavored to be as accurate as possible with regard to the times in which the events of this novel are set. Still, this is a novel, and all references to persons, places, and events are fictitious or are used fictitiously.

Cover concept and design by Jonathan Grisham for Grisham Designs

Published by WordCrafts Press
Cody, Wyoming 82414
www.wordcrafts.net

The Rose and the Whip

a novel

JAE HODGES

WordCrafts Press

"If the whole of history is in one man, it is all to be explained from individual experience. There is a relation between the hours of our life and the centuries of time. . . . Each new fact in his private experience flashes a light on what great bodies of men have done, and the crises of his life refer to national crises . . . Every revolution was first a thought in one man's mind, and when the same thought occurs to another man, it is the key to that era. Every reform was once a private opinion, and when it shall be a private opinion again, it will solve the problem of the age."

Ralph Waldo Emerson, *History*

". . . before I proceed, I shall first set down some prophecies and warnings . . . to show how they have been fulfilled, which are fore spoken of by the mouth of all the prophets."

George Bishop,
New England Judged by the Spirit of the Lord, In Two Parts, 1667

"There is no vision unto you of peace and prosperity in your way, but you shall fall with no small weight of dishonour and affliction which shall be your portion. His people shall have peace, when you shall have trouble; His people shall have joy, when you shall have mourning; He shall appear to their joy, but you shall be ashamed. For your portion shall not be like unto theirs, but the wrath of the Lamb shall torment you, even the long-suffering of God, which hath been great towards you, shall be turned into a devouring fire and into fury to consume you; this shall doubtless come to pass, for the Lord hath said it, in the dreadful day of the Lord, and that day is coming upon you; and the judgments of the Lord, the wicked shall not escape."

Edward Burrough
as quoted by George Bishop in *New England Judged*

For my Husband, Ancel, who stands with me, believes in me, and makes me laugh.

And for my children and grandchildren, so they may know from where and who they came.

And in loving memory of my grandfather, George Stimson, who gave me the gift of genealogy and a love of history.

Foreward

I Once Was Lost

Her name was Lidia, and history has recorded precious little more about her than her one great act of courage. I searched and searched, and found few nuggets from which I could piece together her life. But, she fascinated me.

In terms of lineage, she was the wife of my first cousin, ten times removed. Part of my ancestry only by marriage, and so many generations apart that my mind could not fathom it at all. But, still she fascinated me.

I could sleep at night, quite peacefully, until she came to my dreams. A wisp of light in the dark shadows, a ghost from my distant, so distant past. An outline only. I could distinguish neither her face, the color of her hair, nor the texture of her dress. The sound of her voice a hum, so that I could not tell you if she spoke with ease, or anger. Her words came slowly, night after night, telling me her story, her pain, her confusion, her awakening, her return. When, after months and years had gone by, and she had finished her tale, I could hear her peace.

She came to me searching, she said, for the story of her life. The events to fill in the gaps between those that history has recorded, and an understanding of why. It is these words that I have tried to capture. To write for future histories, future cousins though more and more removed.

The summe of all that I know of myself I now hold in my humble hand. Of this, all is clear to me. History will uphold the events recorded. It is the gaps, the memories betwixt the events I seeke. It is Justice I crave.

I feel at once lost in the enormity of my task. For how do I find what has been given over to time. How do I construct an entire life from a few crumbs. Yet I reason that if ye shall seeke to know, ye shall finde thy way.

For now, thee, deare cousin, know what I know. I am Lidia Perkins. There is no record of my birth, though thee can expect it occurred in the new world. And so, too, there is no absolute knowledge of my parentage, only speculation and wonder that who I was later to become was, or perhaps was not, so far removed from where I had started.

For our purposes, thee shall accept that I was the eldest child of Isaacke, son of Isaache of Hillmorton, in Warwickshire in the old country, and Susanna. Some have claimed that Susanna was a Wise, sometimes a Wyeth, and the daughter of Humphrey and Susanna Tidd Wise. But she was not.

I was wed to my goode Husband Eliakim Wardell on the seventeenth day of October, in the Yeare of our Lord, 1659, in Hampton now in the county of Rockingham, in the state of New Hampshire.

We were quiet people, as history records nothing of us until we had begun to absent ourselves from the Puritan meetings as the leaves began to change their colors and fall from their perches in 1661. The records of baptisms, and the failure to find any record of baptisms, gives us clue as to our standing in the community. We surely fell into the routines of daily life, the common rituals by which good people thrived then . . . which is to say we worked and lived and worshipped amongst the flocks of citizens that history has seen fit to recall. We were content to be lost within their shadows, neither rising above nor falling from the path set for us. We were pulled along, the work plough behind the oxen in the field.

Eliakim and I lived amongst our neighbors, and our Friends, scattered as they were about the countryside. A change came upon us, when I cannot say except that we began to appear again and again within the annals of our community. I know that we were adjudged as poor Puritans and that we both bore the scars of the punishments we received at the hands of our own community, all well documented.

I gave birth to two lovely boys before our troubles reached their fever pitch, and a precious daughter to soothe the sting of my scars.

I know that we were forced from our home, our livelihood stripped so publickly from us. But once we were able to reclaim ourselves and mark our own path, I gave birth to seven more beloved children—six of them daughters who would know the pain and suffering of their mother and be the stronger for it. We found peace in the distant towne of Shrewsbury in New Jersey. And there we lived out the remainder of our time on earth in peace and joy, with Friends if not family all about us. I know we were Quaker.

The events of these truths are proved in court records and other provincial and royal documents, in the immediate testimony collected and presented to King Charles II and oft repeated by others, and even in works of poetry. These I repeat for thee as evidence of my veracity. Other details I will recount for thee, though I can offer nothing to corroborate nor anyone to bear witness to these events as I will related them. Some of the words may be difficult for thee to hear as they are heaved from the thoughts and memories I struggled to protect, and distract me, from the whip. I believed then, as I do to this day, these thoughts and memories would be my very salvation. Thee and I together will search out the person I was and who I would become.

My story must begin with the moment for which history has taken my name upon her lips, and has whispered it ever since. This is not the moment of my rebirth, for that came upon my convincement and turning toward the Light, but it was my moment of testimony.

Perhaps thee and I together can find my place, and the world shall no longer be dissuaded by the few facts that have come to represent my life.

Sentencing

The Fifth Day of May, in 1663...

The court records state:

Lidia Wardell was ordered to be severely whipped and to pay costs to the marshal of Hampton upon her presentment for going naked into Newbury meeting house.

And then, as if it were an after-thought,

She was the wife of Eliakim Wardell.

I stood before the men of the court, but it was as if I was not there, as if I did not know these men. I heard their words, but I could not listen because it was as if they came from a voice or a language I could no longer understand.

I turned my head toward the scratch of a quill against paper, and I watched through downcast eyes as the man in the corner dipped it again in the pot of ink. He was Samuel Dalton. A small and quiet man who sat hunched in a corner, away from the dim light of the window, with a candlestick and paper. The ink pot was well-used and well-stained as he had held the post of town clerk for some years. His responsibilities were great for he was to record the court's words on the unbound sheaths of paper which made up the Wastebook in front of him; he would later work, also by candlelight, to transcribe the notes in a neater hand to a large book bound in leather with blank pages, distinguished for its sole purpose to the court.

History captured the words of the sentence for the charges against me. The room was stifling with the closeness of men. They were agitated at the long list of causes held over from the last court. I was not the only woman being presented on that day.

The Quarterly General Court met for the Easter session, by adjournment, at the village of Ipswich in the Massachusetts Bay Colony. It was a Tuesday. The courts met most often on Tuesdays. When last the county, or Inferior Court, met three weeks before at Salisbury, in the southern jurisdiction of the county of Essex—when last we were fined for our conspicuous absence from the Sabbath meeting—the foreman of the Grand Jury, Anthony Stanyon, postponed the proceedings owing to the number of causes still remaining to be heard as the sun fell below the horizon.

Goodman Joseph Baker kept the White Horse Tavern in his house on the High road. He closed it to paying customers every sixth month when the court met at Ipswich. It was the only building large enough to accommodate the jury men, the clerk who sat in a corner recording the day's business, the defendants who were compelled to appear, and as many louts who could fit themselves within the four walls. It would have been irreverent to hold such a forum in the town meeting house.

The building remains, or at least the shell of it though it is now a house, a home with a family who is so far removed from those times they could only know the purpose the structure once held. The only sign of its long history and import to the town of Ipswich is a plaque lately placed upon its wall beside the front entrance door.

On any other day, a tavern would be loud and raucous, where men and boys of a proper age would gather. Their bellies filled with food and drink; their eyes filled, perhaps, with what they had since lost or given up at home, or with a yearning as yet not understood. I heard the long dead voice of Priest Cobbet singing loud to ward off the evils laying behind the door of the tavern as he passed by in the late of night.

The single room was large, rectangular, and the air hung thick and heavy. The crowd of men gathered within the walls added a bitter and harsh stench, while the events of the day were anything but sweet. There were few windows, and the glass was crude, leaving the outside view wavy and blurred. The new spring light could but try and make its way in to brighten the sparse furnishings. The flicker of candles danced across the walls, playing tricks on my eyes. The usual tables, long and stained after years and gallons of ale spilt were pushed to the walls except for the single table in the back of the room, opposite of the door. Were it winter, and the chill of the outside air sneaking in by the cracks of the wooden walls and ill-fitting doors and windows, the only warmth from the single fireplace would be blocked by the men of the court sitting with their backs closest to the source. There was no need for a fire. Rough-worn benches set in rows were occupied by the men of the jury.

Stanyon stood, the legs of his chair scraping against the worn wood-plank floor, stirring up dust about his booted feet. The list of causes still to be heard contained thirty-two presentments, licenses, fines and other questions of cost. His sure voice broke the silence in the hall as he called the court to order.

Stanyon looked about, first acknowledging those men appointed to sit on the Jury of Trials. Had all of the men appointed at the county court been called to attend this session, there would not have been enough room for those called to give testimony, nor for those who pressed in to hear such testimony or presentments they might find particularly steamy. As it was, the men sitting on the court benches that morning were of Ipswich and the surrounding area only. The representatives from Hampton, to the north, the men who knew Lidia Wardell, who watched me grow to a bellicose young woman, would not likely travel the nine and thirty miles, not likely give up a day and perhaps a night away from their homes, their wives, their own farms, to defend the likes of me.

I reminded myself this scene was nothing more than God's challenge for the day. After all these months, I was no longer meek to the reckonings of these or any men. These were the men who took everything from Eliakim and me. They took our property, our livelihood, our dignity—and at the end of it all they would take our family as well. And for what, there did not seem to be a good answer. These men had a few acres more land for themselves; they had some corn to see themselves and their own families through another cold winter; our pretty beast now carried another upon her sturdy back; our prized heifer would soon present some other family with her first calf.

But my courage was a voice these men could not ignore. My faith they would not have from me willingly.

There was, at least, one other man from Hampton. The foreman of the Jury of Trials was Abraham Perkins. He was the same Abraham who came with Isaacke to settle Hampton, drawing adjoining house lots on the north-eastern corner edge of the meeting house green, near where the First Baptist Church now stands. The same Abraham who lived in what can be assumed to have been relative peace as kinsman and neighbor for my first ten years. Abraham Perkins was a dutiful man, well respected in the community and many of the outlying areas. History records he was a man much employed in the service of his community, and of good intelligence.

To be sure, there were also men from Newbury, a scant ten miles to travel to Ipswich. Word traveled fast about the countryside, and there were many who would want to hear the words and relive the Sunday morning when I dared to trespass upon their meeting house, as naked as the day I was born. The room was choked with men standing, pushing, kicking up more dust from the floor until the room was consumed and there was no clear air to breathe.

Foreman Stanyon spoke my name, the first cause to be heard.

Few in the room would recall the words of William Bradford, the man who led so many of our fathers and mothers across a vast and frightening ocean from tyranny to freedoms untold in a new land. I thought the words still true.

All great and honorable actions are accompanied with great difficulties, and must be both enterprised and overcome with answerable courages. It was granted ye dangers were great, but not desperate; the difficulties were many, but not invincible.

"Stand, Goodwife Wardell. What say you of the charges against you."

Anthony Stanyon was once described as a monstrous fellow. He had a practiced dispassion. None of the features of his brutish face, or the set of his imposing figure hinted at the thoughts then filling his mind. As I stood there, he and I alone in the room at that moment, I thought this man knew Eliakim and me. He was our neighbor since our marriage. He came to the colony before either Eliakim's or my parents; he was at Exeter and Wells with Eliakim's father, and then at Hampton with mine. He used his power and his arrogance to raise himself up among the community. He did not suffer fools lightly, nor Quakers at all, and he surely turned his most vile eye upon me.

He peered at me for a long while, taking the measure of me in. A cap covered my head, my long hair pulled sharply back from my face and plaited tight to my head, not so much as a wisp peeking out from the edge. My temple strained against the pulling of my braid as much as the certainty of the punishment I could expect would soon befall me. My womanhood was visible only by the modest round of my breasts, bound tight beneath the hot wool and plainly colored skirts hiding my strong legs. But I felt he was looking through me, instead, perhaps himself feeling the presence of the other women who came before me; the others who stood before a similarly austere group.

When I failed to respond, Stanyon called the charges against me, and only then did I feel the eagerness in his voice.

The words excited the room. A buzz rose steadily and filled my ears. The dead air moved. Some of these men would consider I was taken up by the devil or some such ailment, for why else should I show myself so in the presence of a congregation, in the presence of God. How many of them were aquiver at the thought of a woman who was not their wife, coming naked before them? Did the insides of their thighs quake with anticipation? Did they imagine their wives faces upon my body? Or, did they simply drivel with the lust for something they could not touch? How many averted their eyes, feeling dishonored and ashamed? Would they feel disappointment if I did not speak, did not make a further spectacle of myself? My eyes burned with the sting of fear and loathing hanging about me. Through the smoke, I looked to Abraham Perkins who sat silent, his eyes settled directly in front of him neither looking at me nor looking away. I could not blame him if, on that day, I was no one to him but a disreputable vagabond woman.

I knew what were his convictions, and what was the depth of his faith, as I stood there. But, I also hoped there was love in his heart. He took his oath, as my father, his brother, did many years before—a test to which Eliakim could not submit. Abraham and his family would have been at peril if they remained close, or perhaps even spoke to me. My father long ago moved from the house next to his, perhaps moving from his shadow in the bargain and thus distancing all of us from him. Seated there, Abraham could claim nothing but allegiance to his oath, to his community, and to his God.

In those few moments when none dared breathe, Stanyon allowed the words to hover for the effect of enticing the jury men upon the benches. I looked from Stanyon to the other men, one to another sitting there in various postures. I searched their blank faces and collected the emotions screaming out from black eyes, the twitch of their mouths, the brush of loosed hair away from their sweated brow, the thunderous tapping of fingers against the wooden table. What did they think of me standing there? Would they see their own wives in me, themselves in my Eliakim? Were we so different?

Out of the interminable silence, my brain conjured a scuffling of boots, men pushing and grumbling. The sound of coughing, the dust or merely a subtle way to attract the foreman's attention. Every muscle in my body tensed. Without hearing his voice, without seeing the hard lines of his face, the formidable thrust of his body, I knew. My head filled with the mew of a frightened lamb.

Speak, woman, or your silence should be seen as a kindred serpent round your neck. Only I hear his hiss. His words would weigh heavy on my heart, his desired prize.

I made no pact with the serpent, and the thought of it brought shivers to my spine. But the shameless deeds of selfish men wrought on my husband, my family, the fear blossoming in his wake weighed heavier yet upon my shoulders.

From my corner, my hiding place, the safety of the womb surrounding me, the women who were my sisters in blood and tribulation, pushed the shadowy figure aside, strode past him with confidence and guilelessness. Rebecka led the way. She was my strength, my rock. Mistress Wilson walked as Eve in the Garden in silence. The three women followed, their waistcoats torn and shredded hanging limp from their shoulders, and their feet bare and bloodied. Mistresses Dyer and Hutchinson stood silent, the stench of their deaths hovering about them.

Stanyon was awaiting an answer. To speak for myself would be as if to lash the skin of my own back. Or worse.

The scratch of the quill drew my attention back to Samuel Dalton as he dipped the tip of the quill again into the pot of ink there on the tiny table. He listened. Surely he made no judgement, for his only job was to write the words others spoke, document the events as they transpired. Keep the record.

When no sound came from my lips, Stanyon spoke again. "As the law will have it, Lidia Wardell is judged for disrupting the congregation at Newbury. The court sentences her to take the whip upon her bare back with all due haste."

The message was clear. The court would no longer be patient with me, or my husband. What protection we thus far enjoyed from our families and friends was in jeopardy. We could expect to hereafter be treated according to the law. And my family would pay the costs along with us.

The Foreman turned to his peers beside him. They pounded upon the table in front of them in unison, affirming their collective decision. Whether the decision was unanimous or there was any dissent, I could never know.

Did not Ezra proclaim through fast we might humble ourselves to God and seek from him a direction, a right way for us, and our children? Alone there, I made peace with my God and, at least in my physical presence, I vowed I would travail not only to please Him in today's difficulty, but to take a fast of my own. A fast from the sustenance of fear, from the food of the boar, from the drink of the cracked cup. I reminded myself, He brought me there and by His side I would stand.

Stanyon turned his gaze to the constable of Hampton, William Fifield, whose duty it was to accompany me for the presentment, read any statement I might have made and of late provided to the magistrate, and execute what sentence the court considered appropriate to the crime.

"The court orders Mistress Wardell to pay costs in the amount of ten shilling six pence, and fees of two shilling six pence, in coin or trade at your choosing."

I turned to the good Constable standing to my left in the shadows and watched as he nodded his assent, his face impassive, and then closed his eyes. I needed no vision to know he thought of me standing before him, a noggin of milk in my hand, the silence of three vagabond women at his back. Our fate was foretold.

Fifield was responsible for carrying out the punishment, and then he would need to request payment for the privilege. I do not believe, when he arrived as the sun rose to accompany me to this hearing, he realized this was how the day would end.

2

Punishment

Recovering himself, Constable Fifield turned from Foreman Stanyon to me, his eyes pleading. He was not more than eight and forty years in age, but the past months had turned his hair to grey and allowed a sadness to fall on his face. I caught the slightest of a twitch in his hand as he fiddled with his hat. He took a step, then hesitated, an invitation to walk out unassisted, through the gauntlet of men who would part in unison with each of my steps. None dared to be close enough to risk touching me, as if the stain of my crime could attach itself to them. I could not say whether any of these men were also present at the Newbury meeting house, and would remember the feel of my skin. Some looked at me, anticipated my movement as I passed so they could follow outside to witness the punishment; some turned away, their attention back on Stanyon as he called out the next cause.

At the door I stopped and looked out over the heads of the gathering crowd, their eyes fixed on me as if I were a plump goose hanging from the rafters. My skin prickled at the thought of feathers being plucked one by one to expose my flesh, their mouths watering in anticipation of tasty fat dripping onto their chins.

The Constable stopped just behind me. I could feel his heaving breath through the kerchief covering my neck. If I lingered there, he would be forced to lay his hand upon me, to push me out of the door and down the few steps. I determined I would not add further to his discomfort. Whatever his position, whatever his faith, whatever his instruction, this man was not my enemy.

I found Eliakim standing before the post, blocking it from my view. His hat shielded his eyes, but I knew they held me and nothing more. He was a tall man, broad of chest but slim of hip. His face could be brooding, but there were those who knew the smile he entrusted to only a few. I knew the tenderness of his touch, the warmth of his embrace—and the anguish in his heart. His presence there comforted me, buoyed my strength, filled me with love, gave me the courage to take the next step.

Swift judgment shall end with swift punishment as God would wish it. Or so our elders would have us believe.

Out there, the crowd did not move away from me; they did not clear a path to the post. Instead, they poured over me, threatened me with their closeness. With so little to amuse and entertain the village dwellers, an unnatural curiosity or interference in the daily lives of people might take hold. Many were willing to trade their work for the chance to see a woman whipped. Those who could not fit in the close confines of the tavern, or those who were interested only in the punishment itself, were congregating about the building. They were anxious, and so I became anxious.

I stumbled and took the three warped and cracking steps too quickly, stopped only by the delicate bones of my hands and knees hitting the hard ground. Fifield came around and reached out his hand. I, in turn, raised my hand to him, a signal I could manage myself. He dropped his arm and his head, a return gesture of respect—or it is how I took it—and stepped back.

My field of vision filled with the shuffling of feet, and for a moment I became confused. I was naked and alone on the ground. Boots kicking at me. My eyes stung with dust, my throat burned. My stomach heaved. Out of the discordance in my head, a humming of whispers, came a voice. A voice soft and kind, and spoken with great feeling.

Rise, child. Thee are not alone.

I rose and clapped my hands together, watching the dust billow from them. I slapped at my skirt; more dust fell away. I steadied my cap and replaced a wisp of hair fallen away back under the tight band. When I felt I was once again presentable, I raised my head and, this time, I looked at the people in the crowd. Each one turned their eyes away as I came to gaze upon them. Shame. Fear. Embarrassment. Excitement. Some I did not know, others I knew well, and still others I knew no longer.

Eliakim moved away before I reached him, with our brother John near upon him. They were friends and companions since boyhood, inseparable then and inseparable now. John married my sister, Rebecka, just weeks before Eliakim and I married. I thought of her, younger than I by four years, but always the more adventurous one. She would be sitting in a chair in the sun just then, left to watch over my two boys along with her two girls. I pictured her nursing one infant while another slept in a basket by her side; the two older children perhaps running about the yard, chasing the flies. I hoped they would not disrupt my young tomato plants.

A wave of panic. I felt the color rise in my cheeks. But, the rest of me went cold. I could not recall, just then, why I was there, covered in dust and prying eyes. My breasts ached with the fill of milk and no opportunity to expel it. Why was I not at home, tending to my children?

The Constable moved nearby, reclaiming my attention. He stood close should he need to intervene, but far enough away there could be no question about his behavior. He looked to me with wonder, sensing something, but his eyes begged me, *please, do not turn this to a spectacle or comedy of tragic events.*

I responded with a smile. If I could turn back time and choose again, I would choose my actions the same. Warmth returned to my hands and face. My mind cleared, committed. I encouraged my body to follow. He nodded, and we walked on.

The post stood just paces from the building—*whereunto she was tied, stripped from the waist upward, with her naked breasts to the splinters—*

What is it, I wondered, men think of when they entered the tavern, tired and in need of drink after a long day of work in the fields, seeing the whipping post there? Was it meant as a reminder of what they could expect if they allowed the drink to lead them to unruly behavior? In Ipswich, the stocks and pillory were near the meeting house on the green, as they were in most towns. But the tavern sat upon a hill above the green, set an appropriate distance away.

No post remains on the spot today to attest to the atrocities which took place there; no sign to give passersby any cause to stop and imagine the scene.

Two years before, the governor desired, so he would claim, by all means available he would show as much leniency as he may while ensuring safety to the community from the intrusion of those people who would be called Quakers. How could the governor, or the courts, or any man or woman say for sure who were Quakers as they passed by their neighbors in the course of their daily routines? If a man did not remove his hat, was he a Quaker? If a woman dressed in plain muslin, was she a Quaker? If two families gathered together in one man's home after the sun set, were they Quakers?

Under the old laws, for his first offense of being judged a Quaker, a man could expect to have one of his ears cut off, for he shall not abide by the talk of the Quaker nor shall he think he might hear the word of the Lord himself. He would then be held at the house of correction until he could be expelled from the jurisdiction at his own charge. If he should come again, he should have his other ear cut off because he dared to continue to listen to the blasphemies of the heretics, and he would again be sent out.

A woman was a different matter. Her place was by her father, or her husband. His thoughts were her thoughts; his actions were her commands. So, if a woman should be found to follow a Quaker, she should be severely whipped lest she believe she is able to think or do as she pleases, and then she too would be held in the house of correction to await her expulsion. A second offense would ensure the punishment was repeated upon her bare back.

For a third offense, whether the Quaker be a man or a woman, they should suffer a hot iron to bore a hole through their tongue as a reminder, no one shall speak against the colony or the Church. If any man or woman should persist in returning to the colony, they would be ordered hanged by the neck until they would be dead.

The memory of Mary Dyer was still fresh in the minds of the colonists.

The General Court repealed those old laws, by order of King Charles II, and replaced them with a law not so revolting to the people of the colony—or, so obnoxious to the Home Government. Under the new law any person, man or woman, who was judged to manifest him or herself as a Quaker would be stripped naked only from the middle up, then tied to a cart's tail and whipped through the town. The constable would convey such vagabond Quaker to the next town to be whipped there, and so on from constable to constable, from town to town until they reached the outward boundaries of the court's jurisdiction. A person was thus given three such chances before he or she was branded upon their left shoulder with the letter R, and once again whipped out of the colony. Any said Quaker who proved to be an incorrigible rogue was found to be an enemy of the colony, and the old laws would take effect, allowing the court to sentence death by hanging.

I ask again, if a man did not remove his hat, or a woman dressed in plain muslin, or if families gathered together in the comforts of a man's home away from the curious eyes and ears of his neighbor, were they readily perceived by the sight of the fearful or were they so easily recognized as Quakers?

But, these men did not judge me a Quaker. Public whipping was a punishment of convenience for a variety of offenses for it sent a clear message to both the transgressor and anyone nearby who might be harboring thoughts of disobedience. Even so, public whipping was not commonplace.

The post was a simple structure, nothing more than a tall tree trunk shorn of its branches and bark, rough with weather and splintered from years of use, long dead but not rotted. A chestnut. The timbers Eliakim used to build our house, our furniture. I used the fruit of the nut to flavor my stews or bake bread when wheat was scarce. Now I learned a new purpose for the abundant hardwood.

I stopped walking less than an arm's length from the post, close enough to see where the sections of the wood were rubbed to a dull sheen by rough hemp ropes. Constable Fifield was close behind me. I felt the beating of my heart and tried to relax my breathing, pay heed to my strength.

He took my arm, neither tight nor rough, and turned me to him. If we were alone, another time or another place, I would have pitied him, for I could see he was pale and sickened by this venture. He was a long-standing member of our town. He was named to the post of constable for Hampton only seven months before, but his spirit was tried, and I could see he trembled at being tried such again. This man would live out his days in Hampton, but would not again hold such a position in the town.

Even were I offered the opportunity to bare myself and save the ruin of my clothing, I would still have chosen to stand without movement. My thoughts turned from the discomfort of the man standing before me to an obstinacy not like my usual character. I remained steadfast there. I prayed, God, give this man the strength to carry out the will of the men inside, for they are protected from the distastefulness of this activity, and he is here alone before me.

He let loose my arm and reached his hand to my throat, taking the loose kerchief and stripping it from my shoulders. His fingers released the bit of cloth, and it floated to the ground just as the dust from my hands and skirt had floated to the ground. The skin covering the bone of my chest was then exposed, and the reality of the situation becoming more clear to us both. The crowd jeered, goading him on. He hesitated but briefly before he reached up again, holding his arm and hand suspended before me, his fingers splayed but trembling.

Here his expression changed. His eyes became fierce and implacable. He grabbed the bodice of my dress, and his claw caught the thin material of my shift just below it. He yanked, but was slowed by the bones sewn in to stiffen the dress and hold my breasts securely and modestly. A second pull, harder this time, to separate the laces and release the worn cloth from my body. The people standing about yelled, fewer this time, but with more pitch.

Still I stood firm and quiet. The front part of the bodice of my dress ripped from its seams, and he held it in his clenched fist. My eyes never left his, even as he dropped the rag to the ground beside him. I felt the last of the protective wool slide down from my collarbone, the sleeves held by a few threads of worn cord keeping it from falling away altogether.

The ribbon holding my shift came loose, and though it remained whole it now hung slack, exposing the cleft between my breasts but held still by my hardened nipples.

The Constable's face flushed with the red fire of rage, and embarrassment, and exhaustion. He put his hand on my bare shoulder, squeezed tight until his thumb pushed deep into the soft space between bones where the purple and black patch would later contrast the red welts. He turned me away from him toward the post, and the jeering was more loud still.

Eliakim was there, sheltered in the sea of faces, arms flailing about, necks craning to see. Our eyes met and I traced the tear falling down upon his cheek. I shook my head with but a slight movement. Do not cry for me. Then he was lost, the good and the evil of the town consuming him as they fought for each step closer to me and my post. Do they crave a look into my eyes for some explanation, or a whiff of fear rising through the pores of my skin? Maybe they clamored for the cold touch of a heretic.

At that moment, I could no more recognize this sad and embittered lot than they could recognize me.

The Constable's hand grabbed and twisted the cloth at my back, then pulled away hard. The force and the angle were only enough to release one of the sleeves. Before the loose cloth could fall from my arm, a second pull, downward this time, pulled me backward enough to require one foot to step back to catch myself from falling. As if in harmony, my sleeves fell from my arms and sliced through dead air to the ground while what remained of my bodice limped to the top of my skirt. With nothing left to hold my shift up, it, too, pooled about my waist.

My full breasts were then unprotected, my back as bare. People pushed and shuffled, packing closer together into an arc to my front and sides for a clearer view of my face when the whip should reach my back. Only then did it really occur to me I had rather large breasts compared to my smallish frame.

Fifield came around, nothing left on his face of the earlier fear or, embarrassment, or pity; all replaced by a pure kind of scorn for me for having put him in this position. His stance became rigid, and he seemed to be confused as if his mind could not decide whether to grab my wrist to tie my hands, or look at me bared before him. I felt the let down brought on by the jostling of a breast too full of milk. Without the mouth of a child to receive it, there was nowhere for the milky white liquid to go except to drip—drip down onto my skirt or onto the ground. I watched as my skirt and the pure dirt became spoiled with the wasted milk.

All eyes were fixed on my leaking breasts. Both men and women. Some were eager for this moment, eager to experience the same shock the good citizens of Newbury experienced those weeks ago. Some must have felt concern for the fate of my children. Some were perhaps merely discomfited to be there, watching. This is what the men of the court wanted when they passed their sentence, this was their judgment on me.

I closed my eyes and felt myself quiver, then shake, first my head then throughout the rest of my body. I drifted from side to side, the blood left my head, and my shoulders began to drop. I felt my body pitch forward, and my mind separated to watch as I plunged to the ground.

The Constable caught me, his hands grasping my arms, though the momentum of my fall allowed my bare skin to connect with his body. The raw intrusion of his bare hand upon my nakedness had the curious effect of releasing me from any modesty. The rush of spring created against my skin, his field-torn fingernails digging into my arms gave me a brief hint of what was to come.

My cap fell from my head—leaves falling from the trees—my plaited hair falling to my shoulders. I heard the gasps of the people all around me and wondered, were they shocked by this good man now holding this naked woman who was not his wife, or to discover my hair glowed a deep red? After all his own trials during this year, I wondered if Constable Fifield would ever be able to hold his head up to the people of the community again. I wondered if these good and pious people would feel justified and vindicated in their belief I was the daughter of the devil, and their actions might prevent me from rising from the fiery depths of hell. It is a rare thing, even now, to come upon a woman with hair of red, and there are no shortages of myths about those of us who have it.

After an awkward moment, he straightened us both. I thought this was really the cost to be paid, his compensation for my submission. From the other side of the post, he reached out to grab my wrists one in each of his large hands, and lifted them ready to be tied.

Was it only just the night before when Eliakim found me sitting on the far edge of our bed, unclothed though I would be vulnerable to the chill in the night air. He was late from his chores, perhaps a thought to making up for the loss of the work on the morrow or, more likely, a feigned delay in the inevitable. The boys were fast asleep by the fire, the embers would keep them warm for some time. But, Eliakim's supper was grown cold.

He spoke—his voice was always low and deep but smooth as fresh churned butter—of the golden red of my hair lingering in the firelight shadows against the wall though my braid was still tied against my head, the last vestige of the woman known to the outside world.

He came to me, released the pins, then ran his fingers through the thick strands, caressing my scalp until my hair fell down upon my bare shoulders. I knew before he moved again he would find the tiniest bit of ear lobe peeking out from the loosened strands, his roughened fingers marveling at its delicate curves. He often told me, in the quiet of a night, it was a shame a woman so beautiful could not show her beauty, and I would smile at my good fortune to have a love like his.

He brushed a tear from my cheek; my way of saying I was not confident in my strength to bear the pain I was inflicting upon him, upon our children and families. I once cried with ease, and he was always patient. But, it was some time since last I cried, and so he was surprised I would now give myself over to the tears. He did not move away from me, only sat beside me and listened to my muted sobs and sad mews.

The morrow would be the most difficult day, for us both. More difficult I thought than the day when all this began. More difficult than all the days before. It was no folly then, and would be no folly now. The decision to take action was mine, and mine alone, but these consequences were ours to bear together. How many times he reminded me however we shall make our life, we would make it together.

When finally I stopped my sobbing, and I looked to him for forgiveness, he asked me, "Why does thou sit here so?" Without waiting for an answer, he moved and pressed his lips against my throat.

"I needed to feel the air against my skin again." I needed to remind myself, and from this I hoped to be strong.

I relented to his fingers against my back, tracing the line of my shoulders and spine. "Thou has a skin of perfect beauty, a landscape I know well," he whispered.

We had lain together for three years, with few nights passed when he did not explore this landscape as he called it. But, on the morrow, the landscape would be marred and changed to something raw and strange. I tried to smile. "Tomorrow will bring thee a new landscape to explore," I said.

"New meadows to desire," was his reply.

I reached out to him, release or invitation I could not quite tell for myself. "We will be fine, together, as fine as we have ever been."

He took me gently, and I could not stop myself from responding, again and again throughout the long night. Whether with his fingertips or his lips, he returned often to the smooth glens and valleys of my back, though he managed to explore every inch of my body with both. I, in turn, used every crevice of my body to bring him pleasure.

When we were both spent, we lay nestled together, our arms and legs wound about each other against our naked skin, until the first blush of daylight. He whispered to me of strength and courage so I might meet my trials without fear and regret. But I found no matter how hard I listened to his words, to the wind outside the window, to my heart, I could not truly be prepared for what was to come.

3

Lidia

I was christened Lidia, so named for the seller of purple and the woman who opened her heart to the words of the Lord. So sayeth Saint Paul, *if you have judged me to be faithful to the Lord, come into my house, and stay...and I will hear the word of God.*

We are taught from early on our family, and our home by extension, is a sanctuary. A place where we may open our hearts and welcome the same in others. A place where we may have no fear nor doubt in ourselves and in our faith.

There is nothing yet found which is definitive in recording my birth or my baptism. And because of this I have lived an existence only in the shadows until my marriage brought the first tangible proof that I was—and who I was.

Because there is no such record, there is no proof of my parentage. History has given me over as the daughter of Isaacke and Susanna Perkins, and I will not dispute this. I will hereafter speak of them as my father and mother, their children my brothers and sisters; my father's brother my uncle.

Isaacke received his christening on the twenty-sixth day of January in the year 1611/12 at St. John the Baptist Church, in the Parish of Hillmorton, in the borough of Rugby, county of Warwick, in old England. In those days, the new year commenced with the Feast of the Annunciation on the twenty-fifth day of March, more popularly called Lady Day as it celebrated the Virgin Mary. It would be well after his death, and the deaths of his children and their children before January first would mark the beginning of the year in the colonies. So it is the years are recorded now as January of the old year, and the new.

He was the youngest son of the youngest son, Isaache, and his second wife, Alice. Although the Perkins family stretched far afield within Warwickshire, the name Isaac could be found only, but found with plenty, within the line in the parish.

The parish itself was of two towns come together. Hull as it stood on the bank and Morton where the church was built, and around which a town grew on a hill rising from the moor which lent its name to the parish. The church still stands, surrounded by the relics of the village.

One modern source might revere a circumstance where few were poor in the village of Hillmorton, and the villagers were able to support their parish as a testament to the Astley family protection from the manor house nearby. Others harbor resentment toward the lady of the manor against whom the peasants of the village rioted in protest of her disregard for their traditions, and thus their agricultural livelihood.

Isaache the elder would well remember the lady's enclosure agreement which nearly destroyed the community in 1606. This agreement cheated the peasants of their commons, their system of crop rotation was disrupted and they were forced to grow wheat on pastureland and pasture their cattle in the hay meadows while their sheep grazed in the beef pastures. If it were not enough, the pathways to the river were enclosed and cut off to them. Without rebellion, the strong farmers, their sturdy wives, and their hopeful children would fall quickly to famine.

The villagers banded together, their shovels and their hoes if not their fists raised, their women afire though they clutched their children close. But rage was not their kindling, violence not their fuel. They chose to abide by the laws of the day, and were rewarded for their faith and belief in natural law. The Chancery convicted Lady Mary Astley a year later. Unfortunately, this did little to appease the villagers and make up for the loss of fifteen houses, and the ravages to goodly husbandry in the area.

Could the elder Isaache have known once upon a time, in the century before him, the Astley and the Perkins families were united—he was descended from the same family who sought to ruin his own, and ensure nothing remained for him in offering to his children.

Whether thanks or blame could be bestowed on the Astley family, neither Isaacke the younger nor his brother, Abraham, as the youngest of a large family, could have seen a distant future except what they might scrape from under the yoke and hoe of their forefathers.

I could leave Isaacke's reasons for seeking freedom and adventure in the colonies to God's providential plan. Or I could wonder whether he might have found himself beguiled by Abraham, his elder by four years. As God tested Abraham, should not Isaacke sacrifice himself as proof of his fidelity and follow his brother to the new world? For if there is nothing to look back upon, then there is only what can be found ahead. And so much the better if under the protection of one whose trust has already been earned.

How like my father and uncle was my relationship with my sister, Rebecka.

There was a cousin, John Perkins, who with his wife and five children sailed in February of 1630/31 on the *Lyon* from Bristol. They are listed in the ship's manifest, which begs the notion of John as a prosperous man able to procure passage for himself and his entire family.

No record remains of the passage of Abraham or Isaacke. If Abraham is remembered as a man of good intelligence, then could not Isaacke have been a man of steady hand? It is said Isaacke's occupation when he arrived in the colonies was as a ship's carpenter. Hillmorton lay on the banks of the River Avon, a navigable lane for both boats and barges, and so it is possible he learned his trade there and turned it to good use in exchange for passage to the colonies, especially if a prosperous cousin would have been willing to speak for him. As a ship's carpenter, he might have signed on to the crew, or served the ship and its passengers in other ways. In either case, an indenture could leave both he and his brother anonymous until they could make names for themselves in the new world.

At Winnicunnet Plantation we find the first records of Abraham and Isaacke Perkins. Though they may have been at Ipswich, where John Perkins settled his family, they were surely at the village of Newbury where the Reverend Stephen Bachiler gathered around him a following of fifteen men and one woman who were moved to leave the comforts there and begin anew in the wilds in the northernmost regions of the colony. Neither Abraham nor Isaacke were with the early number, but both made their way to the plantation, and were counted among those with Bachiler in the blush of the first summer in 1639, lately chartered as the town of Hampton. Both men married by the time they arrived at the plantation, and both welcomed sons within the last months of the year. Isaacke's wife, Susanna gave birth to children in rapid succession with each of twelve children baptized and duly registered in the town of Hampton. If I am to be accepted as the daughter of Isaacke and Susanna, then I must have been born before they arrived at Winnicunnet Plantation.

So I raise the question of my birth. In the Newbury court baptism records there is a transcription of an unnamed child, a daughter, born on the fourteenth day of March in the year 1638 to Lidia Perkins in Newbury. The record names no father.

If the two men, with their wives, passed through the town of Newbury, from Ipswich to Hampton, they would have enjoyed few, if any, privileges afforded to the village's own people. While the Reverend Bachiler owned property there, it does not seem likely he was granted his own church, nor did he have appointment from the court to act on behalf of the new plantation in such matters as baptisms.

Could it be the transcription, in error or in interpretation, listed Lidia as the mother instead of the child? Could it be the manner and fitness of the times should welcome the child but not the parent? Years later, when I was called to appear before my congregation in Hampton, having long been absent, I chose the Newbury meeting house to make my plea. And, so my presence at the Newbury meeting house in the late days of March, in 1663, served as both metaphor for my long absences from the Puritan worship without the priest's sanction and plea for recognition of the suffering of my Quaker brothers and sisters.

As the years passed, Abraham was known to be industrious, well-educated, and of a fine hand. He proved himself a good Puritan, and participated with enterprise in the governing and management of the Hampton community. Isaacke, on the other hand, did not participate overmuch in the growth and development of the village. When called upon to pursue some purpose or sit upon the bench during court proceedings, he obliged as was required by law. But, he did not pursue these endeavors, even though it meant the community would little notice him. I often wondered whether this came as a result of a lingering bitterness from having received no grant of land in the first division or any other recorded, leaving him virtually his elder brother's ward, or a disinterest in or separation from the community. This, unfortunately, is a question with no possible answer. Some have written Isaacke gave over to the Quaker faith in the new world, perhaps owing to his discontent. But, at best, Isaacke tread on the edges of the Puritan faith.

I grew into a quiet and sullen girl, unsure of myself as I am now unsure of who I was, perhaps, in a house divided, brothers drifting towards differing paths, raised by a man who would or could not see beyond his own shadow.

As I stood upon a knoll, some years later, and took a final look upon the upland acres, the last of our hard won property, upon the relics of the Hampton I knew, I thought not of the day nearly two years past or of the town's people who stood by and watched with curious yet unwelcoming eyes as I took the whip against my bare back. I considered then all I am, all I have learned has come from my own heart. I have watched and I have listened; I have thought and I have believed. I have learned my dignity and the skin from my back are fair payment for my freedom and my faith.

That moment would be my ultimate sight of the Hampton as I had known it those first seven and twenty years of my life. As the village grew beyond its boundaries, so Eliakim and I grew beyond ours. How could I not have recognized before then the feeling of being unwelcome, the need to move on to a future unknown?

There I stood, the wind about my face at ease and raised to the morning sun, and my hair loosed and cascading down upon my tainted back glowing in the early light. And there I came to know the man Isaacke as my father, the man I could not recognize as long as I stood with my feet in his footsteps, his hand upon my shoulder.

4

Priest Cotton

...and yet, though it miserably tore and bruised her tender body, to the joy of her husband and friends who were spectators, she was carried through all these inhuman cruelties quiet and cheerful, to the shame and confusion of these unreasonable men, whose names shall rot and their memories perish.

The Constable pulled from his pocket a length of raw leather to bind my hands together. Though the post was stout, my arms could more easily wrap around it than they could about Eliakim's broad and sturdy chest. Did everyone feel a pull to escape punishment, or was this binding meant to ensure I would remain standing for the entire event? Other women had been whipped before, and I wondered, were they all treated to the same assumptions?

But a man cannot know what it is to be a woman. A man is taught to believe a woman is weak—a woman could not possibly bear the pain of a whip or the shame of the scars it leaves. It is a man's responsibility to protect a woman. So when a man finds himself facing the naked back of a woman, his whip in his shaking hand, he must tell himself, *this is no woman*. He must convince himself this is the devil's spawn before him. For how else could he face doing what he would not do to even his horse.

But I know only a woman can look upon punishment and pain as the surest sign of life and rejoice in the joy it precedes.

Before the Constable took my hands to bind them, he looked at me with dispassion though his face was anything but blank. His eyes sought permission to touch me, his raw skin against my raw skin. I imagined he looked in the same way at the three vagabond women when the constable of Dover delivered them to him, tied to the cart, already bloodied, shivering naked in the cold of winter. I wondered, could he look at his wife with these same eyes?

As he busied himself with tying my hands, I examined the short handle of the whip pushed into his belt, the ends of cow hide falling away as the lengths of each thong worn smooth and shining in the morning sun swished about in rhythm to his movements. The cat-o'-nine tails would soon extend his reach, connect his hand to my back, yet without the closeness to feel my skin or even hear as the flesh tore. I pictured a loop on the opposite end and this instrument hanging as innocent from a nail by a door as the winter cloak beside it.

I thought how convenient this would not be the constable's whip, but—and I found grim humor—this should be a community whip. Touched by each constable in succession, branded with their individual marks, their sweat absorbed into the leather. Perhaps the magistrates would desire it set upon their table during each proceeding, a vision to torture the lines of innocent people moving through the court each quarter.

I could see each of the dozen thongs ended with a thick knot. I needed no explanation. This was meant to put a gouge at the site where it hit skin, before the lengths of leather would leave long red welts.

I watched through my mind's eye as each knot hit, leaving an indentation deep enough to immediately fill with blood, before each thong followed and came to rest for a brief moment across the welts from the previous lash. How many thongs to accompany each stripe? Would each account for the number of weeks lost, the number of lecture days missed, the sermons to which we were not subjected? Would each account for the lost wages, the forfeited coin, the seized property now left us in penury?

My face and naked breast were pressed against the rough wood. Splinters were already invading the delicate skin, making their way into the folds, finding the most vulnerable spots. Milk continued to gather at the tip of my nipples, and with no where to go it dried in the warm air leaving a tight film to soon crack and pinch. The post was not quite wide enough for both breasts to rest against it, rather it fit with discomfort between the space separating them, pushing them aside, stretching the skin to the begging wood. Several inches lay between the hard wood and the sturdy bone protecting my very breath and heart.

The good Constable tied my hands loose. Surely he would understand the difference this could make, or perhaps he was never so close to the post himself. To tie my hands thus could ease my discomfort, or it could make the torture more exacting. I thought I would have preferred my hands be bound more tightly, to give my arms and breast little opportunity to shift and scrape. Though my mind might endure the punishment, I could not speak with such confidence for my body.

Still, I was close enough I would need to lean my head back, stretch my neck to turn it. I could look out in but one direction else my nose and lips would be forced into the wood as well. So I lay my cheek against the post and thought instead of the first night I lay it against the soft fur covering Eliakim's chest; the first love I ever felt.

I searched the milling crowd, some moving to be within my sight while others moving away, for a compassionate Friend. I found many surrounding Eliakim and John, protecting them, comforting us all with their presence. We learned all too well not to show ourselves, not to call attention to our presence, not to congregate or show too much affinity beyond the casual concern for one neighbor to another. These were the people whose light shown only in the gloom of night and in the hidden corners of remote houses. And they were everywhere.

A warmth grew within me, and a smile came to my lips.

There was one watcher among the crowd who did not shift or dance or maneuver for a better view. He seemed almost to desire to remain hidden, lost within the field of broad hats. The black eyes of my tormentor bore into me and riveted my attention. The beaming expression on my face froze. Though he did his damage, I would not give him more satisfaction. I did not concern myself with whether anyone else would notice, for it was my only thought he should see the cheer in my eyes.

His face twisted, his brow knit, and his skin paled. He expected something different in my countenance. I saw the tiniest of drops form on his forehead just below the wide brim of his hat. He turned his head away, seeking solace from the crowd, but he remained rooted to the spot with a clear view of what would come next. He often spoke of love in his sermons, and he often gave of his time and energies to the benefit of the community. When he came and knocked upon our door and begged for me to return to the fold of worshipers who followed him in blind faith, he spoke of love for me. Yet there he stood, with no love shining in his eyes, no words of love upon his lips. Instead I wondered, were his eyes closed to my suffering? Did his mouth water at the sight of my pain? Did his loins ache with gratification? Would his wife pay for his love?

Reverend Seaborn Cotton kept a commonplace book, and in it he made notes for his sermons, though none remain, and he recorded family and church records as well. But I find it now curious, in retrospect, to discover he filled this book also with literature, songs, and ballads. If these extracts are any true indication, Cotton's nature feasted upon poetry and prose, much of it romantic and revealing of his fondness for a handsome woman. It is this one example, though, which speaks now the loudest:

Love is a cruel paine
Nay more a torment fell

They who have felt it say
Tis next the paines of hell.

If this be so, then it was torment feeding his lust in equal measure. If love and torment are so closely aligned—and it was my torment he sought just then, I was sure—what perversity would allow him to call this an act of love for a wayward child of God?

Our Reverend Cotton was the son of John Cotton who fled England as a dissenter for want of a place to practice his Puritan beliefs in peace and safety. The younger Cotton was invited to minister to the Hampton community in November, in the year 1657. In those first two years, the good people of Hampton looked upon him as he followed in the footsteps of his father, praised him and esteemed him as a man of thorough scholarship and able preaching; looked to him for not only spiritual guidance but as an example, with his wife and their two children. Who could know then, what darkness I would find in his heart?

I heard behind me the snap of the leather thongs.

A chill came, then turned to cold. A harsh, extreme, cold. Like no winter, or fear, I have ever felt. I could not contain the shiver throughout my body, and I found I could not push it from my mind. An overwhelming need to relieve myself followed. It was the only thing I could think of for some moments, and I feared I would not be able to control it. Perhaps it was only the chill. Perhaps I realized the trap I was then in—there was nowhere for me to go, nothing for me to do now but endure.

My stomach clenched, my buttocks tightened, my thighs closed. My teeth chattered. Only the post kept my head from shaking.

The men of the court could not force my confession within the walls of their justice. They could not provoke my contempt with their words. Out here, they could tie me to a post, strip me of my clothing and wrench my testimony from my body.

5

Eliakim

The Reverend John Cotton, Mistress Anne Hutchinson, and Thomas Wardell with his brother, William, were all amongst the more than two hundred passengers who arrived in Boston harbor on the eighteenth day of September in 1634 aboard the *Griffin*, a square-rigged sailing ship of some three hundred tons of primed wood and iron cannon. They were long tired by weeks at sea, and had since forgotten the impatient days passed in the pitiful village of Deal near the southern point marking the convergence of the North Sea, the English Channel and the River Thames where they waited, anchored safe in the Downs until the gales came from the west to carry them away from the English shore.

Their bodies may have been carried to the colonies by the seas, but it was their common dissent from state interference in their spiritual beliefs carrying their souls. These men and women sought their religious liberty for themselves and their children in the new world. History calls them non-conformists.

The elder Cotton and four other ministers fled to the safety of the New England colony from persecution of the unpardonable offenses of being dissenters and Puritans. Though the escape was made with much difficulty, the decision to do so, at least for Cotton, was not. Only months after his marriage, Cotton went underground rather than appear by summons before the Bishop of London whose mission it was to suppress the Puritan practices. This was the English Inquisition in full force.

For nearly a year, with only moments of stolen time here and there with his family, Cotton travelled under the protection of other Puritans throughout the south of England until he determined his future could only be in the new world. Reunited with his bride, now large with their first child, they made their way to Deal in Kent, to board the ship. As far as Atlantic passages go, the *Griffin*'s was uneventful. They set sail on the first day of the sixth month, and thus made their way in just seven or eight weeks before landing at Plymouth in the Massachusetts Colony. Colonial Governor John Winthrop met the eminent Cotton's arrival with the invitation to be appointed the first minister in the principal city of Boston, so named for the many settlers from the village of the same name as their birthplace in old England. Following Cotton down the plank from the ship was his wife, and his first child, a son he aptly christened and named Seaborn. To this renegade minister of God, this was a sign of His pleasure of the future which began with an ocean voyage.

Also coming off the ship were the Hutchinsons, Mistress Anne, her husband and their eight children. The Hutchinsons were followers of the Reverend Cotton in his pastorate at Saint Botolph's in Boston, in Lincolnshire, despite the distance from their home, a good twenty-five miles up the coast of the North Sea in the village of Alford. Following his lead, Mistress Hutchinson championed Cotton's spirit-centered theology, but from an adversarial pulpit, which led to her excommunication from Cotton's new church in the colonies and her eventual banishment.

Also from the village of Alford were Thomas and William Wardell. Though both were skilled in their respective labors, they did not have the means to pay their passage, and so sought a sponsor. It may perhaps have been through their connection to the Hutchinsons the Wardell brothers, along with two young women in the village, were able to secure a position in service to Edmund

Quincy, a wealthy merchant in Northhants, a county far to the southeast of Lincolnshire.

Thomas Wardell remained in Boston after his indenture to Quincy was cleared, plying his trade as cordwainer. He was married to Elizabeth Woodroffe, one of the two young women from Alford, and there they welcomed a son.

Eliakim Wardell was born on the twentieth day of the ninth month, in the Year of our Lord, 1635, in Boston, in the County of Sussex. Tradition holds Mistress Anne Hutchinson attended the birth.

After three days of the cold November, Eliakim was baptized by the Reverend John Cotton at the First Church of Boston where Thomas was admitted just eleven days earlier.

Through another connection with the Hutchinsons, Thomas and his family followed the Reverend John Wheelwright as he departed Boston amid tensions growing at an alarming rate, and made their way with twenty devotees through the wilderness north to the falls of the Piscataqua River where they gathered a church beyond the reach of the colony. Wheelwright was long the vicar at Bilsby, in Lincolnshire very near to Alford, and was a brother-in-law to Mistress Hutchinson. Though he was a close associate of John Cotton, his brand of teachings of the Puritan doctrine led to a conviction for sedition by the Massachusetts Colony courts. He, like the Hutchinsons, was banished from Boston in 1637.

Their destination, where two tributaries met, one a freshwater and the other a tidal saltwater, provided all the game, vegetation and fish the burgeoning community needed to sustain themselves away from the security of the colony. Once the home of the Algonquin people who called themselves Sqamscott, the natives of the area were forced to move their settlements from their big water place by the European colonists who laid patents on the lands.

It was already November in 1637 when Wheelwright and four others were disenfranchised for little more than their disruption of the church and public order. Yet Thomas, with his dear Elizabeth,

Eliakim, and his sister Martha among them, followed through the deep snow and bitter cold to a better place where they would be free once again to worship according to the promise of their long and difficult crossing.

There, in the town they called Exeter and later in Wells where the Wardells continued to follow their pastor, Eliakim grew strong of body and certainty of mind through the teachings of Mister Wheelwright. Thomas died there, in Wells, in December of 1646, leaving Elizabeth to fend and care alone for their four children.

In March of 1647, Wheelright would have arrived upon the doorstep of Goodwife Wardell to announce his order of banishment was retracted. She would have greeted him with warmth and fond memory of him sitting with her as she endured her husband's last breath. He would soon be removing back to Massachusetts, to Hampton, thirty-five miles south along the ocean coast where he was to be welcomed back to the colony with a grant of assistant pastorship. Without Thomas, the Wardell family's sole tie to Wells was the Reverend Wheelwright, so Elizabeth would not find it difficult to follow him once more.

I knew Eliakim as a child of twelve years when he arrived in Hampton village with his mother, two younger brothers and a sister, and our new pastor. To ease the burden on her family, Elizabeth agreed to allow Eliakim, a boy with the soul of a man, to work the Wheelwright farm as an offer in the spirit of Thomas' long and faithful service. The pastor's home was on the east side of the meeting house green border just before the turn off toward the sea, not far from our own houselot on the north edge of the green. Not a day would go by when Eliakim's path did not cross mine as we grew from children into our adulthood.

In Hampton, Eliakim and John Hussey would grow to be brothers in every way except by blood. John Hussey was the son of Christopher, a well-respected widower in the colony, but one given to his own thoughts on the subject of faith. A son-in-law to the Reverend Stephen Bachiler, among those first to arrive at

Winnicunnet Plantation, the elder Hussey was familiar with the sacrifices made for religious freedoms. He, therefore, was a cautious man who learned to balance his faith against the safety of his family. Neither John nor Eliakim remembered the tensions their faith wrought on their fathers, and as boys were driven more by the hot blood flowing through their veins.

Eliakim was good and faithful in his service to the Reverend Wheelwright, and others of the community. So, when Wheelwright decided to return to England in 1655, he gave over his property for Eliakim to occupy. By then, he was tall and strapping. Though his hair and eye were like the color of charred wood, and he did not seek out conversation with any but those with whom he was close, lending some to look upon him as prickly and rebellious, he was soft in his voice and touch and his soul was warm and quiet. It was then we began to talk of marriage in whispers in the tall salt grasses.

What began with the Reverend John Cotton and his disciples, came to be fundamental to Eliakim under the further paternal influence of Reverend Wheelwright, Goodmen Christopher Hussey and Jeffrey Mingay, and others of similar mind about the community. The hypocrisy which later took hold was foreign to them, and puzzling, but Hampton was their home and there Eliakim and I would make our home as well.

Our patience was blessed again in June of 1658 when Eliakim, then a man in his twenty-third year, received a respectable piece of land from Mingay, as he lay sick and nearing his end. This land lay to the left of the bridge over the old Taylor river on the road to Exeter. Mingay's grant consisted of ten acres of upland in the community lot, a fair and fresh piece of the great meadow, the salt marsh nearby to Goodman Stanyon, and finally two acres and a half of swampland. He granted also his share of the cow common for the peaceful respite of one ox. Mingay's last decree was his wife should give Eliakim what she would for the value of a farthing, and a yoke of beasts though she should take liberty to claim for her own comfort and need the young or the old ones.

With this generous gift, Eliakim could well establish himself in a home and his own means to provide for the future of a family. He approached Father and Mother to seek their blessing for us to wed as soon as he could build us a house and harvest his first crops. It was too late in the season for planting, so he would have to wait until the following spring and summer, and we would celebrate our marriage with a fine harvest in the autumn.

So he left behind his youth and he welcomed the struggle which lay ahead as he, with the help of John Hussey and others of his friends, was quick set to building a house to one day blaze with the fire of a home and a life and a family constructed with the pain and sweat and tears of his own mind and hard labor. It would prove to be a long, hard winter, but Eliakim would learn all he needed to survive.

6

The First Lash

I had seen men whipped. I had seen women take the whip, too. I saw the anguish in their faces no matter the strength they had to bear in silence. I saw them twist and writhe, buckle and fall. But I could not know for myself before then the sensation of leather tearing through skin.

For days before I struggled to remember the pains I endured in my life. Could any of them give me even the faintest of ideas of what a lash across my back would feel like; and then what would five, ten, or a score of lashes require me to endure? How would I separate the physical from the mental or emotional pain? How quick I was to forget the pain of childbirth, and my mind eager to embrace the result; anticipation for the next time, how quick would I recover only to jump in to it again. I found anticipation kept the thoughts forward in my mind, but expectation of the worst I could imagine would ultimately help to ease the first shock of pain.

Would I scream? Or would I whimper? We like to think we can withstand our troubles with dignity, but how can we know before the time actually comes? So much in the past few years taught me to be strong, to think away my fears, observe and learn from those around me. Perhaps I could know what to expect because I heard how others received the whip, and thus I could wash away the fear of it. But I could also be curious about it, eager in a way to experience what could torment some and make others stronger.

And, so it was the Constable let loose the whip—*and then sorely lashed [me] with twenty or thirty cruel stripes.*

A *whunh* sound reached my ears first. The thongs rippling through the air. The crack, like thunder after the flash of lightening, came next. Tree branches breaking away under the stress of a dry wind torrent. It was sharp and sudden. No matter what I expected, the force of leather meeting flesh broke into my thoughts, wrenched me back to the post, back to my place at the center of a riotous mob, my breast and heart bare. An echo in the breeze. Distant thunder. The scream deep in the night from a dream so real, and so disturbing, it wakes you in a cold and clammy sweat, and lets you only reach the edge of an exhausted slumber for the rest of the night.

Despite my mental preparations, and my brain acknowledging the report as the thongs were let loose, I was taken by surprise when the whip's tongue lapped at my shoulder. I arched my back impulsively, pushing my belly to the post. The wood splinters were a piercing intrusion into the delicate skin. My cheek scraped against the harsh wood. My hands twitched against the ties. A hoarse whisper escaped my strained neck and opened mouth. I heard nothing except the blood rushing to my head.

A dozen thin leather thongs met the skin beneath my right shoulder with an almost charitable introduction. The bone jutting out there was the first to register the sensation. Then all around it a blurred kind of feeling. It all faded and I traced the leather fingers as they searched with a kind of heaviness pulling down the curve of my back to the top of my buttock before they fell away completely leaving little more than a tickle.

I held my breath, waiting for the skin to tear.

I felt the coolness of the breeze brushing against my bare back. If the skin were torn, I would be left with a sting from the air entering the open wound. But there was little stinging. There was no drop of blood forming where the tear ended, then pulled by the heat of my skin down my back.

I expected more, and I found myself disappointed. Was this the measure of the Constable's full strength, the extent of the passion growing just minutes earlier, expelled in the first lash? The night before, as Eliakim and I slept, he held my unblemished back against him, and I resigned myself to the barbarous strikes that would break the skin and leave me forever scarred. But these weals of softer lashes would heal, and leave no lasting marks upon my back. Without the marks it would be as if I escaped punishment.

If this was all I was to receive, then this trial would pass with little note. Again, I was disappointed.

7

Hampton

Eliekin Wardwell and Lidia Perkins were Joyned in mariage. 17: 8 mo: 1659.

The Seventeenth Day, in October, in 1659...

October is a beautiful time in Hampton in the Massachusetts Colony. The leaves are turning, and, though they will soon die with the winter's cold they are for a short time the most splendid of reds and oranges, yellows and browns. I would often, of a morning during this time of year, rush to complete or maneuver my morning chores so I could walk alone just to let the colors swim about my eyes. There was a peacefulness on the path with the trees surrounding, bending over as if to create an archway, calling me to enter. The denseness of the trees blocked the sunlight, but breaks in the branches and leaves waving with the wind left spots of light to lead the way. I listened as the wind raced over my head, like water falling to the left and the right of me. The trees parted and opened at the glen by the pond, the colors were as vibrant in the reflection of the still water as in the glow of the new morning sun. There was a rock there, shaped as a seat, where once the Indians who first lived in the area would grind corn and grains and nuts into a meal or flour. I would sit there for a few moments, alone of anyone with whom I must share my thoughts.

Our contract was made in Hampton as we were required to register our marriage in the town clerk's civil book. According to the custom of the times, the clerk published the bann, the notice of our intent to marry, to the meeting house door before each of three consecutive lectures in order to avow to our plan to make an orderly union. At the start of each of those lectures, the clerk rose and further announced the names of each of the couples whose banns were hanging then on the door.

On lecture day, it was the younger Reverend Cotton's habit to expect the townsfolk to await his arrival before entering the meeting house, separated into groups of family and friends, men and women. While we waited, the men would congregate in the front of the building while the women would stand close, especially as the air became more chilled, to the side where they talked in solemn whispers near the entrance. Even then, Eliakim and I would find some way to catch the eye of the other and exchange a sly and knowing smile.

On the lecture day when our names would be called for the first time, the men stood about, stamping their feet in the dirt like brave and restless stallions, and I stood among the women huddled close with our cloaks drawn tight about our shoulders or younger children held close for their warmth. Rebecka, married not yet a fortnight before, stood with me, our mother and sisters apart from her new husband and his family, our father and brothers.

When the Reverend Seaborn Cotton and his wife and children arrived just minutes before Goodman Henry Smith was to ring the nine of the clock bell, he passed through the crowd greeting the women with a clever smile and a few of the men with a hearty handshake. His wife, with her infant son held tight in her arm and her toddling daughter in tow by the hand, passed the threshold of the main door. Only then did one of the men call the town folk to enter just as the bell rang out. Inside the door there were two men standing, one to the right to motion for the women to be seated together in the east end of the south side of the building, and the other to the left to direct the men placed on the west end of the building according to their prominence within the town. In the meeting house there were no pews, rather we sat upon hard wooden benches turned to face the center of the north end of the building where the scaffold, also called the pulpit, stood raised above the floor level so the parson could look out upon his flock.

Eliakim sat near the back owing to his refusal to take the town oath, and thus be called a freeman and have membership in the church. Men who refused this honor were still expected to attend the weekly meetings, but could not have a voice in the community nor the responsibility of participating in its management. I could not look to him when our names were called out, so I tried to fix my eyes on my sister, Hannah, nearly three and one half years of age then. She sat squirming in my lap and I thought of each of my brothers and sisters as they grew and proved themselves able to remain respectful so they could be allowed to sit on their own in the gallery. Mother sat beside me, holding her youngest child, a girl Mary who was barely fifteen months, on the ends of her knees tight against her growing belly; the birth of her eleventh child would scarce be two months away. This would be me one day, soon I hoped. I was glad to be there, be a part of this community, glad to have such good examples around me.

On the second lecture day, when our names were called out, I dared to raise my head and wished to give my full attention to the minister. I felt I should soon stand beside the other women, but I held no notion what I would say. Rebecka sat beside me. She was the next eldest of the Perkins daughters, no more than a child of sixteen, yet married before me. I could count on her to always know what I was thinking, which allowed me to remain silent and in a place I could be far more comfortable. Surely, she carried the same thoughts just two fortnights before. She fought hard to stifle a giggle, and I was forced to squeeze Hannah tight with one hand while I eased my other hand free to pinch Rebecka so she would be quiet and not draw our mother's, or anyone's, attention. She only giggled more, and I was left to smile at our private quip.

By the third of the lecture days, I gave up all thoughts. Eliakim and I were to be married the next day. No one came forward to make objections, but then who would? I remained in my father's house too long, he would complain, and did I mean to try and remain a maid at his expense despite my advancing years? He would be happy to shed himself of a mouth to feed even though I more often made myself useful with the care of his large, and still growing, brood. Mother would need only to look at him during such outbursts for him to recall his tongue and praise me for being the dutiful quiet daughter. But then he would turn to attend to something else, and mutter all the while.

He could be a hard man, and it would be many years before I understood he bore the burden of his own deeds and demons in silence. It was the suffering which made him hard, and I wished I would not find the same fate.

Mother, on the other hand, spoke without end of duty and responsibility. She was all along patient with Eliakim as he made his own way, so he could well provide for me and our own large family.

But what of love? Surely there was love between my father and mother, though I never saw them so much as touch even by an accidental brush. Looking back, I was naive though not ignorant of how things were between a husband and a wife. Mostly thanks to Rebecka and her incautious eagerness; she did not know it yet but she would birth her first child the following summer, less than eight months away.

So the prospect of marriage was both exciting and fearsome. Eliakim and I found ways to sneak away from the prying eyes of the town and our families, but we did not venture so far as to become too familiar. He would not push me when I was not yet ready, for he seemed to know my mind better than even Rebecka. This is what I came to believe was love. Sitting there, on my last day as an unmarried girl, I could think of nothing else but how he would come to know me as a woman and how it left my body to tingle.

The next morning we presented ourselves to the clerk, for unions in those days were civil rather than religious events. I returned to my father's house to complete my chores for the last time. Later in the day, Eliakim appeared to help me take my few belongings to the home he built for us.

My silence was deafening even to me as we rode, side-by-side for the first time, in the cart carrying us to our new lives and the home I had yet to see. Though I became comfortable with him over the years, on this particular day I found I could say nothing. What was a woman, a wife, to say to her husband? It seemed the childish stories we rationed to one another no longer mattered. We should be talking of important things, of grown adult things, of married people things. I spent most of the journey trying to remember such occasions between my father and mother, and my disappointment grew with each turn of the cart's wheels when I could think of nothing between them except his declarations and her acquiescence, his gruff ways and her soothing excuses. Eliakim was equally silent. Perhaps he was battling the same questions for he had not the benefit of a father in his home for many a year to guide him in these matters.

We arrived as the sun sank low in the sky, but by the waning light I saw the most perfect sight. The house was a simple rectangle structure with wide clapboard sides and a steep pitched roof of thatch. There were side gables and a narrow roof overhang. Eliakim explained he added a loft within the steep roof pitch extending over the large single room below, opening just about the fireplace made of stone. This loft would provide us with a nest where our new love would grow and sprout wings like the birds I so loved to listen to in the early morning hours when they and I were the only creatures awake. Later, as the balance of young and old shifted, the children would be given the perch as their sleeping compartment while Eliakim and I would take up the space nearer the warmth of the hearth.

He brought the cart up to the door, which was placed at the center with a small window to each side. He reached his hand out to help me down. I climbed into the cart without his help when we set out, afraid his first touch would leave me somehow fearful. But this time, having sat beside him for the ride, despite the quiet, I felt more at ease and I took his hand. This was the first time we ever touched. He squeezed, though not hard. My body reacted quicker than my mind, and I squeezed back.

He stepped aside and motioned for me to enter my new home. Just as he described, there was but one center hall, the large fireplace directly in front of me. It was larger than the one Father built, and Eliakim was very clever in shaping the chimney of boards, covering them with a thick layer of clay, and then plaster to give it a very refined look.

He outfitted the fireplace with an iron-forged crane, jack, and set, and hanging from the pothooks was a large, cast iron Dutch oven with the most delicious scent of rabbit stew coming from it. He said with a great smile he used baby carrots from our own garden. Eliakim lived on his own for more than a year, and he learned to fend for himself. From this oven I would practice what I learned of cooking from my own mother and make many fine meals of broth, bean porridge, and hasty puddings.

I turned about, letting my feet dance upon the wide planked hardwood floors, and looked at the multi-paned, double-hung windows with shutters of plain wood on either side. Finally, I went to stand at the edge of the fireplace by the rocking chair Eliakim made just for me. I ran my hand over the delicate carvings decorating the top. I had no difficulty imagining myself sitting in the chair, rocking with a babe in my arms. My feet beneath me gave way, so overcome with joy was I, and I dropped into one of the two simpler spindle chairs at the table dividing the room. Eliakim planed the top with such care I knew not one splinter would find its way into my hands. Two shelves hung from the mud plaster walls to the left, with two plates of wood, two horn cups, and two pewter knives.

Farther left, a ladder leaned against the wall leading up to the loft.

To the right of the fireplace and the table was a large empty space. I turned to Eliakim, and he could see tears starting to fall down my cheeks—tears of happiness—but I was confused by the empty space. For as long as I could remember, my father's house was full, not a corner empty of children or bedsteads or boxes containing those necessary things of everyday life. He knew immediately what troubled me, and he drew me into his arms and whispered into my ear we would soon fill this space with so many beautiful children.

He took both my hands in his, and he looked into my eyes. I was captivated. His voice was a melody to my ears. "We have no assembly here to look upon us," he said. "I take thee Lidia to be my wife. I promise with Divine assistance to be unto thee a loving and faithful husband so long as we both shall live."

The words were so beautiful I repeated them without hesitation. "I take thee Eliakim to be my husband. I promise with Divine assistance to be unto thee a loving and faithful wife so long as we both shall live."

Our marriage promise thus fulfilled, we lay together, his rough farm-worn hands clutching me tightly, securely. I felt the heat rising from him, and I felt the flush of heat rising in my own body. And so we started our lives with ne'er a thought except to our good fortune. We were innocent, then, of the fever spreading outside our coverture, and we could not have imagined how we would be caught up into it.

8

John Endicott

Not two fortnight before our marriage, on the twentieth day of the seventh month, in September of 1659, three individuals were brought into custody in Boston. I did not know these three—two men and a woman—and I cannot say Eliakim had not cause to meet or converse with them at one time or another. But my acquaintance with them did not lessen the impact of what occurred, and what then wrenched me from my innocent happiness.

News of this sort travelled swift through the great distances of the colony. Since our marriage, Eliakim and I busied ourselves with settling in to our home and daily work and did not meet with anyone except at the meeting house where such gossip would not be tolerated.

Shortly after our marriage, Eliakim went to the village for supplies and there he met with a Friend and neighbor. He brought the news with a pot of vinegar from town and we sat at our table, the sun fading outside while the candlelight raised ominous shadows in the corners of the house. He reached across the table and held my hands as he told me what he heard.

The governor, who was then John Endicott, was required also to officiate certain of the court sessions. He demanded to know why the three had come again into the jurisdiction from whence they were before banished, their return on pain of death.

"We come in obedience to a Divine call," they said in unison.

Despite the authority of the law, the Governor and his fellow magistrates shrank from the blood-stained deed and looked down from their platform upon the three who stood tall and straight if disheveled.

Endicott spoke quietly but deliberately. "I desire not your deaths. Take liberty and speak for yourselves."

His offer was met with deafening silence, and so Endicott ordered the gaoler to take the three away and return them to the prison house.

At the meeting house on the following day, Minister Wilson of Boston, with not a thought to the souls of men, exhorted the rulers to act against the three who came amongst them. Wilson, with Priest Norton who was another of like mind, turned their backs to tenderness and love, they devoted their eloquent speeches to a corrupt or unworthy purpose, and they wickedly excited anyone who would hear them to hatred and revenge for the diabolical doctrines and the horrid tenets of the cursed sect called Quakers.

Inflamed by the priest and the reaction of the crowd thus kindled, the magistrates sent for the three to be brought again before them.

Governor Endicott was one of the earliest patentees of the Massachusetts Bay, arriving with his family in 1628. He was the longest serving governor under the old company charter. Said to be of a stern manner, many spoke of his prudence, especially in secular affairs. Here he hesitated, and he spoke faintly as if he feared he would wake God to what he was about to say, and then he too would find himself below and soon drained of his own life.

"We have laws, and have through many ways endeavored to keep you from our colony. But, the whippings, the imprisonments, the cutting off of ears, and finally the banishment on pain of death did not keep you from us." His gaze then bore into each of the three before him, in their turns. After a pause, he continued, "I desired not your deaths." Then he bowed his head, and closed his eyes as if he were in prayer. His lips twitched, and so the hairs on his mustache danced. Raising his head after a moment, he once again found his voice, and this time he boomed, "Give ear and hearken to your sentence."

William Robinson, the first of the three, determined then to speak, interrupting the Governor's words to request he be permitted to read a statement he prepared the previous night which set forth the reasons for why he did not depart the colony. No one can know why he chose that moment to speak, why he did not speak at the previous offer of the Governor.

Endicott, incensed by the interruption and the man standing before him, said, "No, you shall not read it, nor shall the court hear it read." Instead, Endicott took the paper and read it to himself and no other.

When he was finished, he raised his eyes to Robinson, and without preamble directed the gaoler to take him back from whence he came and from thence, on the appointed day, to the place of execution.

Endicott turned then to Marmaduke Stephenson and, without hesitation, pronounced his sentence in the same words. Taking his lead from his Friend Robinson, Stephenson launched an address on the court without giving pause for the Governor to chide him. Stephenson warned the men sitting behind the bar of a curse evermore upon them should they put these, His three servants, to death.

As the gaoler led him out of the room, Stephenson called back to the magistrates, "In love to thee all, I exhort thee to take warning before it be too late, so the curse may be removed. For assuredly, if thee put us to death, thee will bring innocent blood upon thine own hands, and swift destruction will come upon thee."

Finally, Endicott who was now haggled from these trying exchanges, turned to Mary Dyer and pronounced the same dire sentence. Without compassion, Endicott listened to her meek but undisturbed reply. "The will of the Lord be done." When she was again silent, he merely waved his arms at the gaoler to take her away.

All three were to be hanged by the neck on the gallows until dead one week hence, on the twenty-seventh day in the month of September.

Were this the end of the matter, the sentences would likely have been carried out without another thought. But, Stevenson's prophesy hung like a thunderous cloud above the court, and there rose an excitement and a sympathy among the townspeople of no ordinary nature. Rather than accept the ruling of the court, even under law, the townspeople flocked to the open prison windows, amazed and marveling to hear the ministrations of the three inside, which went on without stop night and day.

When Endicott heard of this spectacle, he paled with a fear where none before overtook him. This did not, after all, change matters. Priest Wilson was heard to say, "Lest there be any doubt about the deliberations, hang them, or else." He repeated these words over and over, and he drew his finger again and again across his throat to make clear his preference for the means of their execution.

On the prescribed day, the prisoners were taken in a procession of two hundred or more men armed with flintlock, sword, pike, and halberd, and not a few horsemen besides to ensure no rescue or escape. Their escort paraded them through the streets to Boston Common, led by drums beating so loudly one might claim to have heard them all the way to Hampton.

I pulled my hands from his and raised them to my face. I was horrified at this news, but I had no words to express it. From between my fingers, I looked at my husband, my protector, and I asked, "Yet were they saved?" He lifted himself from the chair, heavy did he appear, and he turned away, not wishing me to see his face as he went on to tell of the hangings of the two men.

"And what of the woman?" I asked, tears beginning to well in my eyes.

Eliakim took my hands in his once again, and continued his tale.

Mary Dyer stood alone and watched the lifeless bodies of William Robinson and Marmaduke Stevenson suspended before her, their eyes were open and staring blankly over the heads of the watchers and spittle trickling from between their purpling lips; their martyrs sentence of death carried out under the taunts and scoffs, the low and vulgar language of the Priest Wilson of Boston.

She ascended the ladder, calm and bearing a contented look on her face. The hangman tied her feet with her own cape, put the halter around her neck, and covered her face with the handkerchief of Priest Wilson himself, while the autumn breeze let sway the bodies of her companions on either side of her.

Before he could move to kick away the ladder and send Mary to her joy in eternity, a rider came galloping up. This man yelled and waved his hat about his head, "Stop, stop, she is reprieved." He pulled his horse, lathered from the frantic ride, to a stop and swung down to the ground with the governor's paper clutched in his fist.

It was Mary's own son who interceded on her behalf and convinced the governor to stay her execution. As he pulled her down, she protested for she had eased her mind. The reprieve required her return to prison for no more than forty-eight hours at which time the magistrate thought the prudent course, given the excitement roused amongst the village throughout the whole affair, would be to commute her sentence to banishment but with return a second time surely upon the pain of death.

Two days hence, when the gaoler brought her out of the prison and set her upon a horse, the magistrate spoke to each of the horsemen selected for the task. The first sat upon a rare white with eyes the blue of sky, attentive as the magistrate instructed him to take the vagabond some fifteen miles toward the colony at Rhode Island. There he and the two following him were to leave her under the charge of the fourth and last horseman to be taken the rest of the way out of the jurisdiction. The magistrate bade the horseman allow no harm to come to the woman whilst he shall lead the group.

The next horseman sat on a young chestnut of vibrant red roan. His face blended with a mixture of fire and vengeance. A sword hung from his belt, he was at the ready and eager to resolve the prosecution shortly ended.

Next came a handsome blue-black morgan, the black about its eyes and muzzle sweat-shined. Its rider sat astride two saddlebags, the leather worn but stained as black as the horse's coat. Looking back over his shoulder at Mary, who was put upon an ancient buckskin bay mare with her hands tied and hooked around the pommel, he called out to her the journey was fortuitous for his bags contained wheat and barley, which he intended to trade at the next town, penny for penny, for oil and wine.

The last of the horsemen came up beside Mary on a salt and pepper gray steed who pulled at his bridle and stomped the ground, impatient to be away. The magistrate called up to him and nodded. No words were spoken.

And so, Mistress Mary Dyer departed the colony, her life intact, her faith intact.

I dreamt that night of Mistress Dyer.

9

The Second Lash

The interval following the first lash seemed long, though it perhaps was no more than a minute. My first thought was he meant to give me time to regain my strength before the second thrust. Perhaps he needed the respite. This was not the first time he was called upon to use the whip, nor was it the first time his hand held the whip which tore into a woman.

My arms clung to the post as a small child clings to the leg of her father, begging for forgiveness for some small misdeed. If I could have released my hold, and then acknowledged forgiveness would not be forthcoming, I would have stood straight and begged for the punishment to be swift and just.

I was shaken by a whimpering spit from behind me. The leather tongues lapped at my back.

The second lash was much like the first in its lack of enthusiasm. It was a backhanded thrash, the thongs connecting at the skin over the ribs on my left side and taking a more horizontal path which allowed them to fall away much sooner. An infant bear cub strikes out in blind playfulness as it imitates its mother. But it has no strength to do harm, or inflict pain. It is only just learning and has but a glimpse at what is to be its true nature.

Again I was disappointed. I felt cheated somehow. Deprived of what I had earned and anticipated. Where was the fury promised just moments ago; why did I long for the sensation as I traced the thongs reaching out to my body, and then they as neat fell from it? I had no illusions my punishment should be lessened because I was a woman, nor was I somehow better equipped to handle this or any kind of punishment. I fervently hoped the Constable felt no measure of pity, and allowed such pity to guide his actions.

Then I understood, and I cursed him for his lack of strength.

Another lash, then another, much the same. I felt the blood rising, seeking an outlet from which it could weep. But, my skin was tough, my heart strong, and so it retreated. What was before a whisper, was now a laugh at this pretense of barbarity.

I opened my eyes almost believing I would find myself at home, my arms about Eliakim in a loving embrace, my son running and weaving in and out from between my legs, whooping and screeching. My other son cooing from his cradle, polite, begging for attention of his own.

Instead I found people grumbling and spitting, some with disappointment in their eyes and others with fire and rage. Some lost interest and moved away, the proceedings no longer worth the loss of a day in the fields. Others closed in as if they had a mind to strip the whip from the constable's hand and finish the job themselves. These others inspired a fear in me I had not yet felt at Fifield's hand. The blood lust in their eyes poured over me, and I had naught with which to stanch its flow.

Frantic, I thought, could the constable not at least make a better show of this.

My thoughts were interrupted by the crunching of footsteps, heavy and clumsy, closing in from behind me. They were not like Eliakim's sure and stealth foot. Or the timid, hesitating steps of the Constable. I knew without seeing his black eyes these footsteps could only be those of my tormentor. With the veil of protection around him waning, he would bolster his courage with arrogance and risk approaching me, but only from the back. The bitter and burning taste of betrayal rose from my stomach.

Was it the heat of his breath against my neck? Did he speak, or was it the wind carrying a sound like voices without words to my ears? *Shall I pray for you.* Then the slightest of a touch to my bare arm and I was reminded of the devil's mark.

Man's hands upon a woman's body. A father's touch, when she is but a girl, how it would be gentle to comfort and protect, or hard but fair to teach her how she must suffer and learn. Then a friend's touch. She knows what you know, feels what you feel, and her touch is a knowing that requires no words. Later, her husband's touch can be tender and loving, though calloused as working the land will do. His touch can be warm by a winter's fire, or cold made by the distance of time and loss of passion. Or hands made hard by anger. If he is a lover then his hands are eager with a hunger for excitement, passionate as they explore every inch, every curve, every hidden treasure. Yet, still they might be hesitant, fearing what they might find, confused by the changes in the landscape.

But what was a stranger's touch?

This was unlike the violation I endured at the Newbury meeting house. When I was a child, the town leaders declared every townsman shall kill a wolf, and carry its head to the meeting house; he should nail it to the little red oak tree nearby. For his troubles he should be paid ten shilling from the town's coffers. In this man's sinuous mind, was I the wolf. Would he relish in the thought of hanging my head from the old oak tree? Did his eyes glisten and his mouth froth at the jingle of the coin in his pocket? Unlike the touch of the constable's hands in the execution of his duties for which he could be forgiven, this was personal, meant to be our secret. How would he look upon his parish from here after? How would I look upon him?

The bile halted within my throat. As much as I could want, I would not spit or hiss my contempt at him, or any of them.

Were I judged a Quaker, I would have been tied to a cart, the whip flying through the air in time with my steps as if I were dancing with death. But I was not judged a Quaker. Yet, how was this any different? Would we all not have the same thoughts as the executioners carried out their punishments? Would we all not hope for mercy, or perhaps embrace the barbarity of it all? Would we not cry out, or would we be able to remain strong and silent throughout? Would we not feel each lash, or shut our minds to them altogether?

This much I could know. Women are bred to endure, and endure in silence if we will it. The men of the Newbury meeting house groping, this man's furtive touch, the constable's whip. They were nothing. Pain, like a rabid man's pleasure, is fleeting.

10

Mistress Mary Dyer

The winter months after our marriage passed without haste, and for me it was a joy to lie every night with Eliakim. His hands upon my body, and mine upon his. We whispered into the nights of our dreams of prosperity and children. We talked of how we would teach them to be good citizens, have faith, stand firm for their beliefs, and Eliakim talked of them finding the Light. We knew of the dangers mounting within the colony, but we never spoke of it. He told me of his discourses with God, how they talked as father and son, often when he was alone working at his chores in the field or barn, or when he rode alone into town. I listened in wonder for these things were never said in my father's house. If someone listened with care about the town, they might hear things in the hidden corners or empty paths, but I chose not to heed such talk—it was of no interest to me then—so now these things were new, and it was my husband who spoke them. I listened first with rapture, then later with curiosity. Finally, I began to understand.

Each month I waited in anticipation for the first signs, and I watched Rebecka's belly with growing trepidation; her marriage being a fortunate event since many a young couple in those days would take the whip on their back if they could not pay the fine for having relations before marriage. When my chores were done, I sat in my rocking chair, comforted by the fire and my hands busy with sewing little gowns and caps, adding to the growing pile of clean and folded linens I kept packed away in chest at the foot of our bed. I hoped this would somehow inspire the rest of my body to respond. But as each month passed I grew more concerned, more fearful of disappointing my new husband with my failure in my most important responsibility to him. Each lecture day I endured the talk of other women, their cooing to each other's infants, their anticipation at their own coming births. My mother soothed my mind and reminded me of the lapse of time between her own marriage and my birth. She did not speak of losses, and I did not ask. She reminded me of her eleventh child born just four months earlier. Finally, she bade me not give over to vanity, *two are better than one: because they have a good reward for their labour*.

Eliakim and I came together for more than a child.

I continued to pray, though I wondered if God would answer me in the same way he seemed to answer Eliakim's calls. I worried His silence should be my answer. Finally, after more than five months of marriage, I was able to tell Eliakim we were with child.

As the bloom of spring became the heat of summer, I worked at my chores with a steady hand and a sturdy back, and was not plagued by any of the sickness of which some women complained. I attended lectures each week and was several times tempted to pride myself in the compliments I received from the other women.

But, while we rejoiced, we could not know yet the full extent of how others were suffering.

Mistress Mary Dyer inevitably appeared again in Boston some seven months after she was left at the perilous mercy of the fourth horseman at the outward edge of the colony to find her own way out on foot. Governor Endicott heard of her return, and sent for her immediately.

She appeared before him on the first day of the month of June in

1660 as calm as the last time. He leaned forward and looked down upon her from his perch. He wore a black cap, the hair beneath it almost as white as the falling band tied tight around his neck, covering his broad chest, and trailing down his back. "Are you the same Mary Dyer who was here before?"

Undaunted by his position and his tone, she replied with cordiality, "I am the same Mary Dyer who was here at the last General Court."

Determined, Endicott asked, "you will own yourself a Quaker, will you not."

She straightened herself the more, reaching her full, but diminutive, height. "I own myself to be reproachfully called so."

From behind she heard the gaoler speak out of turn, timid. "She is a vagabond."

Endicott looked to the gaoler with scorn, distracted by the outburst, then returned to her with a fierce gaze. He did not wish to be cheated again, and so he repeated the sentence before handed down. "You will return to the prison house, and there remain till the morrow at nine bells of the clock; from thence you must go the gallows, and there be hanged till you are dead." The echo of his words hung limp in the heat of the room.

Unmoved, she replied, "this is no more than what thou saidst before."

Endicott's sagging cheeks beneath sagging eyes appeared to flush with this, a woman's, audacity. He leaned further forward, lifting himself out of his seat, and spoke in a quiet, but harsh voice. "But now it is to be executed, therefore prepare yourself on the morrow at nine of the clock."

He thrust himself back into his chair so hard the feet scraped so loud against the wooden platform even he was startled. He signaled to all in the room the exchange was then finished by turning his attention to some papers before him. But by divine providence, or some other cause, the gaoler hesitated, thus allowing Mary the opportunity to speak again.

"I came in obedience to the will of God at the last General Court, desiring thee to repeal thou unrighteous laws for banishment on pain of death; and my work now is the same, and earnest request; although I told thee, if thou refused to repeal them, the Lord would send others of his servants to witness against thee."

Endicott's thin pale lips began to quiver betwixt his bristling mustache and the narrow tuft of a beard, and his eyes opened wide, his pupils became black dots and the whites of them contrasted against the red of his face.

"Are you a prophetess?"

To which she replied, "I speak the words the Lord speaks to me, and now the thing has come to pass…"

Cutting her off, Endicott slammed his hand upon the pulpit causing the cups and papers there to rattle, and he yelled out, "Away with her, away with her."

The next morning, as promised, the gaoler took Mary from the prison house and presented her to a waiting band of soldiers. Instead of the Common, they marched her for another mile onto the Boston Neck. But just as before, drums beat ahead of her, and drums beat behind her; the cacophony of it was such no one heard the words she spoke throughout the entire trudge.

As before, she arrived at the old elm tree chosen to serve as the gallows, and as before she climbed the ladder and allowed the hangman to place the halter around her neck. As he did this, a man spoke from the crowd. "She was here before with a sentence of banishment upon pain of death, and now she breaks the law in coming again." Raising his voice so all would hear, "She is guilty of her own blood."

Without a handkerchief to cover her face this time, she looked down upon the man and down upon the crowd who had come to witness this, her second execution. She spoke slow and clear to everyone who would listen. "I am here to keep the blood-guiltiness from thee, desiring thee to repeal the unrighteous and unjust law of banishment upon pain of death, made against the innocent servants of the Lord. Therefore, my blood will be required at thrust hands who are willful to do it. But for those who do it in the simplicity of their hearts, I desire the Lord to forgive them. I came to do the will of my Father, and in obedience to His will, I stand even to my own death."

"Will you repent? Be not so deluded and carried away by the deceit of the devil," she heard the priest who stood nearby ask.

"I have naught to now repent."

He then asked, "Would you have the elders pray for you; would you have the people pray for you?"

She looked him straight in the eye. "I know never an elder here. But I desire the prayers of all the people of God."

Before the priest could respond, standing with his body pushed forward and his two arms by his side ending in tight clenched fists—for he surely was sharp to do so—another voice came from the crowd. "And, do you think there are none here?"

She looked about the faces all staring eager for her reply, and recognized some of the townspeople with whom she was previously acquainted. In their eyes she could find no bit of compassion now. She said with sorrow, "I know but few here."

Once again the priest asked, some hope in his voice, "Would there be but one of the elders to pray for you?"

Without acknowledging him, she said, "Nay, first a child, then a young man, then a strong man, before an elder in Christ Jesus." None could escape the implication.

Only Mary and the men closest to her heard any of the dwindling exchanges as the hangman approached the ladder. Her feet fidgeted in anticipation, and she said, "Yea, I am in paradise these several days, and to eternal happiness I shall now enter."

With these, her last words, the hangman pushed her sharp from the ladder as the crowd came to an ominous hush. Her neck snapped with an audible pop, and her body shuddered and twitched from her shoulders to her feet for some moments. When finally her eyes bulged, her mouth fell open and her tongue distended, the hangman picked up the ladder and turned to mount his horse. His orders were to leave her there to hang like a flag for the townspeople to take as a signal. Some said they saw a crown descend upon her martyred head.

And thus, Mistress Mary Dyer departed this life the first woman executed for the crime of being a Quaker.

We talked of this event, Eliakim and John and I, in the stifling heat of summer, when on the sixteenth day of June in 1660, while my sister Rebecka lay sleeping peaceful with her beautiful baby daughter in her arms. In honor of John's mother, they named her Theodate.

11

Goodman William Marston

After the execution of Mistress Dyer, the summer months kept Eliakim and I busy with chores about the house and garden, barn and fields. In the early morning, the sun just risen and the air still carrying a chill, I walked among the chickens, collecting their eggs in a basket hanging from my arm, cooing and talking to them as I imagined I would with my babes.

In the barn, Eliakim milked our cow, brushed our prized saddle horse, and babied the heifer he had received from the Widow Mingay. She was by then Goodwife Hussey, married to our brother John's father those past eighteen months. The heifer was ready to breed, and we looked forward to a new calf by the next spring.

As we prepared to expand our garden to include beets and lettuce, I harvested the carrots and peas. Eliakim nurtured the young bean plants and corn stalks in the fields, and I fostered the cabbage heads, onion and pepper plants in my garden. I bent and stooped without thought, then straightened myself, putting my hands to my still flat and taut belly, and let pass a fear of over-straining myself. I was strong and healthy, and I felt with all my bones this child would be strong and healthy, too. I kept the house, made bread, and experimented with different stews. We were magnificently happy.

Goodman William Marston was another of the original inhabitants of Hampton, a neighbor and a Friend. He arrived from

Newbury in the second summer of 1639, and received a small house lot tract grant for farming in June 1640. He bore the title of Captain though nothing remains in history to record the deeds which should cause this title to be bestowed. From 1650 on, as the court records show, he suffered many times to relinquish his lands for reasons not recorded. He was said to be goodhearted and kind, a Godly man, but his repeated calls to court show he sought only to be treated with fairness and did not shy away from what he believed to be right.

He and his wife, Mary, lived peaceful in Hampton until her passing early in the spring of 1660. It was then he perhaps removed to Salem, and acquainted himself with the local Quaker community. He was in Salem with Southwick and Shattuck and Buffam, and others whose names are remembered only through their many appearances before the court. By the time we began to suffer from our own absences from the Puritan worship, Marston was back in Hampton, with a new wife and a farm not far from our own.

Though advancing in years, Marston was still of good health and strength, and he was of pleasant bearing which drew people to him. Eliakim visited him often, and helped him with his farm and other chores when he could spare the extra time. In return, Goodman Marston often appeared at our door for an evening of friendship and companionship. After inquiring as to our good health, and settling himself at our table with a bowl of hot chicory, he regaled us with stories of Hampton in the earlier years; how he stood by Jeffrey Mingay, Christopher Hussey, and even William Fifield to bring strength and integrity to the town and its growing population.

A carpenter by trade, the town's leaders called on Marston on numerous occasions to construct buildings and other structures to the benefit of the community, including making additions to the home of the teacher, Mr. Dalton, and building a town mill. These tasks he accomplished by the side of Abraham Perkins. So busy was he, and valued for his skill and the quality of his work, the town once extended their contract with him for the mill for a whole year so he may be free from his other commitments to finish this project.

In those days, the local priest, not God, called believers to worship services, and the law required attendance of every person whether or not they pledged their loyalty to the community, or became official members of the church; and whether or not they were inclined to the good health or means of conveyance to get them there. Absenting oneself from the public ordinance was recognized by the priests and the courts as failure to give both the respect to which they felt entitled. As a church and a court offense, a person neglecting this responsibility could be punished by either the priest or the court, or both.

By the spring of 1657, the same people were again and again absenting themselves from worship. Fearful to think other influences were spreading beyond his control, Magistrate William Hawthorne empowered the constables of Salem and other towns nearby to break open houses where they thought persons might be gathering to hear the preaching of the Quakers.

During one of these searches, the constable found William Marston, a man who the town of Hampton respected and relied upon, possessing paper and two books for the teaching of the accursed doctrine. The court fined him ten pounds for the books, which were then taken away, and five pounds for not coming to meetings for the public ordinance of worship, plus another three pounds for his insolence toward the priest. In payment for this last fine, the court seized several barrels of beef.

The priests and magistrates were quick to learn exacting fines and seizing property could be a lucrative business. While the constables of the various towns throughout the colony gathered coin and other treasures with values often reaching one hundred pound or more, the villagers watched as families whose wills were loathe to bend under this pressure became more and more impoverished.

Marston was not to be daunted, and so he protested the ruling against him and sent a petition to the General Court requesting remission of the fine. In his petition, he admitted to transgressing the law of the court but asked for mercy. In the meantime, the good Marston travelled to Salem, bent on delivering provisions to his Friends, Lawrence and Cassandra Southwick who were imprisoned there after one of Hawthorne's raids. For this act, the magistrates sentenced Marston to the cold and damp dungeon prison though it was late October, the weather no longer mild, and he a man of five and sixty years. When the General Court finally granted his petition, and remitted one-third of the fine on condition the remainder should be paid forthwith, he was released from prison and returned to Hampton.

At the end of June in 1660, he came to the house one evening, he said, to tell us of the events of his day in court at Salem when he and several others of his acquaintances presented themselves for being absent yet again from the public ordinance on the Lord's day. By this time, the courts could not keep pace with the demand for their justice. And so men and women found themselves called to answer for absences taken more than a year before. It seemed the courts would search deep into the memories of the priests.

He described for us how he stood beside the wife of Friend Josiah Southwick, with three others, two men and another woman, to be admonished for repeated absences. For this offense, he was fortunate to receive only an admonishment. And fortunate he was otherwise well-respected in the community, for this was not the first time he appeared before the court for such an offense.

I sat rocking by the fire embers, my sewing lay idle in my lap, listening to the men's voices behind me, and I thought about the change in the air around us. Goodman Marston continued to bring more of these stories to us, their whispers floating about my head, competing with the night sounds outside our safe house, and I felt more and more I understood why Father placed us on the edges of the community, keeping us apart somehow.

My marriage to Eliakim gave me courage to hope for somewhere we could belong. But it was the very fact these things were discussed in whispers, in shadows, which continued to separate us from the community. These last months we put faces on, pretending, but with each day those masks became more difficult to keep. With our first child on the horizon, we wondered if this community of fear was what we would want for our children.

There was no need for words between us in answer to this question. As the child within me grew large and overwhelmed my small frame, I suffered no little discomfort. Eliakim was quick to pamper me and many a night as I sat rocking, he would ease my soreness with a cloth soaked in a mixture of our precious vinegar and rosewater wrapped about my swollen feet and ankles. As the strain on my back became intense, he would often hold my arm to steady my walk. He even tried to devise a harness to wrap about my shoulders and neck to balance the weight for me. He more and more often forbade me climb upon a horse, and I travelled into the village less and less often with him for concern the rutted paths and long distances would cause some injury to me or the child. This made for a convenient excuse to begin absenting ourselves from the public worship. No one would comment on these concerns as merely God's way of protecting me and my child. Eliakim made the excuse I could not be left alone in our remote corner of the community without danger, and thus he excused himself also from the weekly ordinance.

12

The Fifth Lash

Constable Fifield had tied me to the post facing east. I thought I felt the slightest trace of spray from the river below, but I could have been mistaken as I also felt the air stop moving. Were my sight not obstructed by the width of the post, I might have seen a beautiful one over one-half house in the distance, much larger than ours but of similar construction. As I stood there contemplating the towns, from Hampton to Newbury to Ipswich along what seemed to me to be as straight a path as the drama in which I now played a central role, I could not imagine the irony in this house someday being connected to the house of my father.

As it was, my face was turned to the north. The road in clear view was well-travelled running east to west, the Main road taking a sharp turn to the right just past Call's house to take the traveller down Town Hill to the village center. I had every reason to expect there would be passersby who would surely slow or even stop to glower at these proceedings. Their haunting whispers carried past my face. I could see in my mind's eye the meeting house at Newbury, the one looming so to me as we rode past—the yard empty, another life, another woman—the one daring me to cross its threshold. Hampton was beyond, the place where I might still have a house, but no longer felt I had a home.

I felt the knots hit then, the force of this thrust greater than those before. Startled, I flinched and squeezed my eyes tight. My shoulders tensed, though my back did not fully wrench. My thoughts were torn from the contrasting comforts of my house. I realized the effect Priest Cotton's presence had on the good Constable, and the result would be as if his arm acted of its own accord, less beholden to the rational thoughts of the man to which it was attached.

Fifield was in Hampton since the start, and, like so many, he wished to live nowhere else for the remainder of this life. He worked hard to gain the trust and confidence of the town's people, and he appeared somewhat skilled at resolving disputes. When called upon, he did not refuse the appointment as constable, but surely gave weight to the penalty of five pounds if he should. Rather, he chose to embrace the duties to which he was appointed. But he was a gentle man. A kind-hearted man. Others managed to escape the responsibilities of the town, including my own father. When William Fifield was appointed to the post of constable in October past, the term being a full year, he took it as his duty and his honor to serve his community. He was not a man taken to frivolous thought, and he may have considered the year could be a short one if his responsibilities extended no further than to collect fines and gather town rates. Or the year might be a very long one if he should be called upon to whip and punish, if he could not procure another to do it for him. But could any man have considered this act for which he would have the authority to carry out should mean whipping a woman?

He first held the whip just weeks after his appointment, when he was commanded by Cotton to punish our Friend Marston, our brother John and my own father for their sympathies to Quakers. Just two months later he was called upon to not only convey the three vagabond women out of his township, but to also whip their bare backs before so doing. I think he must have labored the night before over the thought of it. Would he have considered it ironic if the very first of the acts respecting the powers and duties of a constable—and by the time he was appointed there were twenty-seven such duties—should be to whip and punish; to establish, without question, such a responsibility was necessary to maintain the good order and peacefulness of the town?

I felt my skin rip as easy as a piece of my sewing might between my hands. With the three women walking silent through my head, this one lash felt to me as the thirty lashes laid by Fifield upon their backs.

A vision of the town smithy came to me, and I thought, how curious, until my mouth tasted of fresh snow and damp earth, and the scent of raw iron wafted up into my nose. I knew the sensation immediately. Fresh blood.

Not long before Eliakim and I wed, my father handed me his knife and left me alone to skin a rabbit for my mother to prepare for dinner. My new husband would expect me to do these things for him, he said. My brothers would not be there to do it for me, he said. Would I always be a squeamish child, he said.

I often watched the boys handle this task, or Mother, and even Rebecka, but I was sensitive to the woodland creatures and always begged off the responsibility. I never considered how this simple thing might leave me ill-prepared to be a companion, a wife, and even a mother.

I tied the poor limp creature up by its back feet just above the leg joint and cut a ring about each leg below the string as I was taught. I made a single slice from the ring on each leg to the animal's backside. I hesitated, gathered my strength and my nerve, put the knife down, and started pulling away the hide down from the rings. When I reached the tail bone, I picked up the knife once again and was tender as I cut through it. My success thus far gave me confidence, and my stomach leaped inside me no more. Again, I put the knife down and used my now bloodied fingers to pull the hide from the swaying body. As I worked my way down to the poor creature's front feet, it occurred to me how similar the task was to dressing and undressing my infant siblings, and my silent stomach lurched just then up into my mouth. I stopped and took a step back, the skin now dangling over the head of the harmless creature. I do not know how long I stood there, but I heard my mother just then telling me to pick up the knife and cut the head from the spine. Her voice was soft but firm. With no other choice, I completed the task. I shook as I picked up the knife, cradled the tiny head in my left hand, and positioned the knife above it.

The blade slid across my palm, and I felt nothing until the hot blood met the cool air. I felt the metal, cold and hard, my hand nothing more than a piece of meat. As curious as I was afraid, and sickened by what I failed to do, I brought my hand to my lips and I tasted the lingering metal; I spit the blood and taste of it to the ground. The amount of blood seeping from my hand was alarming. It soaked through three of my mother's best cloths. My father appeared just then and he berated me for being a simple child, no more ready to marry than my sister, Mary, who was but a year old.

The edge of the blade was newly sharpened and so the cut was clean and sleek. The sting lasted well into the next day even as I moved my hand not more than was needed, but I soon found the pain was replaced by a curious throbbing as it healed. I watched, fascinated, as each day the scabs formed until they fell away completely and I was left with a thin rope of a scar from the thumb to the little finger.

Looking out beyond the post, I saw a pained look upon Eliakim's face, the tears welling in his eyes. The brim of his hat was not quite broad enough to cast sufficient shadow and prevent any of the gawkers from seeing him and recognizing the signs. Any man watching surely was thinking of his own wife and daughters secured at home, going about their chores as if nothing so dreadful could touch them.

Perhaps this would not be the event some were expecting. Perhaps those who continued to linger were then imagining themselves tied there in my place. How well could they bear the feel of the whip, the weight of the stares fixed upon their naked bodies? Would they cry out or could they too stay silent? Would they repent under the burden, the shame? Were the women now holding their arms to their own chest, protecting themselves, shameful in their caresses of the inner parts of their arms, checking their unblemished skin?

Would the men's hands tingle at holding a whip? Would it exhilarate them to think of beating a heretic, or a woman? Would they search their minds for an opportunity for the law to sanction such an adventure? When did they last lay an angry hand upon another—man, woman or beast?

I am not a large woman. My back from side to side would not even take Eliakim's two hands, fingers outstretched; from my thin shoulders down to the slope of my buttocks, perhaps only three. There was no room for a score of lashes without them laying one upon another. I thought a cross-stitch sampler might be a more accurate portrayal of my back than Eliakim's image of a landscape. In any case, the words left there would not be meant for encouragement; the picture not intended to please. Hands, both large and tiny, would find gentle exploration of these new regions fascinating and at the same time fearful.

So many before me endured the pain, some more than once. I wondered whether there were some whom I knew, some whom I passed in the meeting house or on the street without the least clue. Many taunted the courts, condemned the law by their actions. Some were no longer alive to torment or be tormented. But I knew of none who died by the whip. I would not die by the whip.

Those first lashes were no measure of the Constable's full strength, or the extent of the passion growing in this task.

I did not think, tied there as I was, having just taken those first lashes, I would suffer more than some indignity, some shame at the public display. I did not think, after the most savage of punishments, they could find more ways to prolong our suffering, more to take from us. I did not think, held there as I was, I might later be a prisoner of my own mind.

But, I would not die.

13

The Courts

In the Autumn, in 1660...

Two months passed after Goodman Marston and others were admonished by the courts for their absence from public worship, and the autumn leaves mimicked the catching fire of growing waywardness. The town of Hampton determined it must be curtailed.

If the behavior of the town's men and women was becoming wanton and reckless, if they could not be coaxed by the court's attempts at leniency, if they deterred not of their own volition from their path to certain destruction, the leaders of the town of Hampton would not punish the good people who struggled hard for the community. But they determined, something must be done. If certain of the men and women of the town were lost, then the town must save the children.

The Reverend Mr. Cotton came to their rescue. On the tenth day of September, the town's leaders voted, on the basis of his great influence, to allow Cotton's offer of catechism to the community families. He would teach the children and prepare them to take their places, as they grew to adulthood, among the congregation.

While Priest Cotton attended to the community's spiritual needs, the quarterly court at Ipswich, on the twenty-fifth day of the same month would attend to their legal needs. Seven of the jurors sitting on the bench banded together to make a motion and an inquiry of the brethren and neighbors of the county concerning several persons and whether they did come to the public meetings according to law to hear the word preached on each and every of the Lord's days.

Michael Shafflen, Phillip Veren, the wife of Josiah Southwick, the wife of Richard Gardner and William Marston were named again, though they had appeared just three months before. Again, they confessed to their absence from the public worship, and again they were admonished. Elisabeth, wife of John Kitchen, for twenty days' absence; Deborah, wife of Robert Buffam, and the wife of John Southwick, for twenty-six days' absence; the wife of Nicholas Phelps and Edward Wharton; Samuel Gaskin, for twenty-four days' absence; Daniel Southwick, for forty days' absence.

Take heart, good reader, these names are many, but you will see them again, and again throughout this tale.

November then found the court again full. Elisabeth Kitchen and the wife of George Gardner were fined for twenty days' absence; Goodwife Buffam for twenty-six days' absence; the wife of Samuel Shattuck for twelve days' absence; and Daniel Southwick for thirty days' absence. The wife of Josiah Southwick, Philip Veren and his wife also, the wives of Nicholas Phelps and Richard Gardner. The wives of John Southwick and George Gardner appeared on this day for two separate summons.

As the court worked through the list of transgressions, some dating back months, some years, the same offenders continued to be called forward, and their punishments piled on. Clearly, the lessons the courts sought to teach would have no effect on these restless and determined people.

While the sun rose on the malevolent of the town, the winter dark forest took hold, and a discontent was harboring about the colony.

14

Joseph

The Twenty-Ninth Day of December, in 1660...

When my time was come, I sent Eliakim to ride out to John Hussey's house to fetch Rebecka and bring her back, her own infant child in her arms. John went on to retrieve our mother who was herself big with child, then her twelfth. While he was gone, I paced the great room of our house, which seemed now small in contrast to my girth. I was glad for the quiet, the bareness, because I did not want Eliakim to see my fear. Mother had come through eleven births, and Rebecka her own just six months before. I was healthy and strong; there was no reason to fear for my own life. The baby kicked with vigor, so there was no reason to fear for his life. This left me with the fear of being a mother, the fear of what lay ahead for Eliakim and me, so accustomed now were we to being alone, together.

Nonsense, a voice in my head said, and this was enough.

By the time all arrived, I had spread the straw, fresh from the barn this morning, and the worn blankets I collected from Mother and Rebecka on the floor, and I was kindling the fire to warm my nest. The pain in my back as I started to rise forced the air from my lungs. "It is time," I said, smiling. I had but one charge, and it was to give myself up to this one task.

The voice in my head then was clearer and I recognized it as God Himself, though this was the first He had spoken to me. *As Mary before you, thou should have many more trials than this ahead.*

"Yea," I replied aloud, "I am ready."

And so, at great length, I being left speechless and without breath, my body slick with sweat, the scene before my eyes fading with my exhaustion, He by His own providence found great mercy in delivering to us a son.

I lay there upon the floor, the fire kept roaring, the straw wet and sticky with my own blood, and I listened to the sharp wind whipping against the sides of the house. Eliakim wrapped us both in a blanket to protect us from the night cold, while my son suckled at my breast.

It was the twenty-ninth day of the tenth month in the year of our Lord, 1660 when we greeted our sweet son, Joseph. A very cold Saturday in December. Yet, as the pain in my loins passed into memory, I thought only neither of us would be fit to travel the distance to the meeting house on the morrow for the privilege of having Reverend Cotton perform the baptism. If our trust in our Puritan leaders was then waning, our belief in the grace of God did not, and so our child, as every other in the community, deserved to receive the sacrament marking his entry into a spiritual life.

15

The Seventh Lash

Anger rose from my feet still planted firm on the ground, through my legs and into my back. The heat like flames licked and scorched and seeped into the crevices of the open stripes, winding their way under the surface of my skin, a harsh force taking hold of the inside, burning to my very core, the blood oozing out then creeping down my bare back in streaks and bolts of fiery lightening. I felt not the warmth of my heart, but the searing outrage of this injury and insult. I ground my hips into the post, and I hugged tighter trying to draw strength from the dead wood. My face was ablaze. I squeezed my eyes shut to block out the sun and the faces, the wind and the whispers, so tight flames burst into the blackness behind my eyes. My cheeks tightened. I clenched my teeth until my jaw ached.

And still I would not give them, any of them, the satisfaction of thinking I would break with so facile an attempt. I forced my attentions inward, and absented myself from what these people may do, what they may think, what they may say. I would accept each stripe until the last, each a reminder, each a sacred revelation. Every thought was to keep myself silent.

To myself I repeated over and over, if thy whip is meant to teach me, if my will is what thou means to have, if thee craves my obedience, then I am determined to stand and demand thou should have it only by force. I will give thee nothing.

Eliakim was made, not by the law, but by his love for me to watch as each lash would land upon my naked back. For every compassionate face of a Friend concealed nearby amongst the throng, he would suffer a score of contemptible stares of the feral. For every sympathetic word uttered close to his ear to prevent people from hearing, he would be subjected to the clamor of vile insults. For every brush of a hand or arm about his shoulder in comfort, he would resist the pushing and crowding of the bestial brawling for a better view.

My rage made me a trapped lioness whose only response was to protect my children. How much longer would Eliakim and John be spared the whip? How great was the fear Rebecka felt for her own children? I might survive this, but could my children?

To the empty faces surrounding me, take from me what thee must. Take from me what little is left. But thee shall not take my family. I relaxed my body and I resettled my mind, and I welcomed the next thrust.

16

Wenlock Christison

Early in March, in 1661…

Governor John Endicott heard the raucous at the back of the room. He looked up from his papers, and a cloud descended over him. His eyes narrowed, and his lips twitched at the disturbance. He heard the voice, recognized it, but could not at first see the man to whom it belonged. From the crowd a man emerged, his arms outstretched and his palms opened, and some said a lightness rose about him, parting the unruly mass and sending gloom back as if by a strong east wind. He stopped and stood for a moment, no man near him, no touch upon him. The horde quieted, but they did not close in among themselves again.

Unmoved, the Governor rose from his seat, planted his feet in a wide stance, and pulled his shoulders back, his hands rested upon his bulging middle. "Fetch him up to the bar," his voice was rough and scratchy. The constable standing by rushed forward and grabbed the arm of Wenlock Christison, the wandering preacher. Not unwilling, Christison lowered his arms, a mere man among men, and walked to the side of his friend, William Leddra, over whose trial Endicott did then preside.

Endicott's flaming eyes bore into Christison, his lip quivered. He was anxious to speak further. He pointed a bony, shaking finger at

Christison and ordered him to pluck his hat in the presence of the court. Rather than comply with this order, Christison responded, "No, I shall not." The crowd behind him began to buzz at the dangerous liberty Christison took by speaking without the court's leave to do so, and further in contradiction to the Governor's order. Leddra remained still, his gaze steady on Endicott and his hands clasped before him; his hat was likewise upon his head.

The voice of Secretary Edward Rawson, who sat to the Governor's right in a seat lower but still above Christison and Leddra, cut through the unpleasant heat rising throughout the room. "Is not your name Wenlock Christison."

Christison and Leddra were both released from prison in Boston late the previous year and banished from the jurisdiction of the Massachusetts Colony upon penalty of death should they return. Leddra, choosing his Friends over his own life, returned to Boston not long after to attend to those who were still imprisoned there. Recognized, he was again arrested, and then placed in irons, chained to a log, and left to suffer the harsh winter within the dungeon of the prison house. He expected to stand before Endicott alone. But news of his arraignment reached the outer regions of the colony where Christison was traveling about the countryside. Christison likewise would not take leave of his charge to ever stand by his Friend, no matter the consequences.

"Yea," Christison speech was quiet for such a large man; his voice betrayed nothing of fear at having acknowledged his name despite the risk.

Endicott was still standing, his eyes fixed on Christison, his attention diverted away from the charges against Leddra. With an exaggerated tone of scorn he asked, "Did I not banish you upon pain of death at our last meeting?" The heat from the fire behind the platform on which the men sat could not have melted the frigid breath escaping Endicott's lips. Christison could not determine whether there were droplets of sweat or tiny icicles adorning Endicott's mustache.

"Yea, thee did so." Emboldened by truth, Christison ably bore his testimony, though he knew he would pay with his own death alongside his Friend.

Said the Governor with such ferocity, "What do you do now here, then?" As if released from some hidden torment, Endicott composed himself once again and sat back upon his seat, placing his hands upon the table and clasping them as if he meant to lead the room in prayer. His thumbs were a nervous twitch, though, playing one upon the other, and his expression begged Christison to engage him again.

Christison, who was undaunted by his adversary's poise, raised his voice. "I have come to warn thee against shedding more innocent blood lest the Lord God call for vengeance to come upon thee."

These threats were not new to Endicott, but they were tiresome. He had matters to attend to and did not have time for whatever nonsense Christison would use to waste it. He turned to his gaoler and bade him take Christison away back to the prison. Not nearly finished with what he wanted to accomplish, Christison struggled against the hands then upon him, calling out, "Murder!" as the gaoler dragged him away. Before the two were quit of the building, Eliphalet Stratton, who was known in the town to make the grave-clothes, leaned toward Christison and, matching his stride, said with no little tenderness, "Oh, your turn is next." He broke off with a cheery cackle.

Christison surprised the man with a smile and said, "The will of the Lord will be done."

But the Governor was to have no peace. Instead of turning his attention back to Leddra, he bade Secretary Rawson call forward four more to stand with him. They approached each in their turn and stood just as Leddra remained there standing, their hats all atop their heads.

When the five were lined up in front of the bar and their hands clasped before them, Deputy-governor Richard Bellingham stood and with cunning called out, "Who is it, Edward Wharton? Surely, this is not Edward Wharton."

Bellingham was known to be a harsh supporter of the law as well as a difficult and garrulous instructor on the topic. He served as deputy governor and governor repeatedly, though not until late in his life was he able to secure his position as governor for consecutive terms.

At this, Leddra broke his silence and turned his gaze upon Bellingham, the merest break of a smile coming to his lips. "Thou shouldest not lie, for thou knows it is Edward Wharton."

The mob, before quieted by Bellingham, once again erupted in a stir. Not one of them cried out it was Leddra who lied, and it was he should be carried out and whipped for it. But Bellingham, who would not be goaded, then looked down upon the men, and called out with a smear upon his face, "I jest, for I know very well who this is before us."

Having enough of the farce laid upon his court, Endicott turned to his Secretary and ordered he should draft a warrant of his commitment and his power. Then he rose, and smoothing his doublet, turned and strode down the steps behind him and out of the room. Rawson proceeded to write an order to the constables of Salem requiring the apprehension of Edward Wharton, a formality since having presented himself he was now already in the hands of the court.

Meanwhile, in the prison, Christison was pushed into a chamber which was no bigger than a saw-pit. Made to either stand or stoop, he had no space sufficient to sit or even move his arms except to raise them above his head. The walls were damp and covered in a slime reeking of decay, and the only opening for light or air came through the narrow frame opening in the door divided by thick bars of iron. The gaoler returned in short order with Leddra and Wharton, and the other three, each put to his own like cell. Having secured them all about the winding corridors of the dungeon, the gaoler tittered just loud enough for all to hear, "Warm and feed yourselves, m'lords, tis a long night ahead."

With just their coats for warmth, and their bellies whimpering after a single bowl of cold watery slop obliged by the gaoler, Leddra,

Christison and Wharton set to conversing within the shadows and silence of the long hours between the gaoler's rounds for the only purpose of seeing if his prisoners still breathed. And so, the men conducted their own meeting and provided comfort to one another.

For two days, the gaoler arrived each morning with a new bowl of undetermined origin, and barely a grumble. On the third day, a Monday, the three men in their cells were surprised when the gaoler greeted them, chipper and talkative, and teasing; two would have the pleasure of fresh air, and if they behaved while out of their cells, they might get a noggin of cool water to wet their throats.

"Now, which will he be who gets to stay here?" the gaoler giggled until he coughed with uncontrollable vigor for some minutes before he finally spit and cleared his throat.

The gaoler slammed the key into the lock on the door of the cell to the right of Christison. The hinges creaked as he pulled the heavy wooden door open and Christison listened to the muffled scuffing of feet as the gaoler pulled Leddra out. From the height of the hole in the door, and the angle at which Christison was positioned, he could only just see the tops of the two men's heads as they trod by and then stopped at the cell on his left. The key again rattled against iron. Wharton spoke, but Christison could not make out the words nor whether they were addressed to provoke the gaoler or soothe the minds of those left behind. When the gaoler departed with his two charges tied and trailing behind him, and all was quiet again, Christison lowered himself and braced his back against the cold wall. The toes of his boots were wedged against the stone blocks, his elbows upon his knees and his hands about this numb ears. There he resumed his conversation with God.

The gaoler led Wharton and Leddra out into a crisp and bright morning. The two men raised an arm to shield their eyes, so long in the keep they had been the sun, though welcomed, blinded them. The gaoler marched them through the lane toward the court, and with each step the two men stood taller, planted their feet more firm, and raised their heads higher to rejoice in the fresh air and light.

Once again they appeared before the Governor, his Deputy by his side and his Secretary at his right hand, all appearing refreshed after their day of meetings and preachings. The two men, ragged and dank from three days and two nights in the dungeon prison, stood before the bar, but with equally refreshed looks about their scruffy faces. The gaoler moved off to the side of the room to await his orders; the men of the court sitting above them were silent and intent upon their papers, content to let the two men stand there in silent wonder.

Edward Wharton broke the stillness. "Friends, what is the cause for having kept me from my habitation and my honest calling, imprisoned me without charge, and treated me thus as an evil-doer?"

His question met with only more silence. The magistrates did not raise their heads from their work for some moments. When Endicott did speak, he still did not raise his eyes as if the response was not worthy of the effort of it. "Your hair is too long." Then a pause, "You are disobedient to the Lord's commandant to honor thy father and mother," and putting a fine edge on his words, "You will not put off your hat before these magistrates." A look of affront appeared on Wharton's face, for he was known throughout the community as anything but a dishonorable man. Endicott's head rose and he fixed his gaze on Wharton's stunned eyes, and punctuated his statement with a raised brow and a sweep of his hand.

"It is not so," said Wharton, anger rising red and steaming into his face. He took a step forward, a momentary lapse in awareness about where he stood. With no lack of self-confidence in his voice, Wharton continued. "I do love and own all magistrates and rulers who are for the punishment of evil-doers, and I praise them well for it—" Endicott interrupted Wharton's speech here.

"Come to the bar." Secretary Rawson rose from his stool, and with swift aplomb caught Wharton in mid-stride.

Disoriented but not deterred from his outburst, Wharton retorted, "Yea, and shall I come onto the bench as well, for we all here know thou hast no evil to charge us justly withal."Rawson calm and seeming to enjoy the events, then turned to Leddra who had been standing as a stone statue throughout the exchange. "You, there, hold up your hand."

Leddra turned his head, chin first, to Rawson, but with eyes on Endicott, and without so much as a signal of any kind, spoke in unison with Wharton. "Nay, for thou hast no evil justly to lay to our charge." Just then the room took on an unnatural chill.

Rawson stood frozen, Endicott and Bellingham above him, speechless. With deliberate movement, Rawson lowered himself to the stool again, shuffled about the papers before him, and without again raising his eyes to Wharton, said, "Edward Wharton, hear your sentence of banishment."

Wharton realized this decision was forewarned and the court would not entertain any testimony to support him on the matter. He replied in a soft voice, but with all the vehemence he could muster. "Have a care for what thou dost; for if thou shall murder me, my blood and the blood of those before me will lie heavy upon thine heads."

Rawson repeated the sentence, and continued, "You are upon pain of death if you should not depart this jurisdiction within ten days hence."

This was an extraordinarily cruel and severe punishment for a man with too long hair and a hat, but Wharton received the message loud and clear. For want of some right of testimony, and with as much restraint and reverence as he could muster, he dared to speak again. "I am but a single man with business obligations. I beg the court's indulgence to complete my dealings, and then, if thou should still mean to murder me, I am thine."

Endicott leaned down to confer with Rawson in hushed tones, with Wharton and Leddra watching on in muted silence. After some moments, Endicott straightened himself up, and taking the time to smooth his doublet once again, lifted his bearded chin and his eyes above the heads of the all those who occupied the room. "If we should give this man a hundred days more, it would change nothing."

Wharton, knowing this to be untrue, cried out with much more volume to his voice than he intended. "Nay, I will not go." Lowering his tone, he repeated his threat against the court should his blood be spilt at their hands.

At this, Rawson called forth the gaoler who took hold of Wharton's arm, turning him about and marching him through the crowd to the door. Before going, Wharton caught sight of the Secretary as he picked up the Book of Records laid upon the table before him. Understanding what was to come, Wharton raised his voice and continued to speak to the men closing in around him, giving his testimony to all who would listen, cautioning against any one of them being driven in like manner from his own honest calling, forced out like an evil-doer, for nothing more than hair and hat.

Rawson read from the pages how Wharton did accompany William Robinson and Marmaduke Stevenson, and coveted their memories still though they were dead these seventeen months. Wharton stopped at the door, pulled his arm free of the gaoler's grip and turned back to the magistrates. "What matters of my memories, I have the blood-furrows thee ploughed in my back to show for it already, though thee had no more law for it then than thou dost now."

All three men sitting on the bench realized Wharton unwittingly thwarted the court from its intentions to use him against the other man still standing by, silent. Bellingham stood so hot, intent on regaining control and recapturing the previous mood of the room, the legs of his chair caught on some nail or loose board and near toppled him backwards. He looked at Wharton, still standing by the door with the gaoler near upon his elbow and the throng loose about him, and murmured, "Wharton, depart this court and take your banishment before I order you whipped and returned to prison."

Edward Wharton turned his back to the court and walked out, followed by the gaoler. From outside, they both could hear a terrific pitch grow inside the building.

Inside, the men sat again comfortable in their chairs, and Rawson upon his stool with his papers composed and his quill once again in his hand as he prepared to continue with his duties. It took some minutes before the horde of spectators quieted once again. But the air was still charged and Wharton's words still heavy around them all. Endicott could not, would not, permit those words to take on any power here, not in his court.

"Mr. Rawson, if you please. Continue with the next order of business."

And so, on went Rawson who remained seated, his shoulders somewhat dropped from their previous height, his voice low but with his composure returned, until the gaoler again appeared. Then, he said simply, "William Leddra, you are sentenced to death on the fourteenth day of the first month, this being March, in the year of our Lord, 1661."

Without hesitation in his stride, the gaoler came forward and laid his hand upon Leddra's arm. Leddra spoke not a word, for there was nothing he could add, but walked out of the room with all eyes upon him. In three days time, he would be the fourth whose blood was to stain the hands of the colony.

17

Eleven Lashes

Blood mixed with sweat rose with the temperature in my body, and rolled down my back. Dirt wafted up from the feet still dancing around me. The burden of my body pulled me down; the only thing holding me up were the splinters gripping my breast and belly and arms. My mind went blank. I felt nothing. I smelled nothing. My head filled with the sounds of rushing water, and buzzing bees, and howling winds.

When my anger subsided, I was left with panic. What have I done. How did I think I could bring shame to my family without having a price to pay. I would not blame Eliakim then if he turned and, with John by his side, raised themselves back onto the cart and pointed the old plow horse towards home to leave me there to suffer my indignities alone. Where was my God while I was there tied to a post?

Were these men who judged me so wrong? Surely they followed their hearts and minds, their teachings, their want to protect the good people who wanted nothing more than to harvest their crops and feed their families, and pray they would be met at the golden gates when their earthly lives were at an end. Who was I but a woman of small means and small stature? Why should I complain when others did but take their punishments and pray for redemption?

How could I face my children after this, my folly, my own profanity and selfishness? I should never have thought myself strong enough or deserving enough. Would not my children, and my children's children reap what I had sown there? Would not my example visit upon them time and time again as they must make their own way through this terrible life?

I lost count of the lashes. Through the rushing water, the swarming bees, the winds called my name forth, I did not hear the whistle or the crack or the spit. But I did feel my body writhe and twist as lash upon lash tore at my back, the rough splinters tore at my front. It was as if I were being lashed by two men, alternating a stripe to my shoulders, my spine, my ribs and sides, my buttocks with a companion stripe to my neck, my arms, my breast and belly. Were these men not practiced enough to hit their mark with any consistency?

Humiliation numbed me to the physical pain and I thanked God for it at least. But my thanks were met with silence. Did even God have his limits? Could I be so far gone I would not find my way back, find a path to return me to His graces?

Blackness.

18

Governor John Endicott

"Leddra." Wenlock Christison heard the call as if coming to him from out of a fog surrounding him. He knew the voice, but could not place it just then. "Leddra, do you yet breathe?"

Christison tried to move his head too quick, turn to the sound, but pain shot through his back to his neck and then exploded into his head. Slower, he lifted his head from his shoulder where it had fallen and locked there as he slept. He tried to move his shoulders, but they felt as if bolted to the wall behind him. His mind woke, and he returned from the fog where he had escaped in his dreams to the cold, hard prison. He was wedged between the walls. Moving the lower part of his back away, his hips screamed in agony and his knees cracked as he worked at shifting them to stand. How many hours, how many days? He kicked the hard stone wall with his one foot then the other to wake the blood within them.

"Your day has come," the gaoler called. It was the fourteenth day of March, a Thursday.

William Leddra was returned to the dungeon three days before. Edward Wharton was not with him, and the other three were removed without ceremony or explanation. Leddra told him of the verdicts of his own death and of Wharton's banishment, and the two men prayed together until their voices gave way to mere croaks of unmoving air. Christison listened now as the gaoler opened the cell door, the key scraped against the rust accumulated in the old strong lock, then the screeching of the iron latch, and then rustling. Feet dragging across the wet cobblestone floor. Did Leddra still breathe? Was he not able to stand or walk of his own will? Finally, Christison and the gaoler heard a sort of grunting and then a whisper.

"Unhand me, I am a man and I will have no other carry me."

Christison smiled, and breathed easier. His lips moved, "Friend, God be with thee." Then his head fell back against the wet and cold wall and he slept once more.

Deep in the recesses of his uneasy slumber, Christison heard the scraping of metal on metal once again. There, through the murk a light shone behind the head of his Friend. Leddra held out his hand and Christison felt the words he was reciting, words which did not reach Christison's ears...

The sweet influences of the Morning Star, like a flood distilling into my innocent habitation, hath filled me with the joy of God in the beauty of holiness, that my spirit is, as if it did not inhabit a tabernacle of clay...

and the two men walked out of the house, their arms locked together, their heads held high to receive the cool breeze and refreshing sunlight, their wariness abandoned, their voices in harmony, their eyes closed to the ugliness they left behind.

When Christison opened his eyes, expecting the beloved faces of his friends and his wife and children around him, he saw instead the rancid little gaoler beside him, clutching at his arm and dragging him out of the cell and to his feet. The gaoler spoke no words. To what purpose? He was the only one in the prison. When the gaoler saw his prisoner was alert, and breathing, he bleated, "I am to bring ye to the court again." Christison smelled the sour ale on the man's breath, and he looked at his drooping eyes, red and bloodshot and gazing off into nothingness. The man was several heads shorter, even as Christison unhinged his knees and ankles and pulled himself up to a stoop, and he sported a ragged beard and unkempt hair, both long and matted with dirt and food specks; and his clothes were little more than tatters, adding a rotting stench to the mix.

Christison nodded his understanding. There was, apparently, no more profit in being the gaoler than the gaoled.

The two emerged from the house, by design, to the sound of bells tolling to the execution of William Leddra. Christison wondered where Wharton was just then, and prayed he was yet unharmed. In the distance between the prison and the court, with the sound of justice accompanying him, the magistrates expected Christison would be cooled and brought under, and would thus be eager to preserve his life if he could do nothing for his Friend. But he would not grieve their underestimation of his strength and conviction. So, despite their thinly veiled machinations, Christison marveled at the beauty of the world around him, the fresh air invigorated his mind, and the walk warmed and loosened his body. Leddra walked beside him, still speaking those lovely words only Christison could hear.

Behind the bar, Governor John Endicott and his deputy Richard Bellingham once again looked down upon Christison, with Secretary Edward Rawson curiously silent beside them. Christison, though, was at ease.

Without preamble, Endicott stated as a matter of fact, "Unless you would renounce your religion, you shall surely die."

Not at all daunted or terrified by this, as the magistrates would wish, Christison firm and without reservation replied, "Nay, I will not change my religion even if it should save my life. Neither shall I deny my Master. If I am to lose my life for the sake of Christ and the preaching of His gospel, only then shall I be saved."

The men sitting above him looked from one to another in dismay. Once again, this man dared to trifle with the court with his noble valour for truth.

Not to be goaded into action, whether by right or might, Endicott turned away, leaned toward his deputy, and spoke a few words which Christison could not hear. Turning back to the irritant standing before him, as if Christison were nothing more than a thistle trapped inside the magistrate's breeches, Endicott flicked his fingers away as a signal for the gaoler to return the prisoner back to the piss hole from which he had been drug, "Where you shall surely rot before your trial is set for the next term of the court, two months hence."

When the gaoler departed with his charge locked in his grip, and several minutes of silence throughout the court had elapsed, Endicott slammed his fists upon the table and strode from the building in an implacable rage.

For two days, the Governor absented himself. He paced a rut in the fine carpet in his drawing room. He stood before the night fires, gazing into the flames. He ate nothing. He slept little and only sitting in the hard chair behind his desk. He spoke to no one, and no one dared to interrupt his contemplation. He knew what he had done when he sentenced Leddra to his death—with the King's letter banning executions in front of him.

Although King Charles II was not yet crowned, his restoration to the throne took place nearly a year before when the Convention Parliament in London assembled and proclaimed him king with invitation for him to return from his exile to England. Charles promised, as a lenient and tolerant regent, to pardon his opponents and enemies, and above all to work in cooperation with Parliament.

By the King's command, Endicott should have stayed the sentence. He chose not to. He reasoned to himself he had only just received the letter, and lacked proper opportunity to consider it, to present it to the General Court, or to draft a new law. But for two days, Endicott's mind worked over the matter, replayed the earlier debates with his deputies. Their charter was due for renewal, and they knew accusations were starting to reach the ears of the King. Accusations about their treatment of these people called *Quakers*. The King might easily use these accusations as an excuse to end the charter, and thus end the privileges they enjoyed under the protection of the Crown but far enough removed so as to not be under his watchful eyes.

Endicott returned to the court, resolved to make their excuses, at least until the magistrates of the colony could be fairly heard in London. When he completed his dictation to Secretary Rawson, he snatched the paper from the table, and reading to himself he once again became rankled. What business was it of the King's how they treated these heretics? The King was not here; the King could not see how these creatures threatened the good order he and the other leaders of the community were so diligent to instill for near on thirty years.

The paper rolled and squeezed tight in his fist, Endicott took his leave of the court once more and went out into the street to observe the tenor of the village. He found there not only those who panted with eagerness for the blood of the innocent, but also those who were sorely troubled by its shedding. He walked until nightfall, praying upon the very laws he had sworn to uphold. He considered how they were not only ineffectual at arresting the obnoxious doctrines portended by these Quakers, but they were rather more efficient at spreading them to shock and convert the attitudes away from unnecessary harshness. Vowing to put the matter to rest, and send the letter to the King on the next ship, he returned home and, finally, slept.

As it happened, a ship arrived in port the next day, bringing Endicott's agents from their sojourn to England. But the news was not good. They were dispatched months before to push some preventative measures, measures requiring the colonists to make their appeals only to the Crown. The magistrates reasoned should the apostates be forced to pursue their cause only before the King himself, then they, the magistrates, were justified in banishing them from the colony to do so. Not only were the Governor's agents too late in bringing their case to the King, but Endicott realized his response to the King's earlier letter was also too late. Instead of bringing him an acquiescence, the agents handed Endicott the King's order to repeal the very laws which the colony relied upon to maintain order.

After just sixteen days more locked in the depths of the prison, in the dismalness and cold with no relief, Endicott ordered the gaoler to bring Christison again to the bar. Christison stood before the Governor, his hair yet more matted, his scraggle of a beard covering his cheeks and chin another two inches onto his chest, his coat heavy with dirt and prison stench. Yet, beneath the crumpled hat pulled down secure upon his head, his face showed no sign of being disaffected by those who sat before him, in their mock position above him.

This time, Governor Endicott spoke with little more than mild irritation, but would not extend his gaze toward the prisoner. The others beside him attended stiffly to their thoughts, shuffled papers before them, scratched notes with their quills, or just set upon picking invisible lint from their coats. "What have you to say for yourself? Why should you not die for your crimes?"

Christison raised his eyes to meet his accuser and replied with quiet strength and conviction, "I have done nothing worthy of death, for if I had, I should surely refuse not to die." He continued to reflect upon the men before him with pity.

After some moments, Endicott looked up finally to meet Christison's own gaze. "You have come in among us in rebellion," the words spat from between his pursed lips, "which is as the sin of witchcraft, and ought yet to be punished."

Witchcraft was a grievous sin, but not one for which Christison was before accused. He received this charge as one of baseless desperation. Endicott would need to be more specific than this. "By what law will thee put me to death."

Before Endicott could answer, someone of the jury spoke. "We have a law, and by our law you ought to die." Endicott turned to the jury, a look of uncertainty as to which of the men spoke, but his irritation clear to anyone who should be so presumptuous. The men sitting beside him knew of the King's order of repeal, and yet some of them would not accept it. This day was in rapid spiral toward a tornado of hot air.

Did they think they could debate him so? Christison thought. He looked from one to another of the men upon the jury until each of them squirmed on their bench or turned away, then returned his eyes to stare upon the Governor who sat in silence.

"So said the Jews of Christ," Christison responded with calm and self-assurance, "We have a law, and by our law he ought to die." The irony of it did not escape him.

Christison asked after a brief quell, "Who empowered thee to make the law?" If Endicott wished this to become a game of chess, then Christison meant to make the first move and force his accuser to reveal himself for the law of God or the law of Man.

Endicott still remained silent and reflected with care on his next words. And, again, those on the jury, heated by the exchange and impatient by the Governor's dullness, called out, "We have a patent, and *we* are the patentees. Judge whether we have not the power to make the law."

Christison knew he had positioned himself correctly, and he knew Endicott had lost control of his court. Without leave to speak, Christison commanded, "How, then, do thee have the power to make laws which impugn the laws of England?" The very words emboldened him and his voice boomed. *Check.*

Endicott opened his mouth but only a whispered, "Nay," escaped before Christison charged onward with his attack. "Thou are gone beyond thy bounds, and by this thee forfeits thy patent." He took in air sufficient to fill his lungs. "Are thou subjects to the King, yea or nay? Own thou are, and in thou petition to him he will protect thou." Christison took for assent the silence there upon the bench. "As am I." He paused for the effect of the strike to come. "If the King does not know thou hearts, as surely God knows them, he would see they are as rotten to him as they are to God."

Endicott stopped listening. The court was muted, all faces turned to the Governor, eyes begging for his response to this harangue. Christison stood tall, his shoulders raised and his face flushed. He was not yet finished. "As thee and I are both subjects to the King, I demand to be tried by the laws of England." At the word, *demand*, Endicott returned his attentions to the proceedings before him, but not in time to stop those on the court from once again speaking for him.

"You shall be tried by this bench and jury." Endicott, puppet though he was, would not have underestimated Christison so.

"It is not the law, but you confuse it for the manner of it," Christison scoffed. "If thee,"—and this he directed at Endicott—"are as good as your word, then thee must set me at my liberty for I know of no law in England for the hanging of Quakers." In fact, Christison knew the General Court repealed the laws against the Quakers not even three weeks before.

There it was. The truth was out for all in the room to hear. *Mate.*

Endicott could only hope to salvage his dignity from this point. "There is a law to hang Jesuits."

At this, Christison bellowed for he knew his fate was sealed no matter the outcome of this discourse. "If thee sends me to my death, it is surely not because I claim the name of *Jesuit.*" He threw his shoulders back, took in another lung-full of dead air from the room, and with a quiet roar declared, "I am a Quaker. I appeal to the laws of my nation."

The men of the jury could not remain still. "You are in *our* hands, and *you* have broken our laws, and we will try *you.*"

The Governor sat back upon his chair, placed his hands before him on the table with the fingertips of one hand tapping upon those of the other, and turned his head and locked his eyes upon a fly flitting about the papers strewn before him. He heard Christison's voice, but heard none of the words his opponent spoke.

"Thy will is the law, and what thee has the power to do, thee will do." Turning his eyes to seek out each man independently, Chrisitson continued, "Take heed what thee shall do, for if thee swear by the living God, then thee must a just verdict give, according only to the evidence. If what I have done does not deserve death, then keep thou hands from innocent blood."

Enough was enough. Endicott picked up a paper from the stack before him and began to read, in a voice so shallow Christison thought he was reading for himself, but then he shook the paper as if to scold a naughty child standing before him awaiting his punishment for some meaningless act.

"Edward Wharton sees fit to send a letter to this very court."

Casting his eyes carefully across the room, and to remind the magistrates, the jury and the louts about the room, Endicott commanded just a fortnight ago this man, Wharton, stood before him and was banished on pain of death. He then pulled the paper in close to his face, and he squinted his eyes thus causing his nose to pinch and his brow to converge in the center of his forehead. "*Whereas you banished me on pain of death, I am yet at home, and I therefore propose you*"—and here Endicott looked up and in a scornful way only a magistrate seems to possess, raised his voice and shouted to the room—"*take off your wicked sentence so I might go about my business and occasions outside of your jurisdiction.*" He then flung the paper into the air and watched it float to the ground and come to rest before Christison's feet.

Endicott waved his hand at the men sitting on the jury. At their signal, they turned about to face one another for the deliberation, bowing their heads and speaking in whispered tones. Christison had no interest in reading the moods upon their faces or the positions of their bodies, or even the flaying movement of their arms. Neither did he pay any mind to those who would turn from the group to look upon him as he stood there stone still. He knew the verdict, perhaps before they could.

Some moments passed before, impatient for what must surely be a simple matter, Endicott huffed, then griped, "What say you?" To his agitation, the vote was not unanimous for death, but rather Christison could see there upon the faces of some his innocence and steadfastness did indeed prevail in dividing them and compelling some to discharge him from these proceedings.

The Governor's face filled with rage, and Christison thought the devil before him would begin to smoke and blaze. But as he spoke, the skin of his face verily melted away. "I could find it in my heart to return to my home just now and be done with this business."

Seizing the moment, Christison counseled the Governor, "Go to thy home now rather than stay, for thee are about a bloody piece of work if thee stays here." It was as if only the two men remained in the room, so intent upon one another were they.

"Go to it, again," Endicott ordered the jury without diverting his eyes, "and this time be sure and swift."

Christison prayed. Endicott felt the beat of his heart against his chest, counting one… two… ten… five and twenty… five score… six hundreds and thirty… whittling away the time until the foreman of the jury rose with trepidation, his eyes cast down upon his hands clasped before him.

"Well, what say you?" the Governor's words bore a hole through the jury foreman. His heart pounded, pounded harder against him. "Speak," he screamed. Then, the jury unleashed a confused and uncertain torrent of words, none of which Endicott could comprehend having seen only there was still no agreement on the verdict. Endicott began to sway upon his pulpit as a man who has taken overmuch drink. "I thank God I should not fear giving judgment." With this, the side of Endicott's mouth twitched upward, his eyes clouded and the man welcomed the countenance of a sinister and evil force.

"Then hearken to your sentence," Christison challenged.

Endicott exhaled the breath he had been holding throughout this entire exchange, and proclaimed, "You will be returned to the place from whence you came, and from there you will be taken to the place of your execution where you will be hanged until you be dead, *dead, Dead!* on the thirteenth day of June next."

Christison maintained his stance, his eyes fixed on Endicott, as the gaoler came and took hold of his arm to lead him away. Before turning, Christison rallied before the magistrates, "The will of the Lord be done, in whose will I come amongst thee, and in His counsel I stand, feeling His eternal power, which will uphold me until the last gasp; I do not question it." But he did not stop there. In a frenzy he had not thus far shown, "Be it known unto you all if you have the power to end my life, then I do believe thou shall take not one more Quaker life—for the last man thou puts to death, here are five come in his wake. Thou may know torment upon torment, which is thine portion." Then, for his final words, he raised his eyes and his fist, "For there is no peace to the wicked, saith *my* God.

Wenlock Christison then strode toward the door, leaving the gaoler behind, amidst a sea of naked fear of prophesy in the crowd's stunned faces.

Endicott recovered his composure and turned his attention to the gaoler, and with a look of scorn equal to what was visited upon Christison, ordered, "Take him away."

19

The Cart and Whip Act

This Court, being desirous to try all meanes, with as much lenity as may consist with our safety, to prevent the intrusions of the Quakers, who, besides their absurd and blasphemous doctrine, doe like rogues and vagabonds come in upon us, and have not bin restrained by the lawes already provided, have ordered that every such vagabond Quaker found within any part of this jurisdiction shall be apprehended by any person or persons, or by the constable of the town wherein he or she is taken, and by the constable, or in his absence by any other person or persons, conveyed before the next magistrate of that shire wherein they are taken, or Comissioner invested with magistrattigall power, and being by the said magistrate or magistrates, commissioner or comissioners, adjudged to be a wandering Quaker, viz., one that hat not any dwelling or orderly allowance as an inhabitant of this jurisdiction and not giving civill respect by the usual gestures thereof....

Wednesday, the Twenty-Second Day of May, in 1661...

The foe now had a name.

The legislature called it the Cart and Whip Act, and they said it was designed to be more effective against the growing tide of miscreant distractors from the common worship and the depraved behavior which kept the good folk from showing due respect to the exalted leaders and their follower masses. While the power of the law would be more effective, the result was thought to be not so obnoxious to the Home Government.

Under this new law, one might still remain free as a Quaker, confessed or no, as long as one lived in the jurisdiction, had a home and a family, and was recognized for their contributions to the community. One might still remain free as a Quaker as long as one exhibited the usual gestures of respect to the civil authorities and the townspeople. We knew the simplest of these rules, like a man must remove his hat in the presence of his neighbor, or take care gatherings at one's home did not grow too large, especially if the sun was fading into night. A woman should not cast her eyes direct on a man or speak out, but defer to her husband to speak for them both according to the tenets of the church's teaching.

Around our table, by the flicker of the candle, we wondered had it been so long since the fathers and, for some, themselves and their brothers were branded as dissenters and non-conformists. Could they not recall the persecution which drove them to this colony in the first place? Or was it their own shame at turning their backs on they who came before to seek out ever more heinous activity in the name of protection. What were they hiding, or more rightly, from what were they hiding?

We heard the Governor called for Christison three times more and subjected him to the same discourse as each of the times before. And each time he refused to give in to the Governor's demands to renounce his Quakerism, and each time he welcomed the Governor's scornful response with good cheer. Each time he allowed the gaoler to march him back to the prison.

On the morning of Wednesday, the twelfth day of June, the gaoler arrived and cackled through the silence of the prison. "Christison, do you still breathe?" For ninety days the gaoler entered the dungeon with the same morbid jest, followed by the clanking of the heavy iron keys and the grunt accompanying the effort to turn the rusted lock. For ninety days Christison shifted his position. Since his last appearance before the court, he gave up greeting the man at full stand. He now could only maneuver to a crouch, or a bent stand, or he could lean some part of his body against the wet and slime-covered walls for the width of the cell was no more than length of two of his forearms, plus perhaps a shaftment between the tips of his outstretched thumb and little finger. His shoulders were now tilted, his knees bent, his hands twisted from the pain multiplying daily in his joints and the weakness from lack of sustaining nourishment and sunlight. So, when the gaoler came whistling to the door of his cell, Christison merely turned his head, an ear toward the door struggling to hear of whatever purpose the gaoler contrived to visit upon him.

The gaoler struggled to pull open the heavy door, picked up the pewter dish of slop and threw it at Christison's feet. Christison made no move to catch the falling object, instead he watched as it hit the floor with a clank, spilling and splashing the jelled and greasy contents on his fetid boots. A moldy crust of bread flew out and came to rest on the decaying mounds of past meals and his own waste; he had long past lost any sense of smell.

Seeing he had Christison's attention, the gaoler bent his head toward his prisoner and cackled once more, "Know what day it be?" The prisoner preacher would not be goaded so easily, and he stood silent, trying to focus his eyes.

"Well," the gaoler said, the tenor of his voice changed from its usual mockery. But, there he stopped. Christison had also long since lost any ability to distinguish the man's moods by the tone in his voice, but could only detect the difference in the man taken by drink instead of the man sober. "Guv'nor passed a new law."

Christison saw the disappointment obscure the man's face.

"Cart and Whip Act," the gaoler spat the words at him. Even the dim man before Christison did not need further explanation to know the intent of this new law.

The gaoler lifted his meager torch to peer into Christison's eyes for some reaction, but finding none, he stepped back and closed the wooden door once again. Before turning to leave, though, he spoke the most words strung together Christison had thus far heard from the man in these ninety days. "Do ye s'pose we'll have us a parade with the seven and twenty Quakers joining ye at the cart's tail?"

Then he was gone.

We did not for one bell of the clock think the colony magistrates would be content to only focus their attentions on outsiders such Wenlock Christison, nor could we escape notice merely by avoiding situations which might alert them to our beliefs. What of Eliakim's refusal to take the freeman's oath, or calling out of some priest or magistrate who would inflict a cruel punishment on a bent and twisted woman? What of my offering of a noggin of milk to relieve in some small way someone's suffering? What of my intrusion where I was not invited?

This new law only gave magistrates much latitude to levy their punishment as they wished—short of death.

20

Twelve Lashes

From out of the blackness, the constable strode toward me. Could he know of the guilt taking hold, how I questioned every one of my actions? Could he know I searched my heart and found not him or the other men, but myself wanting? Could he know I felt myself now lost and without hope? Was I the fearful child, and he the trapped animal. Would he mean to exploit my despair and use it as an excuse? All these questions sped through my mind from the moment the fingers of leather left my back and dragged me into the blackness, until I heard his step, his foot twist in the dirt as he raised his arm, and then thrust himself forward with all his might to release the whip again. His most vicious strike yet. The conflagration upon my back seared the already damaged skin. The rage in him thrust the lengths of raw leather deeper into the caverns left by the lashes before it, crossing them and pulling skin away at the same time. The blood flowed as a river not yet charted, turning from barriers to its straight path, twisting its way down my back.

I told myself I deserved this, and worse, for the things I had done.

In my anguish, my vow of silence was all but forgotten. I no longer had the energy to fight, though I desired most of all to hold my pain and my suffering to myself, to burden no one but myself. Instead, the cry escaping my throat was dry and harsh. The sound coming to my ears was so full of agony I felt the betrayal as well as heard it. I could not stop. For some seconds, or it could have been minutes or hours for all I could distinguish time, the wail filled the space around me. A wounded animal, calling out into the night for relief and finding none. Beyond it all was a dead silence I feared more than the whip once more against my back, and so I kept the scream for as long as the breath in me would allow.

When finally I stopped, spent, I felt one leg was wrapped around the pole, tangled in my skirt, clutching it. I wanted to burrow my way into the wood, escape my surroundings, and myself. My back arched away, my hands strained tight against the pole. My head fell back, my neck pulling me away. My hair blew in the breeze behind me. My mouth was still open, but no sound expired. I opened my eyes and searched the blue sky above me, empty of clouds, empty of birds. Empty.

As I made to return to myself, and relax my grip on the post, I lowered my cheek to my shoulder, my forehead scraping against the rough wood, my ears awoke to the sounds of the constable behind me. The leather thongs dragging along the ground. The chafe of wool to leather. The scuffle of boots in the dirt as he positioned himself for the next strike. His words were too muffled to hear, to understand. I thought, he meant them only for his own comfort or, more likely, his own abasement. Could it be he now took my punishment as his own? Was each strike against me, a strike to his own back? Would he ask to take the whip on himself for his part in this crime? Must he now abandon all reason and allow the lash to be ever more ferocious, the punishment doubled now on his account? I thought to draw him to me, let him enter my misery, my guilt, and there we could stand together, side-by-side.

Eliakim was still there. John was still there. The wrack, the remnant of destruction was fixed upon their faces. Would their expressions freeze thus, never to thaw into the smiles I knew so well? No longer concerned for townspeople around them, or whether they would be recognized or judged, they came closer. The crowd moved away from them to make an opened space. Their presence there was all that mattered. Their courage was my courage.

21

Wenlock Christison

But before the Day appointed for his Execution, an Order of Court (probably occasioned by some Intelligence from London, of Complaints against them) was issued for the Enlargement of him and twenty seven others then in Prison for the same Testimony.

Wednesday, the Twelfth Day of June, in 1661…

Christison dozed in and out of a dreamless blank expanse of time. He heard the footstep. Had the gaoler just been here, tormenting him with something about a parade, or had it been days, or months, or years ago? He heard the cursing. He heard the clanking of the lock. He heard a fist against the hard, thick wood of the door between them and him. But it was distant, and so he was not sure it was real. Were there people out there, or were they just crowding in his head?

The heavy door swung open. Christison lifted his chin from his chest, and turned his stiff neck toward a lantern hanging from a man's hand. The light blinded him and he tried to raise his hand to shield his eyes, but it would not move. Without preamble, a voice said, "We are ordered by the court to make you acquainted with the new law. You are to be sent out of the jurisdiction." The voice seemed familiar, something he knew he should remember, but there was no light and he long since stopped caring who came to the door, who delivered a bowl of slop or a crust of bread, who called out in the dark. "But if you return, then you will be whipped from town to town."

Did he hear the words correctly? He thought he heard *sent*, *out*, *whipped*, when he should hear *death*. Deprived for so long without sight or the normal sounds, a cry was not a cry; stillness was filled with the unimaginable. His mouth was dry and his throat closed when he tried to speak. How long since he had spoken? He opened his mouth, stretched his jaw from side to side, tried to swallow but there was nothing. He pushed the air out from his chest, a grunt and then a cough. Some undigested slop came up wet.

"How long?" he asked, losing energy for any other words. His eyes were starting to adjust and he could make out a perplexed look on the face of the man closest to him.

He tried again. "How long have I been…" But, again, he could not go further.

The man continued to look at him without expression, or perhaps it was impatience, Christison could not distinguish his features in the dim lantern light, in the blur dominating his sight.

No one standing there in the dark and cold of the dungeon could remember that ninety days and ninety nights had passed.

The gaoler was not there, but Christison's mind was awaking to realize it had only been minutes or hours since their last exchange. The man before him stood silent and Christison began to wonder was he there alone, speaking only to himself. Taking as much air into his lungs as he dared, "What means this. Have you a new test? A new law?"

Yea. And still Christison wondered if these men before him were nothing more than shadows and ghosts.

Weary of the trickery, he said, "You have deceived most people." He found the sound of his voice, while his throat was warming to the movement, course and rasping like the prison door lock.

A perplexed look came to the closest man's eyes. The others behind him began to shuffle and murmur. Their faces were empty, their voices were hollow.

Christison continued. "They did think the gallows were the last weapon. But, thou have more." It was a statement, not a question.

Who is they? these empty faces asked, their confusion replaced by fear for they knew exactly who he meant and they wished not to have those ghosts called to stand in judgement before them. Christison just stared. Finally the man closest to him replied, "Yea."

Becoming more alert, Christison spied a paper in the man's other hand hanging limp against the side of his leg. "Read it," he commanded. And when the man's voice was once again silent, Christison raised his head and turned his eyes to his. "Thou law was a good and wholesome law, thy said. Made for peace, thy said, and the safeguard of thine country. Are thou hands now become weak?"

Several men stepped aside without a word, opening a path for Christison.

Seven and twenty others followed Christison out of the prison. The magistrates, to make their point, held two of them back and whipped them with twenty cruel stripes through the town of Boston. With Christison and the others walking close behind them, and the soldiers who kept their swords tight to their hips, every one of the parade called out the truth with every step until they were driven out of the jurisdiction and into the wilderness.

22

Josiah Southwick

Monday, the Eighth Day of July, in 1661…

Josiah Southwick returned from old England just behind the change in the law. After his wife fed him, and he slept in his own bed for the first time in months, he listened intent on his wife's words as she recounted the many times she appeared before the court. The last being just a fortnight before. All to answer for her absences from the public worship. He held her tight, and she assured him if he not taken his banishment all the way across the water, they would not be laughing now at the absurdity of the courts continuous begging for their presence.

They talked deep into the night, about England and the would be King. They talked about the new law and what it meant for them and their Friends. They talked about Nicholas Phelps who had returned with Josiah on the ship; in fact the reason they returned at all knowing there was still peril for them if they did.

Nicholas' health was failing, his constitution was not strong and the respite in England did not help. The passage further imperiled his life, but he wanted to return home. He wanted to see his wife before he died, and he wanted to be buried in the colonies, despite all the suffering inflicted on him.

It was some days before the Southwicks received word of Nicholas

Phelps' death, and only then did Josiah determine to leave his home in Salem and manfully march himself with his customary frankness before the authorities to announce his return.

Without the fanfare Southwick expected, the agents of the court apprehended him and, true to the new law, tied him to the cart's tail and whipped him through Boston, then Roxbury and finally at Dedham, then carrying him some fifteen miles to the wilderness where they turned him out.

But Josiah was bold, and he was fearless, and perhaps he was reckless. Straight back to Salem he did walk through the night, until the next morning when he once again appeared to the authorities and informed them he cared no more for what they could do to him than for a feather blown in the air. Agitated, they clapt him up and threw him into the house of correction where they kept him for nine weeks.

When next the Court of Assistants gathered, they called him before their bar. But when he was presented, they sat there in silence, ignoring him. Each of them must have been thinking, *but for the new law this would be a trial for the man's life.* They no longer had the old law, and this made them unsure.

"Take off your hat," Governor Endicott commanded from above Southwick's head.

Josiah looked up at him, their gazes met. "Nay, I will not."

Endicott stared down at the man before him and he saw Stevensen. He saw Robinson. He saw Leddra. He thought about Mistress Dyer. And, he remembered Christison.

Southwick gave pause to see if Endicott would respond, then went on. "My hat is my cross, and I, too, shall bear my conscience with tenderness."

A look of wonder spread across the Governor's face. He found it curious and, yet, he understood—here was a man whose very life was at stake, and he would hazard it more for want of putting off his hat. He would call a man a Quaker for nothing more than this want of keeping the hat on. And for being a Quaker, for coming before him not once, not twice, but many times. And to stand there and insist his hat stay upon his head, no different from other garments covering a man. This is a ridiculous thing, between two men of understanding, they should stumble at nothing more than a hat.

But there it was. It came to a hat. And a hat came to a Quaker. Before he knew it, Endicott was worked up to a tremble. He commanded it again, even though he knew the answer would be the same. His honor commanded it, and God had no part in it. But he did not have the old law, and he could not sentence this man to death as he might wish to.

The Governor lowered his eyes, and tried to focus his attention on these proceedings. Satisfied, or filled with dread, they were the same. "You were to have been tried for your life."

Southwick knew of the change in the law, and he knew from whence it came, and he knew Endicott would walk a fine path between the King's desires and his own.

Endicott resigned. "I have made of late a law to save your life, a mercy to you. But I think, it would be just as well to take your life now as to whip you, twelve or fourteen times at the cart's tail through your town and those along the road to the wilderness, and let you die after." Endicott's disposition improved with this last thought, and a sneer began to appear on his face. "Do you not agree?"

Endicott turned to his Secretary Rawson and signified the order should be made. Turning back to Southwick, he said with a flourish, "It might be an order shall come by then, which may save your life."

What would Endicott have said if he knew on the very day, perhaps as he spoke those very words, the King, newly crowned Charles II, was granting deputation to Southwick's Friend and neighbor, Samuel Shattuck, himself a Quaker, and sending him forth from London to deliver a message to the governor of the colonies.

23

Seventeen Lashes

How many lashes? How many more? Have they not exacted their revenge ten times over? Is my flesh the equal of justice, and what price mercy? Is it spite they seek, but malice the gain? I gave over a pound, and still they demand more. Will I know the end?

I tear and bite at the leather thongs holding me to this post; try what I might to break free from these bonds. I stalk about the dwindling crowd, my face distorted with my rage, my fists balled and ready to hit something or someone. When I get to the constable, and I am standing there so close I feel his breath upon my face, I see the milky white of his eyes. So close he would draw back and away if he were not so stunned by my audacity. I would look up into his soul, and I would see the fear of what he cannot imagine. He would be paralyzed, only his eyes able to move, to look from person to person, implore without a move or a sound, for someone to interfere. I would say nothing to him or to anyone. The expression on my face, my actions, would speak louder than I ever could.

But, I pull at my hands, and I push against the pole. The constable did a good job with the knots. I am stuck here, my arms pinned. My breast bruised and bloodied from the rough wood and splinters. My head pounding from the rush of blood with every lash. My mind is strong, but my body is weakening.

The next lash comes and I take it without a movement, without a cry. Go ahead, give me your best arm, give me your anger. You may break my body. You will not break my spirit. But, I can break you.

The blood flowed down my back and I felt it soak into the skirt still held at my waist. It was warm and sticky, and its stench filled the still air around me.

24

King Charles II

The King sat upon his throne and listened, dogged, as Edward Burrough spoke. The room was full of subjects awaiting their turn to raise some issue or grieve some misdeed, but so quiet Edward feared his breathing was too loud, his agitation too great. The King could dismiss him at any moment if his words were too harsh or not otherwise to the Regency's liking.

"There is a vein of innocent blood opening in your dominions." Burrough waited for some acknowledgement, some sign he would be permitted to continue. The King shifted in his seat, leaned forward as if he could not hear the words the man before him spoke. Burrough had the King's attention. "If its flow is not stopped, it will overrun all."

The last thing the King wanted, after his own tribulations, was for blood to be spilt. Without hesitation, or even want of an explanation, King Charles II spoke in a voice so soft Burrough could see many in his sight strain to better hear the words without appearing too interested. "But I will stop this vein."

Edward Burrough released the breath he held throughout this exchange. He took a bold step forward, a small step for he was still standing before the King, and there were armed guards ready all about. The hook caught, Burrough began to reel in the King. Sweat formed on his brow, and his voice became loud—or so it sounded to his own ears. "Then, if it please His Majesty, do it speedily for we know not how many may soon be put to death."

Satisfied with Burrough, and his command, the King fell back into the chair. "As speedily as ye will." He turned to others present near him, "Call the secretary, and I will do it presently." And so, as the secretary settled himself at the small table brought just then before the King, his quill in hand, his ink pot before him, the King began to dictate his mandamus. Edward Burrough did not move an inch, but stood there listening, his head bowed and his breathing easier. He had succeeded, well.

> *Trusty and well-beloved we greet you well. Having been informed that several of our subjects amongst you, called Quakers, have been and are imprisoned by you, whereof some have been executed, and others, as hath been unto us, are in danger to undergo the like, we have thought fit to signify our pleasure, in that behalf, for the future; and do hereby require, that if there be any of those people, called Quakers, amongst you now already condemned to suffer death or other corporal punishment, or that are imprisoned and obnoxious to the like condemnation, you are to forbear to proceed any further therein, but that you forthwith send the same persons, whether condemned or imprisoned, over into this our kingdom of England, together with the respective crimes or offense laid to their charge, to the end such course may be taken with them here as shall be agreeable to our laws and their demerits. And, for so doing, these our letters shall be your sufficient warrant and discharge.*

The secretary continued to scrawl the customary closing,

> *Given at our Court, at Whitehall, the ninth day of September, in the thirteenth year of our reign.*

Burrough never considered the irony of the King having only recently returned to the throne. He waited for the secretary to finish, while the King continued about his business with the others in the room. On a separate sheet, the secretary, oblivious of anything around him, continued with his writing,

To our trusty and well-beloved John Endicott, Esquire, and to all and every other, the governor or governors of our Plantation of New England, and of all the Colonies thereunto belonging, that now are or hereafter shall be; and to all and every the ministers and officers of our said Plantations and Colonies whatsoever, with the Continent of New England.

He signed this

By his Majesty's Command, William Morris.

The order in hand, Burrough set out for the docks in search of a ship to bear the order in his pocket forthwith across the seas to the colonies. Not finding any ship was outfitted or having business across the ocean, Burrough returned to the King's chamber a few days later.

Charles II looked across the room at Burrough with only slight recognition in his eyes. Looking away from a man standing to the side shaking his head, the King said, "I have no present occasion to send a ship thither, but—if some other may have business and would send one, then I command them to as soon as they would. And, after a moment, who would you have carry my mandamus? Who can you trust?

Burrough had already found a ship whose master was sympathetic, and he knew of one man who could be trusted to convey the order to Governor Endicott's hand. "If it please Your Majesty, Samuel Shattuck, who is an inhabitant of New England and was banished here by their law to be hanged if he should come again to the shores of the colonies."

The King was satisfied with this business now coming to a close. He granted Samuel Shattuck deputation and agreed to pay over the sum of three hundred pound to the master of the ship to set sail in no more than ten days time, goods or no goods aboard.

Edward Burrough departed the King's company in haste, the mandamus and receipt secure in his pocket. He sent for Ralph Goldsmith, whom he found to be an honest Friend and master of a good ship, and gave him the receipt. He then sent for Samuel

Shattuck and entrusted him with the mandamus signed by the King's secretary. Looking both pleased and wistful, Burrough bid them Godspeed, turned and walked away without a look back.

Master Ralph Goldsmith and Samuel Shattuck stood together at the helm of the ship as it set sail from London the following Saturday, the twenty-first day of September, in the year 1661. With a prosperous gale, they expected to arrive in Boston harbor by early December. Shattuck considered the look on Endicott's face when finally he would hand over the King's mandamus. Then he saw himself hanging from a tree, swinging dead from the branches in the cold Boston winter winds.

25

With Child

October, in 1661...

The fall colors descended on the village of Hampton. The water by the shore slapped against course sand and rocks with more vigor. The winds turned cool early, and the days seemed to be shorter than they should be. I discovered I was once again with child. Joseph was just nine months old, and was still nursing at my breast. I was as excited as I was disappointed. I wanted to keep Joseph close, enjoy his infancy, for just a little while longer.

What a blessing, though, to present my husband with another child so soon. And blessings multiply. Rebecka was to have her second child along with me. But things change when we least expect them, and not all change is a blessing.

Old William Marston came to our house more often with news from Boston and Salem, and eventually from Old England. I meant to tell Eliakim about the child, but he was distraught by the stories Marston told by the flickering light of the candle stubs, and he was distracted often. He moved through his chores with precision, but his thoughts were elsewhere, and he said he wanted to protect me. Keep me from harm. He said he felt the innocent blood spilling from his veins, and he knew not what he could do to stanch its flow.

I worried I might burden him, so I kept my secret and waited for a better time.

26

Convincement

If my history began with my marriage, my life began with my convincement. There was no moment, no single event. There was no thunder or lightening in the sky. There was no whisper in my ear, or shout from the hilltops.

There was simply an awakening.

Eliakim began to absent himself from the public meetings, using the excuse of my confinement, and the birth of our first child. The courts were woefully behind, the number of causes growing with the population and the fear among the leaders of the community. So they had not caught up to him—yet. After we heard of Leddra's death, and then Christison's imprisonment, Eliakim began to absent himself more regularly. John was by his side while Rebecka and I continued to attend when we could for our mother's sake, and for our children.

I began to wonder, as I sat in my rocker by the fire, tending to my sewing or to Joseph, or serving Eliakim and our guests, always silent but always listening. At first I struggled within myself, fought the words and feelings then taking up residence in my thoughts. The elders would have us believe only those who would be chosen could receive God's grace and it would be those chosen few who called upon everyone else to follow them to God. Was there another way, and how could I know; would I recognize the signs which might have shown me elected, shown me a path to salvation? As I struggled, I knew I had no part in God's choice for me. I felt I would have no warning, no hint of what I should expect or how I might be asked to respond. If I should be without instruction, if I should be without hesitation, then I must only open my mind and heart to what God would offer me.

During my vocation, I spent many hours during which my hands and legs would move about my chores, but my mind would dwell on how, at meeting, we were taught sin would be punished, plain and simple. Only punishment could make us sensible and thus lead us to hate sin. This hate would finally allow us to separate our heart from sin. This was contrition. But as I listened more to the words spoken in the quiet safety of my house, I began to think of God's grace as something which would one day appear upon my table, a gift, a tangible object I could hold close to my heart, and with this gift God would not wish me to seek hate, even of sin, but instead I should be sorrowful at his disappointment in my sins, and in this way I could seek faith instead of punishment.

For months, when Goodman Marston sat at our table, Eliakim and he with their heads close, their voices low—they did not want to wake Joseph, they did not want to say the words aloud—their shadows danced upon the wall belying their reserve across the table. I sat always apart. I filled the cups when they were emptied. I retrieved the old man's cloak when the night sounds had long past quieted. I observed as Eliakim clasped his hand and bade him be careful of the spirited tree roots rising in his path to topple him as he made his way to the old horse dozing nearby. I listened to every word, and offered none of my own. I thought about what these words would mean to me, to my husband, to my child as he would grow during these restless times, to the child growing inside me. Their words filled me, first with fear and concern because I did not understand. But then the words began to fill me with warmth and peace wanting nothing of me except to open my mind and heart. And I learned. As God would choose my way, I would choose the steps, whether they be light or heavy. My soul was then at rest. This was sanctity.

For weeks after my revelation, I would look up at the sky charmed by the pinpoints of random lights filling my curious mind with orderly presentation. I would look behind me for the sound of a twig being disturbed and fear the footfalls of the devil following me, waiting for me to stumble; a face illuminated and the footfalls of the town priest pushing me to stumble. But I persevered, and I would not turn, I did not waiver. I gave my thoughts over to Wenlock Christison, who was once again imprisoned in Boston for having returned to the colonies to tempt the Cart and Whip Act, and Governor Endicott and his band of magistrates.

I felt the child in me growing, giving rather than taking my strength. And I began to form a plan in my head. It did not take shape with any kind of swiftness, but required the pieces of each conversation, each event, each malignant influence to form it. As the days passed, I became more and more certain of my path, and of my step, and I gloried in the feeling.

27

Samuel Shattuck

The Second Day of December, in 1661...

The ship made port at Boston harbor at first light of the first day in December. After ten weeks of rough seas and frigid winds, the crew was anxious and eager to walk on solid ground once more and so they hurried to lower the anchor into the swaying water. The English colors flying from the mast drew the townsmen and women to the end of the pier, clamoring and shouting across the water to anyone who would answer.

Are there any letters? came the calls. *Have you any letters?* Months went by, and people grew impatient for word from their families and friends back in old England. And every ship meant word from afar.

Master Goldsmith stood astern, his hands upon the railing, his eyes looking out over the town, over their heads, silent. Finally, he answered, "Yea, but I will not deliver them until the morrow, it being the Sabbath."

Disappointed, the crowds of people returned to their homes and their shops, but with whispers on their lips. There were many Quakers come, they saw them aboard, and Shattuck among them. They knew he was banished on pain of death should he return. There was much speculation in the inns and the taverns, and in the beds of the town's leading men, about what could have brought him on this fool's errand.

Shattuck awoke the next morning to the gentle swaying of the sparkling blue-green water all around him. He rose with the sun and the bustle of the harbor folk. He stowed the papers he was to carry deep within the pocket of his coat. He kept his hand tight around them, secure in the words written on them, even as he and Master Goldsmith climbed down the rope ladder, clinging to the side of the ship, stepping gingerly into the small craft beating against the ship's sides below them, agitated and awaiting them. Two rowers held tight to the ropes, steadying the boat as best they could, keeping its motion to the gentle sway of the water. Shattuck was careful to seat himself as he held one of the sides, keeping his other hand in his pocket. It would not do to have come all this way only to have the King's missive float out over the water, sinking into the depths, lost forever.

When the row boat made shore, the two mates scrambled out to tie it off on the iron mooring fixed to the wooden pier, both black with age and wear, slippery with splashing water. Shattuck and Goldsmith stepped out of the boat, the lurching from side-to-side acting in the devil's stride to upset them before they could complete their mission. A hand reached down, steady, lifting. Still Shattuck kept one hand in his pocket clutching the precious paper.

The King's deputy and the ship's master went ashore. Out onto the cobblestones, then to the worn trail taking them to their meeting. Goldsmith stopped, turned and ordered the two men back to the ship. Then they walked in silence and without delay to Governor Endicott's house and knocked, determined, upon the ornate carved wooden door. A man, a servant, opened the door and asked what was their business with his Excellency.

Shattuck spoke, undaunted, Goldsmith retreated back a step. "Tell your master we have a message from King Charles of England for him, and we are obliged to deliver it to none but the Governor." The man admitted them, and bade them wait in the parlor. Both nervous and excited, the two men paced about the room, observing the finery covering the furniture, the floors, the shelves and the walls all around them. Waiting.

Endicott would not be rushed, not in his own home, not even for the King's messenger. He was not forgiving for being disturbed there, in his own sanctuary, and by two strangers—for the servant failed to take their names. He finally appeared and his countenance changed mightily when his eye fell upon Samuel Shattuck.

The Governor was a grave man, a strong man. He knew no equal in the land, and he relished in the rule of fear God had entrusted to him, and him alone. No man, for good or ill, could face his iron will. This is what Endicott thought until he saw who stood before him, eye to eye, nothing to separate them.

His brow was clouded, his eye was stern,
With a look of mingled sorrow and wrath;
"Woe's me!" He murmured: "at every turn
the pestilent Quakers are in my path!
Some we have scourged, and banished some,
Some hanged, more doomed, and still they come,
Fast as the tide of yon bay sets, in
Sowing their heresy's seed of sin.

"Your hat is still upon your head," Endicott commented. Such was the greeting he offered to this man, this Quaker, on whom he pronounced the sentence of banishment some months before.

"And there it will remain," was Shattuck's retort.

Endicott contained his rage only for the King who had apparently sent this man in contradiction to the sentence on his head, and thought *If this vagabond before him would not remove it himself, it would be taken from him.* The Governor motioned for the servant to take the hat off Shattuck's head.

Shattuck did not move, but allowed the servant his orders. Instead, he withdrew his hand from his pocket and opened the folded and crumpled sheets, smoothing them as if their wrinkles might diminish their power. The royal arms imbedded in the seal on the paper was fully displayed. He handed the signed deputation and the mandamus from the King over to Endicott. Goldsmith did not move from Shattuck's heel, his hat still upon his head, as the two men attended to their business.

"By the King's command I bear this message and stand in his stead." Shattuck's words came strong, if low in his throat. He withdrew his gloved hand, and pushed his shoulders back, raising him a good three inches nearly to the height of the opponent before him.

Endicott spent some moments in silence, reading the two documents. Shattuck watched, considering what thoughts might just then be going through the Governor's head. The servant remained in the room but timid in a corner, Shattuck's hat in his hand. They would, apparently, not be offered refreshment or comfort. The room closed in and the air became stuffy as tension built all around the three men standing there in the center.

When Endicott was done perusing the papers, he lowered his arms, though he stood there with his eyes fixed on the floor, gathering his own wits and tempering his anger. Looking up at the two men, one then the other, Endicott called forth the servant and bade him, in a quiet voice, to return Shattuck's hat to him.

Without an explanation, or an edict of any kind, Endicott turned and bade the two Friends follow him. The servant brought up the rear of the procession through the house. At the door, Endicott lifted his coat and hat from the hook, and the servant rushed to aid him, then opened the door. Shattuck and Goldsmith followed into the street, several paces behind the Governor, not knowing to where they were being led. After some minutes they arrived at a large manor. Upon Endicott's knock, the door opened and Shattuck recognized the deputy-governor, Richard Bellingham. Bellingham, in turn, recognized Shattuck, and was quick to turn his smirking face back to Endicott. Before Bellingham could greet him, Endicott stepped forward, forcing his deputy back into the house.

"A word, Sir."

The door closed behind Endicott, leaving Shattuck and Goldsmith standing in the cold December breeze. For some minutes the two men stood quiet, both wondering to themselves what the discussion inside would hold for them. Their ears and cheeks and noses turned red with chill, and Shattuck began to think perhaps they were the victims of a dodge and the two men inside were wont to make fools of them, and the King. But shortly after, the door once again opened, and Endicott exited, leaving Bellingham to stand upon the threshold welcoming the frigid temperatures into his warm home.

Endicott made short work of his response to the King's missive. Without looking at either of the two men, he spoke, his tone devoid of emotion, but strained. "As the King commands, we shall obey." He then strode past the two Quakers in a direction opposite to his own home. Bellingham slammed the door. And Shattuck and Goldsmith were once again left standing in the cold, but this time, with smiles upon their faces.

This was not the reaction Shattuck expected, dreamed about, obsessive, over the days and weeks covered by the journey to this moment. Shattuck and Goldsmith both released their breath, neither realizing they held it since the Governor opened the door. They made haste for the pier where they signaled to the ship for a rowboat. On board once again, they gathered the letters waiting there to be delivered, granted liberty to the ship's crew and the passengers, and gave their thanks to God for their great deliverance.

Back at Bellingham's house, the deputy prepared to carry out the Governor's orders to send riders to summon the judges from the last court: the Worshipful Mr. Simon Bradford from Andover, Mr. Samuel Symonds and Major General Daniel Denison from Ipswich, and Major William Hawthorne from Salem. The furthest of these towns was Ipswich, some thirty-two miles as the crow flew. On even the fastest horse, the group would not be assembled before the sun crested overhead. Meanwhile, Endicott went forth and called upon his secretary, Edward Rawson, and bade him accompany his superior back to his house for Endicott had an order requiring his service.

Edward Rawson was a good servant to the colony. Within a year of his arrival in 1637, at age twenty-three, he served continuously in a variety of positions until his seventy-first year. He held the position of Secretary of the Massachusetts Bay Colony for the last thirty-six years of his service. He was a rotund man, giving the impression he was also a large man. His face was square, owing to the heavy jowls falling to his thick neck. His eyes might be called beady, and his lips took on a natural purse. But it was his thin mustache and narrow beard tuft which connected his peevishness, especially in his service to Endicott, to his manliness.

Rawson, confused to be called when the court was not in session, followed in silence. When the two men arrived at Endicott's house, the servant brought tea and then left the men undisturbed until the other guests had arrived.

When all were gathered in Endicott's parlor, seated comfortably, the King's missive read to all, the room burst with excitement and they all thought to speak at once to express their dismay, and their anger. Endicott, who was standing in the center of the room, raised his hand to signal their silence.

"I have given this much thought, and am resolved to obey," he said, looking at Rawson who, at the moment, produced the order and handed it to a stunned Bradstreet. Bradstreet read the order aloud for all to hear.

To William Salter, keeper of the prison in Boston: You are required by authority and order of the General Court forthwith to release and discharge the Quakers who are at present in your custody. See that you don't neglect this. By order of the Court, Edward Rawson Secretary.

Endicott entertained no discussion, declaring the matter concluded—for a time.

And so, Wenlock Christison, who had lately returned to the colony and been again imprisoned, was released a second time. Though he was again ordered to leave the colony and not return, he determined he would go to Hampton where he knew a man called Marston.

28

Wenlock Christison

At this last named town we hear of [Wenlock Christison] in connection with an Eliakim Wardel, a resident of that place, and a Friend. It appears that Eliakim Wardel, contrary to the law, gave him entertainment or hospitality...

Early in December, in 1661...

I was standing by the fire, stirring our supper while Eliakim bedded down the horses in the barn, when I heard the hard snow crunching under a heavy stride approaching our house. The neighing of a horse followed. Setting the spoon upon the table, I checked that Joseph still slept peacefully in his basket by the fire. The blanket was pulled up to his ears and a lock of hair fallen down over his tiny eyes. Outside I heard a ragged cough, but no knock. Apprehension rose from the pit of my belly, where my second child grew, then Eliakim's voice rang through the night with a greeting of lightness and joy I had not heard from him in weeks. I recognized Goodman Marston's voice, but there was another I had never heard before.

I reached for the plates stacked on the shelf and was grateful we had extras for our guests. I placed them on the table with a fresh loaf of rye, an injun, and a slab of soft lard, and returned to my pots of baked beans and pease porridge. With the strong, hot chicory to wash the course food down, we would hardly notice the fire kept low and uninviting to any other passersby, despite the cold. Too anxious to think of anything else to occupy me, I sat in one of the spindle chairs and waited for the three men to enter.

Eliakim entered first but waited at the door, and was followed by Marston who was drawn to the fire and the appetizing odors coming from the pots and filling the room. The third man was larger than both my husband and our Friend Marston, intimidating but for the love radiating from his presence. His face was shielded by a hat with a lifeless brim, hanging over his eyes, casting a shadow on his face in the dim candlelight. He wore a long cloak, dusted with snow and shabby, I presumed, from weeks or months of travel. His pants billowed at the knees below the ragged hem of the cloak, and his boots covered his stockings.

I rose, but then hesitated. The stranger nodded, not as if to only acknowledge me but as if to seek my permission to remove his cloak and sit at the table where a hot meal awaited him. I returned his nod and cast my eyes down, embarrassed by the smile taking shape on my face. When he removed his cloak and hung it deliberately upon an empty peg by the door, he pushed his hat higher onto his head and then I was able to see his face.

His features did not arouse in me a sense of pleasure or appeal—I felt my face flush at the thought of Eliakim just then0—but his eyes were engaging and he looked deep into mine. I felt his gaze piercing through me. I was made motionless but filled with a delight for a moment, and my thoughts turned to God watching over me, approving of the attention this man, this stranger, now offered to me. When I came back to myself, only then did I notice the long and pointed nose hung over an equally long and pointed chin. He reached up his right hand in a motion so smooth and so gentle and touched the brim of his hat.

These pleasantries done, I offered him the chair closest to the waning fire. While we ate, Marston told us of how he spied the man walking alone along the road to Hampton. When he reined up his horse, he was surprised to recognize his Friend Wenlock Christison. *Friend, what brings you to these parts in the snow and frigid winds, and why pray-tell do you smile so cheery,* Marston asked as he eased his stiff and aching legs and back to the ground, determined to walk a ways with the man.

Christison told him what had lately transpired in Boston, and how he meant to visit many of the faithful before he turned south to his home. *You were to be my next stop*, Christison said as he clapped Marston on the back in friendly greeting.

Marston replied he was just on his way to visit young Wardell. *Pray, accompany me there and meet the young man. He will surely welcome you into his home, and provide you with a fire to warm your feet and hands, and a meal to warm your heart and belly.*

Marston offered his honored Friend the use of his horse, but Christison whooped and reminded Marston he had many more years than himself and he would not have the elder man's injury weigh on his conscience. Besides, he added, he had spent so much of the last year in darkness and stench he preferred to walk in the fresh air and light, warm or cold, snow or sun.

I listened as the men talked, refilling their plates and cups until all the food and chicory was gone. I stoked the fire just to the keep the embers hot. And I watched as Joseph continued to sleep in the basket at my feet, seeming undisturbed by the new voices. I thought about this man, and I felt sick for his poor wife and children, never to know where he was or whether he had risen each day to the new light. I imagined Eliakim and I, and wondered if we did not have the strength or the courage to keep our faith with such rigor as he. I, at the least, would require first a strength of my own character.

I was always timid, rarely speaking out unless another bade me answer directly and for myself. I thought about the remark Eliakim once made, early in our youth. *Why*, he asked, *did I walk always with my eyes cast down, and my lips pursed in a frown*. I remember I could not at first answer, thinking to myself I had never noticed this, and therefore never gave it any thought, but then wondering was this a flaw, and worse yet, a flaw needing correction. Now, after years of self-torment, I can only consider it whence it comes to mind but have not truly changed because of it. I came lately to the Quaker faith. I was a mere child in the sense of my growing spirituality. Too young, too eager, too unsteady on my weak and wobbling legs. If I spoke aloud my thoughts would I be quieted and told to listen for I had nothing important yet to say?

And of our marriage. Could I withstand the days, or weeks, or even months of separation Christison and his family endured? I thought of Eliakim's fingers entwined with mine as we walked together. I did not think to sit so close to him, yet the heat of this leg mixed with the heat of mine when we are side by side in the wagon. I did not think to reach out for him in the night, yet I woke to find my arm across his chest, rising and falling with his gentle sleeping breath. I did not think to move my body with the music and rhythm of his when we came together as man and wife. We were connected, body, mind and spirit.

The feeling of sickness turned to respect and admiration, not only for the man and the hope he inspired, but also for his wife and the sacrifices she made for the anticipation of a better life, and a better love.

Marston departed soon after we finished our meal, begging our forgiveness for such a hasty retreat, but the night came and with it a more fierce cold to accompany him on his trek home. And, besides, his young wife would be worried for his safety, he added with a twinkling eye and a mischievous grin.

Christison accepted our hospitality with pleasure, and stayed on for the night, determining to continue his journey only after a full night's rest and the comfort of our warm fire and victuals. As the night drew on, we found ourselves desiring to keep each others company for as long as possible, so we wrapped ourselves in blankets and huddled close so our whispering breaths would at least warm our faces.

Friend Christison regaled us with stories of his travels, his triumphs and his tribulations; his arrest and conviction the year before; his acceptance of the death sentence and his surprise when, instead, he was released not once, but a second time when he lately returned to the colony to finish his work. He was calm, though I felt his excitement as he retold his tale. How many times he must have told it. How many people must have welcomed his voice and his ministrations.

As the two men talked deep into the night, I listened, my whole attention occupied with Christison's words and the lull of his cadence, and my imagination returned always to his eyes. When his voice and his stories were spent, we left him to sleep by the embers and we repaired ourselves to our bed. We held each other more tightly than was usual, not so much for the cold but to share the hope this man brought. When we awoke, we found our blankets once again upon us, a roaring fire in the hearth, hot chicory, and he gone.

We spoke to no one of our midnight encounter except John and Rebecka. But we discovered not long after even the most well-kept secret can escape and return to haunt.

29

Another Lash

The next lash came too quick. I closed my eyes and I let my mind follow the leather cords down, sinking, hanging and at the same time pooling in the dirt and dust. My eyes closed and searched the blackness, finding nothing, finally resting there, consumed. I listened and heard not the whispers, not the birds twittering, but the movement of the air, the rising of the dust and my own breath.

I concentrated on taking air in through my nose, and in my mind I followed it down through my body, filling the cavities within me, to my belly. I imagined a fluttering there, my body remembering but mourning the empty space. When my belly was full of air, bursting, I pushed it out through my mouth and I listened as it came rushing. I did it again, and again, until I was transported somewhere other than a pole, on a spring day, in the town which was not mine, surrounded by those people who were not mine.

From somewhere far outside of me, some place and some time where I was standing and watching as my body was beaten and broken, I stood in the misting rain and watched as the next lash came bearing down on this poor woman's back. She screamed out of the grim recesses of her own mind. My heart burst for her pain. Then the rain came. The drops fell upon her naked body and washed the blood and the dirt and the sweat away, leaving her back as smooth and as soft as the day before.

30

A Pretty Beast

Eliakim Wardel, of Hampton aforesaid, having received Wenlock Christison into his house in the name of a disciple, your Court quickly took note of him, and having fined him for so doing, a pretty beast for the saddle was taken for the fine, worth about fourteen pounds, which was far less than the value of the horse....

Tuesday, the Tenth Day of December, in 1661...

And so Eliakim was summoned to court, the first of many such occasions. No record exists of his having been called before this, and no surviving court documents record this event, so we must rely upon the words of others in this testimony. I can hear, even now, the shadows of the voices of the men of the court as they thrust their gaze altogether down upon Eliakim and cast his sentence in unison.

"Your man has been set free."

At first, Eliakim did not know of what the magistrate spoke. He expected his summons was to be for his absence from worship. Seeing no reaction, the magistrate repeated himself, with more emphasis to his words. "Your man has been set free."

With still nothing of recognition in Eliakim's eyes, the magistrate then asked, "How do you come to know a man called Wenlock Christison?"

Not more than two or three weeks passed since Christison was released from the prison in Boston and made his way to our home. Beyond what he told us of the King's decree to release all Quakers, we knew nothing more of the court's business. Neither had we seen nor heard from or of him since.

Eliakim knew at once he was being led to a trap, and so he remained silent, though there was no denying the flicker of acknowledgement of the name in his eyes. The magistrate repeated himself once more. "Your man has been set free."

The room was full of men. Men of the court. Others who were called for various and sundry charges, petitions, or complaints. All were silent, waiting. Breathing. Sighing. Coughing. Fiddling. Grumbling. Finally, the magistrate spoke again with no more inflection or emotion in his voice than when he first spoke at Eliakim. Without preamble, "The court finds you shall pay fourteen pound for the crime of harboring a Quaker."

Eliakim prepared no written statement from which to read and present his testimony. If he spoke any word, no matter how calm he spoke, it would be taken as contrary and considered an attack on the court worthy of an increased sentence. Yet, Eliakim chose to plead his case, show them the way of things with his family, beg for their indulgence. He told me later the words were liberated from his mind, and flowed free from his lips, before he could think to stop them. "Good Sirs," he said with all the humility he could muster, "I do not have the coin to give."

Pestered now, as if by flies plaguing the air, the magistrate waved his hand and said with a blankness in his eyes, "Then we shall find other means to settle your debt." Was there a smirk upon his face, or was it simply Eliakim's imagination.

Given his leave of the court, Eliakim pulled the reins from the tie post outside the tavern, mounted our pretty beast, and made for home. He walked at a slow pace, talking to the horse, talking to the wind, or talking to God. But it was futile for he received no answer then. *What*, he asked himself, *was he to do on the morrow*?

We had our livestock, enough for our modest purposes, but not sufficient to lose even a calf or a chick. But a horse, even the old nag whose only task was to pull the wagon, could not be spared if we were to keep our farm and fields. At home, he told me of his pleading, and the magistrate's sentence. A beast it was to be. The choice to be the constable's.

Eliakim determined he would not leave the house or the barn, or me, the next day. He did not need to wait long when Constable Henry Robie, who otherwise kept an ordinary in the town, arrived. Eliakim met Robie at the door, not giving him the opportunity to knock or offer any greeting.

"If it pleases you," he spoke thoughtfully and perhaps with some embarrassment, "I have come to claim the beast by order of the court."

"It does not please me," was all Eliakim said. They both stood silent for some time, Eliakim looking at Robie, and Robie looking at his feet. Finally, Robie returned his hat to his head, which was dusted with a sparse snow fall just begun, turned and walked to the barn. Eliakim, without cloak or hat, followed through the snow still covering the ground from the last fall.

I closed the door against the chill wind and watched from the window as both men entered the barn side-by-side, the distortion in the glass made their stiff strides and their otherwise straight backs twist and contort. There was nothing but cold and snow passing between them. From a distance, anyone might not be able to distinguish the owner from the visitor. Within only minutes, both men walked out, but now Robie led our prettiest beast passed the hanging doors. He would not, or could not, look upon Eliakim or me as he mounted his horse once again, ticked his tongue twice, and turned himself toward town, our beast in tow.

Eliakim returned to the house and took his cloak and hat from the peg, and left without a word. Several minutes later I heard the little cart roll by, and I saw through the window the old nag pulling Eliakim toward town.

The rest of the day passed, seeming interminable. My mind was not on my tasks. I rested my hand upon my belly, the secret within me, more than was usual. Even Joseph played with uncommon quietness. I could not dispel the quickening feelings of a raging anger mixed with nauseous waves of fear and foreboding. Eliakim was but one foot within the door before I was upon him. He took a step back, his face more calm but his eyes haunted. He put his two hands upon my shoulders, and I opened my mouth to—what, ask where he had been, what he had been doing, how could we earn enough to feed ourselves and our children without our work horse? Before any words passed from my mouth, he took one hand away and put his finger to his lips. "Do not speak. We do not need to suffer through the event again by talking of it."

Though there were other of our animals which could have satisfied the fourteen pound cost, the constable chose the best of what we had. On the morrow, Eliakim said, he would go into town and bargain for the balance owed to us.

Could we then have believed the constable made his choice of our livestock on his own, for what purpose such a choice we could not fathom. Rather, we came to understand he received orders from a more fitting authority to find the finest specimen we had to offer, and leave it to us to beg for the court's mercy in leveling the debt. It was then we knew to never again underestimate the Reverend Cotton's influence over the court.

31

And Another Lash

The crack. Another lash came sharp and clean, like a knife cut through lard. But I felt it not, at least not within my body. I was betrayed. I was angry. The words flew through my head faster than the blood flowed from my wounds. The images of the faces of people around me, people who once vowed to protect me, people who begged my indulgence, begged the return of my faith, begged me in turn to betray my husband and my family. Until there was only one face left.

Would you have me be weak, I asked of the image before me. Would you have me fall before you, my turn to beg?

Yea. I would have you bow, I would have you beg, I would have you break here before me. You are but a woman, he said with scorn. *What else shall you do when you are beaten?*

At this I laughed, hearty. I may be only a woman, perhaps a plaything you wish to take, a child you think to bully. Rallied by my courage, I kept up the dialogue in my head. But you, sir, are a tiny man, a speck of dirt beneath my feet. You take when you stand on the pulpit. You take when you lead the sheep about, a truncheon in your hand. You take when you send others commanded to do your bidding. You take then hide among the crowd and watch with a fire of lust in your eyes. But you give nothing.

I imagined the face before me stunned, strained with anger, a deep flush rising in his puffed cheeks, stuttering. He, for once, had no words.

My voice was clear. I, too, can give nothing.

32

They Promised Him Land

Later in the Month of December, in 1661…

Eliakim came in from the barn, his cheeks red, his hands near to frozen. I bade him sit at the table while I poured him a bowl of hot chicory to warm his hands, and another of hot stew to warm his belly. I saw him not at all throughout the day for he stole out of the house early before the sun even cracked one sleepy eye, to make the long ride to Salem where the court was sitting. The ride was made longer on the back of our old nag. When he returned home just as the sun again began to close her eyes, he went straight to the barn and saw I had done the milking, laid the straw, and fed the livestock. He spent a goodly time out there and I imagined he was sitting in the empty stall where our pretty beast stood just the week before. Though I was anxious for the news, I let him have his time. When finally he came into the house, his face told me everything I needed to know. There was little his eyes could hide from me.

We sat together, I holding Joseph as he nursed quiet at my breast, Eliakim holding his head in his hands, his eyes staring intent into the stained and smoothed grain of the wooden table on which his elbows were propped. Two bowls of chicory, two bowls of stew growing cold in the winter chill no blaze of the fire in our hearth would quell. In his own time, and his own way, he told me of the events of the day.

He went to the court, unbidden, and he waited quiet in the back of the room, listening. He saw Goodman Marston, with his son and several others he knew, some well, others only in passing for their mutual acquaintance with Marston. With no opportunity to speak afore the proceedings, he thought he would ride back with Marston when their business was completed.

The foreman called the court to order, and read the list of causes held over from the last sitting. Some of the causes were dispensed quickly and without fanfare. Licenses renewed, fines levied against undisputed transgressions, a confirmation of sergeant of the foot company. Others were well ordered but lengthy in their discussion. Inventories of estates of the deceased, ordering of highways laid or repaired, property disputes.

Still others added heat to the room. Eliakim listened more intently as a young man named John Porter, the younger, was committed to the house of correction until the next Ipswich court for his profane, unnatural and abusive carriage to his natural parents, and abuse of the town's authority. While the clerk finished his transcribing of John Porter's statement, another man, who Marston later named as John Burston, burst into the court in a very uncivil manner, interrupting and affronting the court with his bellowing. Eliakim said he raised himself from his position on the bench so he could see the raucous better—hearing it would not be a problem.

The man in his scolding claimed the court were robbers and destroyers of widows and the fatherless. Before any of the men who sat upon the court could move or speak, Burston went on to accuse the priests of devining their truths for money, of false worship. Here, Eliakim said, the foreman commanded this man should be silent. Instead of sitting down, or leaving the court's presence, Burston instead raised his voice louder and took it upon himself to command silence. The court, wishing to continue its work committed him to the stocks, and he was dragged away, through the crowd and out the door, still bawling until his voice could hold out no more.

Eliakim had, until then, been waiting for a lull in the proceedings so he could rise and present himself. But after these two outbursts, he said he relaxed himself back onto the bench, his back against a wall, to wait for the men of the court to return to a state of calm. It was a dangerous move, interrupting the court, so nearly two score of cases came and went before Eliakim at last found a moment when his boredom, fear, courage, and anger all goaded him to stand and speak.

Here, Eliakim did as they bade of him. He begged for the return of our beast, another to be offered in its place to satisfy the fine. He said they listened with quiet restraint and without interruption, though this was another disruption of their day. When his argument was done, he said he was surprised to hear the foreman speak with little hesitation, and some bit of amity, and he promised him land.

The foreman did not give more, and in fact returned his gaze to the list before him, and called out the next cause before Eliakim could raise any other point.

As Eliakim turned to walk out before the foreman might change his mind, he thought where stock remains valued only as long as its health suits its purpose, land will outlive us all. Settling himself on the ground against a nearby tree to wait for Friend Marston, he told me he took faith in this gesture, believing at the end of it we would have the better deal.

Again, we were simple to trust their word when they had already shown their deed could no longer be trusted

33

A Vessel of Green Ginger

Marston found Eliakim waiting outside, huddled in his wool cloak, his gaze blank, one knee up with his arm and head, chin buried against his chest, resting upon them. After greeting each other heartily, as if neither was lacking another bite taken from their already thin arses, they mounted their horses and made for Hampton, a more congenial threesome there never was.

As they rode, Marston related the scene in the court after he watched Eliakim depart. Several more causes came and went until the foreman called forward the eighteen people, himself and his son included, to answer yet again for their frequent absences from the public ordinance. Seven others were summoned, but failed to appear. The accursed group held the same people called forth so many times over the last eighteen months, Marston said, he was starting to look upon these men and women as family, and wonder did the court not tire of seeing the same faces before them so often. Standing there, side by side, were also the five witnesses summoned to attest to these various peoples' absences.

All were convicted, none having any argument to make against the truth of the charges. Fines levied in silence against the others, the foreman came lastly to Marston and his son. Here, he offered on his own and his son's behalf, as Eliakim did just a week before, he did not have the coin to pay. Perhaps it was the lateness of the day, or the fatigue of the court, and the foreman resigned to find some other means of payment. Instead of resolving this in Marston's presence, the foreman dismissed the lot of them and was swift to move on to the next cause. Marston went on to say, he and his son followed the others out of the court to disperse to their homes and livelihoods once again.

Some days after, Eliakim and I found our way back to our routines. Our happiness once again prevailing as I let him know of my secret, and he, in his turn, let me know there had been no secret for he knew my body perhaps better than I.

Eliakim went to the salt marsh where there was often better hunting of waterfowl and other wading birds. I expected him late, but laden with a sack of peat to dry, leaving us with salt to flavor our food and bricks to burn when the wood pile became low. On occasion, Eliakim would treat me with saltwort, a pretty plant with a stem pleasing to chew or pickle for an even more delectable treat, and oysters whose cleaned shells adorned my shelves.

I heard footsteps outside, and thinking he returned earlier than I expected, I put Joseph down on his bed of straw and wool, and went the door. Instead of my husband cleaning the marsh mud from his boots, I found left upon the ground before our door with no warning or explanation, a middling sized clay vessel. I recognized the jar from neither our stores nor those of my sister or mother, and so plunged my hand into it to discover the dried root of green ginger. I knew old William Marston kept green ginger for his ailing stomach, but there was nothing else to tell me from where the contents had come or who may have brought them. The kind man would have gladly bestowed such a gift on us had he been aware of some ailment in our household, and especially if the ailment visited itself upon Joseph, for he doted on the little angel as any loving grandfather would have cause to do. But just as sure as he would give of himself and his own stores, he would not have done it silently, or at least without a tussle with the boy's unruly hair.

I left the vessel untouched by the door until Eliakim's return, hoping he made some bargain with Goodman Marston, but more fearful of the mystery surrounding its appearance.

As it happened, Eliakim came upon the old man's place, and Goodman Marston told him of how the constable visited him earlier in the day and plundered, as payment of the last fine upon him, a pot of his green ginger stored in the cool recesses of his barn. Eliakim stayed with the old man for some time, helping him about the house as he often did, before returning home to find the very pot placed upon the ground before our door.

"Who brought this pot?" he asked when he entered, knowing as he did what the vessel held and from whence it had come. In truth I had forgotten about its presence there, having been set about chores within the house all throughout the day, and the weather still chilled enough to keep me and Joseph, and the growing child within me, close to the fire.

"I can answer neither, Husband," I replied, and told him what little I knew of it. He relayed Marston's story, and we knew immediately

> *...to make up the overplus...officers plundered old William Marston of a vessel of green ginger, which was taken from him for some fine, and sent it into Eliakim's house, where he let it lie, and, as his own, touched it not.*

"So, the spoils of another will be my repayment for our pretty beast, when they said they would give land for the difference." He was silent for a moment, thinking. He turned and took me in his arms and looked deep into my eyes. Our touching was not unusual—we enjoyed each other heartily, by only the light of stars or the moon—but it was rare that we thought to touch for the sake of a touch during the daylight hours. On this occasion, I could feel the strain within his fingers and hands, and I realized his fear became my burden as well.

He spoke, but from a distant place. His voice was as soft as always. His eyes, though, took on a vacant, drifting appearance. He was not speaking to me, but I felt he spoke to the room, to the village, to the world. "If they think they can draw us into their game upon another, our neighbor, our Friend, then we will not allow them. We will not lay finger upon this pot by way of accepting either their taking it from the old man or as the balance due from their taking of our beast."

"Yet we can not return it to Goodman Marston either," said I, my voice trailing behind his.

In those days, the wage for the clergy, for his services rendered in his preaching and conduct of the weekly meetings, was paid from a tax levied upon each man. The priest's rate was his to control and collect as he wished. For those who could afford to pay in coin, the exchange was made each week by passing the tithing dish. For others not so fortunate, the priest could exact his exchange through other means.

We came to believe it was a blasphemy to pay for the privilege of hearing God's word, and so Eliakim would usually pass the dish on without adding weight to it. Before we began to absent ourselves and draw the attention of the court, Eliakim would be called upon to perform some chore about the meeting house or about town in exchange for the privilege of the twice weekly sermons. These chores he did with no complaint. If it were to benefit his neighbor, then he would gladly do unto them as he would expect they to do unto him if we should find ourselves in dire need. In this way we maintained a cordial, if stiffened, relationship with our priest, the Reverend Seaborn Cotton. We were not the cream of the community, for we did not have the prosperity. Eliakim chose not to take the oath which would have made him a Freeman and given him due status in the community. But, neither were we want for attention for desperate misdeed or blasphemous speech. And thus we thought to be protected for our lack of interest to leaders of the community.

It was a surprise, then, when we awoke to find the vessel of green ginger gone from its resting place beside our door on the morning following the next meeting. Though we missed many a meeting, and were called to court as testament to the community's notice of this, we still attended on occasion to see our mothers and others into whose lives we took an interest. But the events of the last weeks troubled us exceedingly, and though we spoke not of it at all, I knew it marked a milestone in our lives.

From this day, we would not ever return to worship with Priest Cotton, or in the presence of the others of Hampton village.

There was no question why the vessel was taken. The only question was why Cotton would choose now to take his rate by this means, and why he would take it under cover of night. Why would he not take yet another opportunity to chastise us, or beg for me to attend meeting even without Eliakim by my side?

34

Twenty Lashes

My legs were weak, my arms tired from being raised and fixed about the pole. I no longer had the strength to stand, and so I leaned there, falling into the pole, my knees bent and crumbling beneath me. My red hair hung down in matted clumps of wet curls limp upon my bare shoulders. The welts criss-crossed on my back, starting to rise through the blood drops rolling downward. The top of my skirt was soaked through, drying in a sticky clot to my buttocks. My bloated breasts were mangled against the pole, cuts and tears, crushed and stripping the frail skin away. My nipples were hard and cracked with dried milk. My eyes were closed to block the sight of people and places which no longer inspired any love or thoughtfulness.

My husband stood back in the dwindling crowd, but I needed not his physical presence. I, alone, had the key to the lock on his heart. My children were at home, playing in the garden, laughing though I was not with them. My sister was there to protect them at least as long as she could, as long as the town fathers would allow her; she was protected herself only by her husband and his father.

My deeds were done. My peace was made with the only God I could care for. I welcomed the lash, and cherished the pain it wrought.

There was nothing left for my tormentor to take from me.

35

Simon Bradstreet

Governor Endicott waited some weeks after he obeyed the King's mandate for the sensation to pass away to a level of quiet grumbling. The fervor, he noted, tended toward support of the action rather than the outrage he and his fellow magistrates and clergy felt. During his reservation to discuss the matter at all for this time, he gave overmuch to thought and whispered discourse with a select group of men in the shadows of his own home and fire, and reached a conclusion: King Charles' mandate must have been fueled by his jealousy of the colony's loyalty to their Lord Protector, Oliver Cromwell, gone these three years past. He also raged with an obsessive fear of Charles willing to lend an open ear to whomever and how many complaints might gather against them without their presence in London to argue against the charges.

On one of these evening debates, Endicott turned to his friend and fellow magistrate, Simon Bradstreet. "We must send a deputation to the King. If his displeasure is left to flourish, then our charter may come to ruin."

Bradstreet nodded in agreement, for he was of a moderate feeling, believing he of all the group there gathered could mediate the colony's position and perhaps even sway the King's temperament at least back to the center of things. But before Bradstreet could speak of the plan formulating in his brain, Endicott declared Colonel

Temple would first go with all due haste to acquaint the King with the colony's attention to having set the Quakers to their liberty.

Colonel Thomas Temple received favor from King Charles upon his return to the throne the previous year and was permitted to remain Governor of Nova Scotia. Endicott did not forgot Temple's proposition to transport all Quakers to his community in the north, and rid the colony of their presence. Though the colony magistrates voted to accept the proposition, the court deputies denied it and it died on the floor of the legislation. Still, Temple could represent the colony and temper the King's feelings, should he lose his objectivity to the horde of rumor-infected mongers.

Bradstreet remained silent as he listened to Endicott speak at length of Temple's accomplishments and thought, were not his own achievements equal in distinction? From the time of his arrival in the colonies, did he not act in all respects for the benefit of the community? Assistant. Magistrate. He even considered, in the deep recesses of his own thoughts, he would one day be rewarded with a governorship.

His wife, Anne Dudley, was of a pleasing nature and distinguished in her own right as daughter to the first governor of the colony, and a poet of some acclaim. He was the father of a healthy brood of children. He built a generous home in Andover. Did not people of the community comment on his modest opinion, his preference for considering the whole of the community rather than a few of its more controlling faction? Could he not be heard arguing against legislation if it would punish people for speaking out, in the tradition of his own father who was a vocal nonconformist? Concluding his self-aggrandizement, was he not a man with whom one could or should trifle? Once his mind was settled on a course, he would give his all to see it through to the end he desired.

Bradstreet was not a large man, and as he aged he grew stout and fleshy about the face. His smallish mouth emphasized his rare smile, though he looked upon his company with tolerance and forbearing. His eyes, too, were small and peevish, but not without a softness.

If you could see anything in his visage it might be strength, with a touch of fairness, shielding a heart not hardened but controlled. Bradstreet bore no great love for the Quaker people. Their growing influence and disruptive behavior throughout the colony, more than their distorted view of God's good graces, vexed him continuously. There were enough troubles across the countryside without adding challenges to the very leaders who endeavored to protect them. Any act to appease these people would surely return to plague the good citizens of the towns and villages.

Bradstreet's disappointment began to rise within him, though he would be loathe to ever show it, especially among the present company. But he found himself very much wanting to be a part of the delegation to the King.

So lost in his own musings he did not hear Endicott calling to him. "Are you quite well, Bradstreet? Your color has risen most noticeably. Should you not retreat from the closeness to the fire, and take a sip of brandy?"

Bradstreet, his attention returned to the room and noticing the looks of concern all about him, replied, "I am quite fine. My apologies. Please continue."

"I said," Endicott restated, "I should think we must also send two agents to follow Temple. Once he has put down the King's anxieties through the rumors of these Quakers, we will need to ensure the vibrancy of our charter."

Turning to Bradstreet again, he went on, "You shall go to act on the colony's behalf and shall take the good Reverend Mr. Norton as your spiritual advisor." Turning his speech to the whole of the room and its occupants, he continued, "We are deeply concerned for the blood of the innocent and their cruel sufferings through the invasion of these abhorrent peoples."

Once again, Bradstreet drifted toward his own thoughts, so wary was he of the talk of blood since receiving the King's mandamus. He, if no one else, would leave things to his God who judgeth righteously. And so, he accepted the role of agent and his instruction to learn the extent of the King's suspicions against the leaders of the colony, and above all to represent its good people as the King's most faithful subjects in hopes the charter would not suffer for these trivial events.

Later, as he lay beside his goodwife, Anne, he considered the supposed dangers of the mission Endicott entrusted to him. As agents of the colony, he and the Reverend Norton might be prone to persecution once they set foot upon the ground of their old country. He thought for some time, there in the quiet and peacefulness of his bed, about the last words from Endicott before he departed the company of men.

As surety of the government of the Massachusetts Colony, Endicott promised all damages suffered by those peoples detained in England by cause of their banishment should be made good. Bradstreet was to be the messenger of this promise. What cause would men who looked upon him as the symbol of murderers of the King's subjects, men who recognized no law or authority from him, have to trust in his word? As he drifted to sleep, Bradstreet resolved he should lay his security in the patience and peaceableness of the principle laid before him—the innocent and suffering who themselves were guided and directed not to avenge themselves—and commit his cause to God who alone could render every man according to his works.

Simon Bradstreet, in the company of the Reverend John Norton, sailed on the tenth day of February, in the year 1662, carrying with them the frigid winds and icy waters of Boston harbor as they made their way into the open seas. For a time, they were accompanied by a pair of great humpback whales. Bradstreet thought of the last weeks, and especially the days leading to this moment. He believed even more strongly in this, for him, would be a journey of truth. Bradstreet watched as the two jumped and rolled up out of the water, and splashed back down in playful motion, the blows like trumpets announcing their arrival.

While Bradstreet might embrace his calm, in his pocket he

carried a letter from Endicott to the King. The last words he kept in his memory for they disturbed him greatly.

> *Although wee hope, and doubt not, but that if his majesty were rightly informed he would be farr from giving them such favor, or weakening his authority here so long and orderly setled, yet, that wee may not in the least offend his majesty, this Court doth heereby order and declare that the execution of the lawes in forces against Quakers, as such, so farr as they respect corporal punishment or death, be suspended until this Court take further order.*

Bradstreet also recalled his mission, if no other, was to endeavor to take off all scandal and objections which were made or may be made against the colony. This included himself, and no disguise or act to palliate the proceedings of the governor's promise and reasons for sending him on this expedition would change the touch of his hand in these circumstances.

36

Dover, in New Hampshire

February, in 1662...

Rebecka and I sat each upon our stools close to the fire for she was near to her confinement, and I was not far behind her. This was one of the coldest of the February nights, and we contented ourselves with the heat washing over our infants in their baskets at our feet, and soaking into our bellies hanging over them. We talked of the difficulties we shared, and the fears we shared, and these were our excuses for not having been to worship or to meeting. These were our excuses for distancing ourselves from our mother and father, our brothers and sisters.

In truth, I had begun to sense a coldness about me which could not be explained by only the winter chill. 'Tis true many of the kind folk of the village greeted me still as they had when I was but a girl. But many others who were newly come to the village, and even many of those who had known Father since the first days of the plantation, now turned their eyes away as I passed. Many of the women turned their backs to me at meeting, setting themselves apart from Mother and Rebecka and myself. I saw the pain spreading across Mother's face each time, though she said not a word. In the quiet of the shadows of the night, Rebecka and I talked of having ourselves only to depend on. In the light of the day we smiled, and we offered ourselves to the community as they would have us.

It was not yet dangerous for us, for we still walked about the village or drove the cart freely about the countryside, but there could be no mistaking the whispers in the air and the looks of penetrating fear from beneath the hats and caps pulled down to shield eyes against the blinding light of the sun bending off the pure white snow. Yet still I walked with my head held up and my shoulders square, if my eyes be still cast down. I could not know what men's and women's minds held, but neither could I be forced to turn back from my purpose. Come what may, I felt I would be protected, if not in body then most assured in soul.

Rebecka and I talked of the blood bond we shared, of the blood to be spilled when our time would come. How I would certainly come to her aid despite my own impending confinement. Would not it be wonderful if we were to birth together, side-by-side, our blood mixing and bringing not only us, but our two children closer? But we were two months apart, or so we judged from the size of our lovely protrusions. And, here we did laugh, though we kept our voices low to not disturb the men at the table. None of the others brought their wives out into the cold, for there was little protection for them, even at our fireside, when they came to sit at our table, and this left Rebecka and I to ourselves.

We listened for a moment, the word *spirit* having caught our attention, and just then I felt the heat from the fire rise and warm my legs then my arms and finally come to rest upon my cheeks. Rebecka noticed my flush, smiled, and reached out to my arm to feel the heat for herself. "You are thinking of your child, Lidia, it shows upon your face."

I returned her smile, but did not tell her it was not to the child my mind had turned.

Edward Wharton was there, at his peril still banished, with old man Marston and his son who were a constant presence in our home. And others, names and faces I've forgotten in the haze left of those days.

Wharton came from Dover, he said, where he met three newcomers from old England. They came up the Piscataqua river, even as ice flowed under frigid winds. But they chose to risk the cold and the ice, to make their way to the town God bade them go thither.

I did not know Dover, but I listened when folks spoke about the convergence of the Piscataqua and Cochecho rivers, and the great falls marking the center of the village. The latter river name, they say, meant rapid foaming water. I could only imagine the scenery through which these rivers flowed, the rushing sound of water over rocks, falling down over ledges, crashing into a waiting pool. I saw myself standing amidst the pool, the water slowed by my presence, swirling about my bare legs, my skirt at first held high to keep it from soaking through. Though it was winter, the water of my imagination was warm. I was then naked, my clothes folded neatly on a fallen log on the bank. I stood there, with the water lapping against my rounded belly, my swollen breasts, beguiled by the roaring falls so close I felt I could reach out and let the water wash over my hand. I felt hands take hold of my head and my back and lower me down gentle into the water. But I was not afraid.

It was there the three travelers stopped, for it was there they could speak with some freedom, and there they could find purpose in the tidal shifts marking the community.

Wharton met the travelers at an inn where people he knew would reason with them and their own faith and hope. They stayed but a few days, but received so many who were want of confession to their truth.

On the last day, though, Priest Raynor of the town thrust through the door and the crowd, who warmed themselves as much with ale and meat as with the ministrations of the travelers, distressed to a great degree. One his flock came to him and said there are such people come to town with much discourse of their religion. This man feared, he told Raynor, he could not contradict what these travelers said, and he wished heartily for his priest to come forward and protect the enlarged following from what surely would cause them to run aground.

So, Raynor broke in upon the four people who sat within the common room of the inn, their backs toward the blazing fire and their smiling faces greeting his arrival. Ignoring the people sitting and standing in close confines around the table, Rayner said to them, "Why have you come amongst us?"

George Preston, the other man who sat beside Wharton, bolstered as he was by the crowd about them, replied they had been amongst them for many a day without concern for being molested. He invited Priest Raynor to join them and they would have a fair discourse. At this, the priest became incensed, and while he composed himself, his wife, who had stood behind him throughout this introduction, came forward. With a deep scowl and a furrowed brow, she asked the group of her towns people standing about which they liked better, her good husband or these vagabond Quakers who wanted only to rouse their nervousness.

Replied one of the townspeople, "We shall tell you true after your husband hath sat with them and listened to their speeches."

Raynor, fretted now beyond apprehension, fairly pushed his wife aside with a heavy hand, and repeated his first question. "What hath brought you here when you know the Laws of the country are against you?"

At this, Mary Tomkins, one of the two women in the party, stood and faced Raynor and looked him direct in the eye, but not without kindness and perhaps some confusion. "What hast thee against us?" she asked him, and then took a step forward to him, close enough to smell the sweet woody scent of sassafras. Would that he could purify his blood so easily.

Priest Raynor took a step back, putting a comfortable space between them. "You deny the magistrates, and you deny the ministers, and the churches of Christ."

Mistress Tomkins would not be dissuaded, answered his charge, "Thee sayest so." She paused, and looked about to judge the tenor of the feelings in the room.

The priest went on. "And, you deny the Three Persons in the Trinity." But his eyes did not well belie his confidence in this truth.

The two men, Wharton and Preston, and their other companion, Alice Ambrose, leaned their heads in together and whispered. Mistress Tomkins was not disturbed, though. In fact, these last words seemed to enliven her.

She raised her arms to the crowd in a welcoming gesture meant to check the tension rising in the room, but said in contradiction, "Take notice, good people, your priest falsely accuseth us." In the roaring silence taking hold of the room, Mary Tomkins' voice, though it be soft and quiet, arrested every movement, every breath. "The Godly magistrates and ministers of Christ we own. The church of Christ we own. Thee is correct there are three God hath bore record to in Heaven, but they are the Father Himself, His Word, and His Spirit. This is the Trinity we own. I ask thee to prove a Trinity of Three Persons as you say."

The priest looked about, searching the faces he knew for the trust he believed he cultivated over the years. His eyes passed from man to man, and woman to woman, and each met him with the same questioning gaze. Never did anyone question Priest Raynor. "I will prove it," he declared.

George Preston rose from his seat on the bench, a protective move toward Mistress Tomkins, and spoke then in a voice also quiet but strong and encouraging. "Men cannot be told, they must be led, but with reason. Thee sayest so," his eyes opening wide, his head nodding forward, "but we ask thee prove by the Scripture thee holds close to thine heart."

Raynor's wife moved closer, nudging him, which served to compose him and complement his confidence. Priest Rayner addressed Preston, man to man. And here he quoted the words he had read time and time again. *Who being the brightness of his glory, and the express image of his person.* In Raynor's mind, he knew Christ was divine, as God was divine, Jesus would be both God and man.

Raynor might have settled into a discourse with Preston at this point if one of the town's men did not choose the brief pause to speak up and challenge his priest with his own knowledge of the Greek translation of the very passage Raynor quoted. "Yea, but it is not person but substance."

Preston again attempted to stir the dialogue and not the paradox. "Thee sayest so, but canst thee prove the other two."

Priest Raynor turned to the learned man, his countryman. In his eyes, if anyone except Wharton was to notice, was the spark of a plea. "Yea, there are three somethings." He realized only then he had allowed himself to be cornered, without escape except by humiliation or violence.

His wife, who was still standing close beside him, moved away to avoid the enraged man's swinging arms, and stood unmoved as he stalked to the door. Before he quitted the crowd, Priest Raynor called out to the people whose faces he saw pressed against the outside of the window they should go away from there.

Mary Tomkins followed him out into the lane and called after him to come back, and she condescended he should not leave his people to the wolves. Raynor neither turned nor slowed his pace away from the growing mob. When she returned to her place at the table in the common room of the inn, with her companions about her, she need not have said for all to hear, "Was it not a hireling who flees from his flock?"

Eager now to end their time at Dover, the travelers soon departed and passed into the province of Maine to where they were next invited.

37

Twenty-One Lashes

There were few left in the crowd. The day was grown late, and the excitement was long since wavered. Gone were the whispers. Gone were the accusations and the judgements floating upon the air, looking for the open ears of those who would choose to listen.

The lash landed upon the top of my right shoulder. No longer vicious, no longer suited to torrid pain. Perhaps a hand came to rest there, and I was no longer able to distinguish a finger from a thong. I was no longer able to even flinch. Instead, my head fell forward, my cheek slid down the side of the pole, and my chin pulled toward my bleeding breast. My eye lids fluttered letting in the faintest of light and the faintest of passing visions.

I cannot say if the people I saw in those moments were truly there or were lingering images in my tired and confused mind. I saw Friends to be sure, and upon their faces were looks of sorrow and love blended together. Their eyes were fixed upon mine, holding me there, giving me their strength by the only means available to them.

The other faces I saw there held a mix of rage, vexation, acrimony and spite. It mattered not whether I knew these people—their eyes, too, were locked on me, and I felt their hands itched to tear what flesh was left off my bones. Were they want to understand what transpired before them, what held them planted to the spot and would not release them back to their homes and their families and their daily routines?. Were their lives forever altered, even should they escape the horrors of this beautiful May day, no matter how many days and weeks and months and years would pass?

More than their eyes, the expressions on their faces would burn into my own memory. I could pretend I was somewhere else. I could open my eyes and relax the muscles of my face. I could smile and greet these people as if I were passing them in the lane. But this would not fool them, nor would it give me any satisfaction for what I was then suffering. There were no answers to be found in the crack of the whip—for any of us.

38

Fortuitous Causes

March, in 1662...

The blossoming spring brought more than blooms to our tiny hamlet of Hampton. As news arrived of the tensions in Boston and London across the seas, the tenor about the village breathed of change and a boldness not before struck so close to our families.

Rebecka gave birth to her second daughter with the loving help of our mother and our sister, Susanna, who was not yet ten years of age. Though my belly was grown large, Eliakim carried me with slow and gentle progress in the cart to Rebecka's home so I could be there, if only to clasp her sweating hand and encourage her with words, which were the only thing flowing freely from my own body. I chided Rebecka, with a laugh, the first breath of spring took her out of the house the day before, but had not seen fit to carry her to meeting, and this, surely, awoke the child within her, and this, her blessing, would be the result. Rebecka Hussey was born on Monday, the tenth day of March. At Mother's behest, Rebecka did carry her newest child to the baptismal celebration on the next meeting day.

A fortnight later, Rebecka's sister by marriage, Hulda, presented herself to the courts to complain about the unseemly speeches made to her by the wife of William Cole on the cause of her and brother John's father, Christopher and his wife, Ann. More than three years passed since the Hussey patriarch took the widow Mingay for his wife, but for some the grudges were long held. As with Goodman Marston, the town of Hampton well respected Christopher Hussey, appointing him many times to positions of responsibility. Eliakim's companionable relationship with both the elder Hussey and his wife was as parent and child. In the earlier days of the town, the men such as Marston, Hussey and Mingay were more cautious of their questions on the Puritan faith, striving to balance their feelings against the risk their deeds might wrought. In this way, they were able to protect their families where conflict seemed to thrive. But, as tensions grew, and their patience and prudence could no longer match the tempers flaring, without reasonable instigation, these men began to look elsewhere for their security. Not long after Hussey's marriage to the still young widow, Christopher became one of the original proprietors of the island of Nantucket, some thirty miles off the southernmost coast of the colony, with the hope of a refuge should it become necessary.

Here we, Reader, first meet Nathaniel Boulter. He was in the colonies for many a year, first at Exeter with Eliakim's father and mother, then at Hampton as he followed Bachiler and Wheelwright much as many had early on. In his younger years he was much in the court's sights for drunkenness and a series of claims both for him and against him, which fixed his character in the townspeople's minds. But by March in 1662, Boulter went quiet within the community and remained so for more than three years. Perhaps age gave him over to a new level of piety or at least a less rebellious nature. We knew of him and may have attempted to greet him with kindness on the proper occasion, but we would not have known this man well, and so we could now give him the benefit of the doubt in his transformation from his earlier course manner. On this occasion, Boulter presented himself to the courts, accused of withholding two calves, two muskets, and a bushel of Indian corn which he was engaged to take from Goodman Edmond Greenliefe in payment for some fine.

Finally, to round out the three fortuitous causes which made their way to the court on a lovely spring Tuesday at the end of March, we find William Fifield was accused of illegally taking away a horse out of the custody of the law. Though no case could be made by the marshal of Ipswich, who made the claim, and the cause was withdrawn, the notches on the pole so to speak were starting to accumulate.

39

Salisbury Court

John Hussey and Eliakim Wardall were fined, each according to law, 6li. 10s. for twenty-six times absence from public ordinance on the Lord's days.

Tuesday, the Eighth Day of April, in 1662...

Neither of us was surprised when the summons came. Nor were we surprised to hear John was also summoned. Eliakim and John were more regular in absenting themselves by then, though Rebecka and I found it in our hearts to attend meeting so long as we could celebrate the baptisms of our children. The court transcripts record only the presentments, and often for the number of meetings missed, but are thin in providing any clue as to when the absences occurred. This summons may have been for absences beginning only a few months before, or longer owing to the delays caused by a meandering court system; it may have been for all the absences thus far, or only those consecutive since our last attendance. The magistrates may have counted absences by the day, or each independent absence for weekly meetings on the Lord's day consisted of preaching in the forenoon, and catechism in the afternoon; aside from the Lord's day, the priests were also compelled to preach midweek. If both the husband and the wife together were absent, the fine took into account only a single day as the wife was nothing more than her husband's appendage. But if the wife was absent alone of her husband, she was fined for her own action.

In any case, the appearance of our Friend Wenlock Christison in December past, may have prompted quicker attention and opened the eyes of the court and the church to our transgressions.

On this occasion, Rebecka and I were both spared the summons, perhaps owing to our conditions, Rebecka having just given birth the previous month and I nearing my own confinement. Salisbury was some eight miles from Hampton village. Rather than concern myself with why the constable did not come for me, I was only grateful I was not called on to make the uncomfortable journey. I did, though, beg Eliakim to take me and baby Joseph to Rebecka so she and I could comfort and amuse each other whilst our husbands stood before the magistrates and the jury.

Throughout the day, Rebecka and I fawned over our babies, did what few chores which would not strain or burden our weakened bodies, and talked of every topic we could imagine. But we did not talk of the trials, and we did not speculate what more cost they could put upon us. It was only a few short months since they took our pretty beast, and I could not think they would exact yet another steep price.

Eliakim and John returned not so late, and my first thought was I should rejoice they returned instead of finding themselves in the stocks or, worse, the gaol. We were able to pull a small supper together for ourselves, and after Rebecka and I satisfied the hungers of our children and put them down quiet before the fire, we asked the men to tell us everything. "Pray leave nothing out."

John was the first to speak, and he let us know our father was sitting upon the grand jury. As with mothers and daughters, and sisters grown close, the three of us felt a bond with one another. This was not so with our father. Where we might have grown to respect, if not love, one another with age and wisdom, Rebecka and I did not feel any such bond with him. Though she never spoke of him, I knew it was anger she harbored, in her youth and to this day. I, on the other hand, began to look upon him differently. There was distance to be sure, but there was also kinship in the silence we shared. I watched Rebecka—her face was calm and she seemed distracted, as if she didn't even hear her husband's words. But I knew her well. Her thoughts were of fear and betrayal.

Eliakim settled onto the stool, and reached across to stroke my hand lain motionless upon the table. How could he know what had just come into my head, and what I could not know myself?

Looking at me, and perhaps only talking to me, Eliakim picked up the tale where John left off. The journey to Salisbury was pleasant. The two men left before the dawn, intent to stop as they would want along the way. If they were to be taken from their chores, there was no reason why they should not receive some joy in the matter. They fished at the Dodge pond and broke their fast by the falls of the Hampton river, listening to the crashing of the water against the outcrop of rocks at the bottom of the stacked boulder wall over which the still freezing spring water rushed. The falls are not so high, nor so immense as I would come to find in Dover to the north, which lent them a delicate and more picturesque escape. The colors of the trees and leaves were not so vibrant as they would be in the fall. But, there was a peacefulness about the place I would cherish.

I smiled, pulled away from my thoughts, and realized how well he knew my mind.

"We passed by Gove's farm then," Eliakim went on, and waved a greeting to their acquaintance, but did not stop to talk for they meant to stop also at the Perkins house and give their regards to our mother and father. They arrived and were greeted happily by Susannah, and the gaggle of little ones still running about the Perkins farm. Here, they learned, as they drank hot chicory against the early morning chill, Isaacke would also be going to Salisbury to sit on the jury for the day's proceedings. Isaacke knew nothing of the summons, nor did Eliakim and John know of Isaacke's task.

John added here the silence between them all, sitting there at the table as family, was very awkward. At this, Rebecka raised her head and a small grin broke across her face. "Do not fancy you were the cause of his uneasiness, my love. Silence in Father's house has always been so."

At this we all laughed, for our husbands knew this as well as did Rebecka and I. John went on, describing with a great gust how the children broke the strain, and the four were able to find other more friendly topics to discuss. They soon departed, determined to ride the rest of the way together. As men. As family. They continued on, though in silence, and stopped only once more to pluck a copper from their pockets and pay the toll.

Seated solemn in the back of the tavern in which the court sat, Eliakim and John awaited their call to the bar. They did not have a long wait, fifteen causes heard, appointments made, excuses registered. Captain Thomas Wiggin, the magistrate on the bench, called out their names and the two men rose and walked to the front to present themselves.

Wiggin looked at them with hardness in his eyes. His spiritual convictions were so strong he would not, no matter how he might look upon the men standing before him, suffer the disrespect of the church.

"John Hussey. You are the son of Goodman Christopher Hussey are you not?"

"I am, Sir," John said with a smile.

Wiggins did not return the pleasantry but mumbled, "'Tis a pity," then moved on. "Eliakim Wardell." Eliakim was not so easy in spirit as his brother, and so he only looked forward, eyes blank, and said not a word. His last appearance in the court, begging for remuneration for our pretty beast, still bit harsh at the back of his neck.

What was going through the mind of Isaacke Perkins as he sat, unmoving, with his two sons before him? Did he think them reckless? Or did he envy their boldness? Did he fear the connection—who among the men sitting on the bench or waiting their turns knew these two men were his sons? Did he rue the marriages he had once blessed?

"You are fined, each according to the law," Wiggins boomed from his pulpit, "five shilling for every absence on the Lord's day." The public ordinance made failure to attend meeting a civil matter. It seemed a steep price for faith. The clerk's quill scratched against the paper. Twenty-six times absent. Six pound ten shilling.

Wiggins looked up from his paper and glared at the two men before him. His disgust leveled on the table as the gavel slammed hard against the wood. The clerk shuffled papers in the corner. Isaacke Perkins coughed. Both men looked to him, and the three nodded. Sitting next to Perkins was William Fifield.

The coin Eliakim paid from his pocket before he returned home, but ever strong in our belief God would provide as He saw necessary. Some might have thought these costs would better have been paid to keep warmth in our humble home, the winter past was a long and frigid one. The snow, too deep at times, buried many an early spring bud. But we were frugal and this time, at least, we would not seek comfort from those of our community who were still friendly toward us lest our two babies suffer needlessly in the hardship of our own making.

Costs run deeper than the coin gone from our hands.

40

Foreboding

The next lash burrowed its way deep, more severe for the scarcity of unmarred flesh remaining on my shoulders, back, and buttock. The whip caught my hair fallen against the bleeding wounds, and stuck there, and twisted it in the thongs, pulling my head back as the lash left my shoulder and fell away down my back. I heard the tiny bones of my neck crunch and my throat lifted and strained, forcing my mouth open into a wide and pitch black cavern. I railed equal in its harshness. The words poured from my mouth were none I had ever spoken, before or since, words of which I had no knowledge. Words which no civilized woman should ever utter.

But they found their mark.

When the screaming stopped, when the chirp of the birds hidden in the trees all around once again reached my ears, I was in my home, laying on a bed of fresh straw before a blazing fire, a blanket of new wool covered me and my suckling child.

We welcomed William on a crisp Thursday morning, the twenty-third day of the third month, in the year of our Lord, 1662. May is a bonny time in the colonies. The breezes fair, spreading the scent of heaven all about. The wild azaleas, clusters of bright pink and pure white against the blooming greens of spring, found their way to our open door. Eliakim took Joseph out to the coop to wake the chickens so I could find a bit of sleep. Mother was seated at the table, her hair fussed, her eyes drooped after the long night. Rebecka lay in our bed in the loft with her two young daughters, softly snoring.

By the crackling of the fire, and the gentle rising and falling of my body as I faded into and out of a broken slumber, I watched myself as at a distance walking into the meeting house on Sunday next, my new babe wrapped and held tight to my bosom. There I sought to receive the one and only baptism into the beginning of his new spiritual life. Before me all the village mothers, their babes in their arms, hosts to a covenant of grace. Their backs were to me, their attention on the priest standing before them. They were listening with rapture to his words. But they were obscure to me.

I was suddenly afraid, and I felt the glow fading from my face and my body becoming heavy, a burden I wrapped about my shoulders.

The priest moved his gaze from the women standing before him to me, apart from them, my feet rooted to the wooden planks.

"You are not a believer." His accusations were a hand slapping my face. Another voice screamed, "Your silence is your insolence. Speak."

But I could not. And I was ashamed. Faith, repentance. Are these just words stuck in my head, kept from reaching my tongue? This was my covenant with God. "Please, take my child, by His grace, we should be made heirs according to the hope of eternal life."

"Go from this place. You shall not receive this sacrament. You shall not stand by these women, bring your child into the presence of their children." The silence crowded me, screamed at me, spun me around until I was dizzy. The priest turned his attention back to the other women standing there, immovable as wooden posts. No sound came from any of the infants in their arms.

I never set foot again within the four walls of the meeting house in the village of Hampton. I grieved then and there for what would come to be. William, his life was to be cut short and he faded into a mere shadow of his brothers and sisters, reaching out but never grasping the grace he deserved, but was denied.

Hanging there, hanging on to what life was left in me, I watched as we would eventually say our farewells to Rebecka and John and move on without them; as Father would pass his quiet life into quiet death; and as Mother would find peace outside the colony. When this was all over, we never would see them again, any of them.

41

Bradstreet and Norton

The End of April, in 1662...

The ship arrived in London harbor, and the captain and crew attended to the business of docking. Colonial Magistrate Simon Bradstreet and Reverend John Norton waited until they were bid take careful step on the plank. Hands reached out to assist them, but they both waved these gestures off. They could manage well enough on their own. They hailed a coach, waiting as two of the ship's crew handed up their trunks for the coachmen to secure to the sagging roof.

Norton settled himself onto the plush velveteen seats. He reflected on the fact there were no coaches in the colonies, only the hard leather saddles or the splintered buckboards. His mind was filled with praise for their good fortune to be returned to the civilities of their former homeland.

But when Norton turned, Bradstreet was not being handed up into the coach, nor was he even near the opened door. Norton leaned over, curious as to where his colleague got to, and peered out. Bradstreet was there, two or three paces toward the back of the coach, with a man whom Norton did not recognize. The look upon their faces was neither congenial nor alarming, but Norton immediately felt ill at ease. He looked about and, seeing neither footman nor coach drivers standing near, he calmed his restlessness so as to hear the words between the two men.

"Did thee have a hand in the hanging of four servants of God, for nothing more than receiving your name of Quaker?"

At this, Norton forgot himself and he called out from the coach door. He heartily denied any wrongdoing on the parts of his or any of his patrons among the God-fearing subjects of the King who bid him come to London.

Both Bradstreet and the unidentified challenger did not realize their conversation held an extra pair of ears, and so turned, first stunned then not a little embarrassed at their words which carried even those few paces.

George Fox knew which of the two men held the power in their cause, and so he turned away from Norton to face Bradstreet again, and continued his questioning. "By what law did you put our Friends to death?" In a moment of silence passing between Fox and Bradstreet, the moment in which Bradstreet calculated how much he would say in answer to these charges, Fox thought of Robinson, and Stevenson, of Leddra, but especially of Mistress Mary Dyer; all his disciples, all who suffered at the hands of the colony leaders.

Bradstreet shifted from one foot to another. As if the names had been spoken aloud, he too recalled the faces of these departed souls. He had not on every occasion been sitting on the court bench when these rulings were passed, and so he could not own all of these deeds, but instead he replied with all the innocence and pride he could muster, saying he was a magistrate, and as such he represented all the colonial magistrates when they acted on the authority of the English law against Jesuits.

Bradstreet had not present during the last exchange, between Governor Endicott and Wenlock Christison, when this same argument found no footing. But the story was thoroughly relayed to him by Deputy Bellingham. Having failed at once to give proper acknowledgment to this man's insight and knowledge of the events across the ocean, Bradstreet chose poorly in his risk at using the same explanation here.

Fox allowed the corners of his mouth to ease upward, the smile barely perceptible to anyone but Bradstreet. "And did you believe the men—and the woman—you hung were Jesuits?"

Bradstreet's innocence was more marked now he realized he was caught. He was compelled by his own honor to admit then, "Nay, I did not believe this."

"Yea, then, if thee had put them to death by the laws of England which would allow the punishment of a Jesuit, and yet thee confess they were no Jesuit, it is plain by your own will and without law you would put them to death." In this moment, Fox spoke not to or of Bradstreet alone, but of all who had participated in the death of his Friends.

Fox watched Bradstreet's face change as he spoke these words. When the discourse had begun, Bradstreet held his head high and showed no fear in his eyes. Now, with these few words spoken, the skin of his faced sagged as if Bradstreet were aging before his eyes. His shoulders fell and were then rounded instead of square and broad. His eyes flickered side to side, and his mouth twitched at the corner.

Finishing his thought, Fox verily spat, "You have murdered them."

Bradstreet was clearly affected by the charge, but his mind was quick to grasp the impact it might have on his quest to ensure the strength of the colony's charter against this unpleasant business. Here, he forgot completely Endicott's promise to mollify such as these people. His response then only testified to his growing discomfort with this exchange. "Have you come here to entrap us?" Forgetting the comfort he drew from the distance he enjoyed from other men, he then looked about for a savior or a circumstance which would allow him to turn from this man, climb safe into the sanctity of the waiting coach, and the fellowship of his advisor, and continue on to his business at Whitehall Palace.

"Thee has caught thyself, and by thine own admission should

thee be brought here to answer for the lives of those good people. Thee has no need to fear me," Fox went on, "but if I were Robinson, father of William whom thee saw to his death, standing before thee here, thee should be strenuously questioned and I could not protect thee."

Seizing on the quiet with which the man now looked upon him, Bradstreet made to turn away toward the coach. But he stopped, his commitment to Endicott entered on his mind. Instead, Bradstreet looked back to Fox and said, "There is no persecution now, here, between you and I."

Bradstreet and Norton went immediately to Whitehall Palace, anxious to be quit from the docks, and from the emerging menace of the crowd. They let fall the curtains over the windows to block the view they had both been anticipating after so long an absence.

Instead of enjoying the sights, Bradstreet leaned back and ticked them off one by one from memory. When they left England for the colonies, a new palace was planned, still to be called Whitehall, and he was anxious to see it and how time changed the landscape. He recalled St. James' Park. The tree-lined walking lane. The Horse Guards barracks to the left. The Banqueting House there behind them, reaching up to cloud-filled skies. The Holbein Gate with its four-towered gatehouse. The Chapel.

These memories comforted him once again.

When the coach came to a stop at the massive doors of the main palace, the two men stepped out to the outstretched gloved hands of a footman in extravagant livery on either side. The dust brushed from their clothes, their hats resettled upon their heads, the disturbing encounter forgotten, they were most flattered by the reception they received.

George Fox went away from the meeting satisfied with the thoughts he infused in his contender, and hoped they would not soon leave him.

The very next morning, as if by providence, Fox received a bundle of letters from the very ship he greeted the day before. As he read the words of his Friends and such acquaintances who would inform him of events in the colonies, he learned there were persecutions anew—even as the agents were at the very moment assuring the King of their felicity.

Taking his hat from the peg by the door of his house, George Fox put the letters into his coat pocket and strode out into the new day. He took the long walk to the Whitehall Palace, vowing to return to the steps each day until Bradstreet and Norton were come to enter or depart.

The two men settled into the London routine easily. They visited with old friends and renewed acquaintances over ale and stew in the taverns. They conducted their business as was their charter, and endeavored to diminish the damages to their cause and to themselves as much as they could do without overstating the concern and thus drawing suspicion.

While Bradstreet worked the patricians, Priest Norton excited himself on any number of occasions by bowing deep, despite the ache in his aging knees, and no less reverent to the Archbishop than he had to the King. The Episcopalian bishops to whom he endeared himself were no great lovers of the Quakers, and Norton pleased himself to find many could be counted as allies. But he found they could not countenance cruel persecution either. To their questioning, Norton found it sufficient to remind them he had not taken any direct part in the bloody trials, nor—was he quick to add with a look about his face of true sincerity—did he advise such a course of action.

Between the efforts of the two colonial emissaries, the Crown's support was secured for a means to keep the Quakers vexed, if not permitted to put them to death outright.

But over the course of the weeks, they became comfortable, and lazy under the protections they there enjoyed. Nearing the end of their business, Bradstreet and Norton stepped through the large heavy doors of Whitehall Palace out into a blinding sunshine, and there they should have considered the omen of such a disturbing change in London weather. But they did not. Instead, they descended on light foot and lighter heart down the marble steps to their waiting carriage where Bradstreet heard the call from behind him. He stopped, thinking another of his dear old friends might have want of some company for the evening.

Bradstreet's smile turned downward as he spied George Fox moving at a quick pace toward him, waving a packet of letters in his hand and begging his leave for just a few words. A footman was already handing Norton with delicacy up into the carriage, who was too far away, in any case, for Bradstreet to call out to without drawing unwanted attention. No one else was about to call upon for assistance in avoiding this man with whom he did not wish to be caught again. Seeing himself thus in danger, he began to flinch and to skulk.

"Sir," Fox addressed Bradstreet not without a proper amount of condescension, Bradstreet thought. But without another word, Fox thrust the packet into Bradstreet's hands.

Bradstreet looked with a puzzled expression at the packet in his hand, then he raised his eyes to Fox. "What would you have me do with these…sir?"

Fox replied, his face stern, but his manner continued to be respectful, "Choose any of these letters, and read any selected passage, and you will see what abounds through them all."

Without means of escape, and fearing any refusal would turn him out to criticism, abuse, or even assault, Bradstreet rested his walking stick against his leg and selected a letter, and with the tips of his fingers was careful to unfold it. He read in silence, then refolded it. A disturbed look began to form on Bradstreet's face. He selected another, and again moved his eyes across the words. One word. *Calamitous*. He read through a third and then a fourth before deciding each would bare the same damning claims. Fox watched as Bradstreet's face tightened, his lips pressed, his eyes narrowed. The color in his face all but drained away. If the King had not seen these letters yet, it would not be long.

Bradstreet folded the last of the letters and returned the packet still tied with a neat string to his patient companion. Without a word, Bradstreet took his walking stick once again in his hand and turned. He walked as quickly away as he could properly do.

Fox called after him, "I leave you to the Lord, whose vengeance is His alone."

In the silence of the carriage, Bradstreet could not stop the voices in his head from reminding him it was he who confessed to Fox before the witnesses milling about on the docks those weeks ago to his hand in the death of Quakers. He must own this, mistake or no, but for the first time he felt fear.

He knocked upon the roof of the coach and shouted for the driver to go not to the inn, but to the docks. Norton looked at Bradstreet, but was stopped from speaking by the indescribable dread marking his face.

Bradstreet booked passage for both the men on the next ship sailing for the colonies. He would have many weeks to contemplate his failure.

42

Simon Bradstreet

Summer, in 1662...

Simon Bradstreet returned to the colonies to the searing heat of an early and prolonged summer. He carried the King's letter memorializing the twenty-eighth day of June. In the letter, the King permitted the men of the colony to make a sharp law against the Quaker people, but one consistent with, or at least not contradictory to, his earlier mandamus. In tenor, the words might be thought most kind and conciliatory. Through the intervention of Simon Bradstreet and John Norton, the King accepted the professions of his loyal subjects across the sea, just as he had accepted the pleadings of Edward Burrough nine months before. The King acknowledged the anxious and frightened musings of both the magistrates afar and the Quakers hovering on his doorstep, one cancelling out the other, while leaving both to resolve the problem amongst themselves.

As Bradstreet returned to his duties, his mind weighed heavier on the plight taking hold in the colony since his return from London. The Reverend Seaborn Cotton was like to feel the same burden of fear and consternation, which he may have captured in his sermons and thus noted in his commonplace book. Of the church meeting on the eleventh day of August, Cotton wrote

> *Whither women who profess theyre inability to speak in publique may bee admitted to comunion with ye church by the reading of what they comunicate in writing. This is owned as ye judgment of ye church...It was also agreed to by the Church that whatever Church members of ours should attend ye meetings of Quakers & ioyne with ym therein, ye It was scandalous & offensive to the whole body.*

The time was ripe, and could not have been seen as more providential, for Reverend Cotton to acknowledge the value and importance of women in the communion ceremony, which in those early days took place on each and every Lord's day. But women did not simply profess their inability to speak, they were expressly forbidden from it specifically in the meeting house, and generally in public. If they could not speak, could they fully receive communion? And if they could not fully receive communion, were they in disobedience to the Lord's commands, left without means to remember Christ and examine themselves and pray for his coming; were they left outside the Lord's doorway, and thus vulnerable to the ravages of heretical wolves? I can see Cotton offering this as appeasement to the women of the congregation with modesty so they, too, could present themselves and be saved, not in contradiction to the law, but in recognition of their place in unity.

That Cotton obfuscated his conciliatory gesture with a warning to avoid joining in with the Quakers, whose circling about the good people of the town, lying in wait for them, was nothing short of scandalous and offensive, shows the sympathy he coveted with the courts—where the court shall lead, the church must surely follow.

43

Lashes

The tongues of the whip found the rare remaining patch of untouched skin at the small of my back, near where the gussets of my waistcoat would lie and flutter so slightly as I walked in the breeze to the barn or to the common—or to the meeting house. This was all my mind registered as I left my physical presence and retreated more into my memories.

My identity among the community, my face, my hair, my beliefs, my heart, no longer of any consequence to these proceedings. To the constable, whose arm was then recoiling, slackening for a brief moment to gather energy and strength for the next swing, I was little more than the post to which I clung. To the few townspeople who continued to move about in aimless circles, I was no longer a tender and chaste young woman. With my buttock as exposed as my breasts, I was the Jezebel among them, and they strained to look upon me in this way rather than listen to the message I carried even then, as I still stood among them.

I thought if I shifted my legs too much, what was left of my clothing would fall to the ground and I would bare what was left of my body and soul. And I thought of the irony of it. The act of being naked in public no longer the crime, but a measure of the punishment. There would be no escape for them, clothed or unclothed, the message would be the same.

44

Reverend Seaborn Cotton

October, in 1662...

The legislature drafted a new Cart and Whip Act. The King's letter along with this new law were put before the court at Boston on the eighth day of October, in 1662, to the rousing acceptance of all in attendance.

One week later, William Fifield was sworn as constable of Hampton.

Five years passed since the town selected the Reverend Seaborn Cotton to aid our teacher, Timothy Dalton, in his final years. Cotton was ordained and called to the town to begin his labors as minister in November of 1657. Dalton was then in his eightieth year. For the next four years, Cotton stood by the teacher, waiting, publicly revering him as he would have revered his own father. Dalton was known to be unsympathetic to the Quakers, and could be cruel in his exhortations of them, both in his teachings and in his conversing among the faithful about the village, even begging those who chose to hear the ramblings of the Quakers to suffer for their ideas and spitting out the distasteful bile he claimed filled his mouth to even speak of them. But history left nothing to suggest Dalton would seek out the punishment of those who would stray from his teachings. One could be cruel in word, but have sympathy in deed. Perhaps he believed it was the court's place to dispense civil justice while he was limited only to dispensing spiritual pacification. During those four years, Cotton's indignation at Dalton's failure to raise his fist above his voice festered and grew and took hold of any spirit his father, old John Cotton the dissenter, might have left behind. So, when the Reverend Dalton passed on a snowy dismal day in December, in the year 1661, Cotton was no longer composed and he could no longer contain his wrath.

Eliakim and I watched over the intervening ten months as the ire in Reverend Seaborn Cotton gave vent to designs outside of the court, first with Eliakim and I as the object, then one by one our family and Friends.

The grand jury sitting at Hampton presented old William Marston along with Eliakim and I, and John and Rebecka for absenting ourselves from the ordinances of the Lord's day. It would be several months before we were called to court for our sentencing.

Mistress Elizabeth Hooten and her daughter, lately expelled from Boston and then Dover, stopped at our home where we gave them shelter for many a day, enjoying the stories of their travels and hearing the Word spoken with such eloquence. For this, Priest Cotton commanded Constable Fifield to detain the two ladies and exact a fine amounting to a few bushels of corn and several flitches of bacon.

Then, Priest Cotton was angered by William Marston's repeated presentations to the court for absences from worship, his sharp tongue and his wayward influences from Hampton to Salem. Further frustrated by the court's deficiency in it firmness in dealing with Marston, Cotton ordered our Friend, despite his age and growing infirmity, to be whipped with great relish for nothing more than his sympathies with the Quakers.

And, the beatings did not stop there. Thomas Newburn and John Leddel, well-known Quaker itinerant preachers, with Edward Wharton, were passing through Hampton from safe house to safe house and came to the home of John and Rebecka where they passed several hours in comfort. Then, to our great surprise, the three made their way to my father's house where they were sheltered happy for the night among the pack of children. When Cotton received this news from one of his many spiders, he ordered both John Hussey and Isaacke Perkins, by then beyond his fiftieth year, to be whipped. On the appointed day, Rebecka and I, along with our mother could not bring ourselves to watch. Eliakim stood with only Goodman Christopher Hussey by his side to bear witness, all the while seething with passion and fury at their treatment at the hands of William Fifield. Fifield could not know these events would set the tone for his entire appointment as constable.

45

The Wife of Robert Wilson

November, in 1662...

She was married to Robert Wilson on the twelfth day of the sixth month in 1658. It was in the same year, little more than a fortnight before, when she first appeared to the court. This first time, she was among twelve people who convented together at the house of Lawrence Southwick, and she escaped prosecution though her mother and brother were not so fortunate.

Whether her future husband held her same beliefs is not clearly reported, and some have said he did not. Never was he called to court for any activities, Quaker or otherwise. And it seems it would be unlike a good Puritan to agree to wed a woman whose beliefs would differ so greatly from his own, and perhaps, like Isaacke Perkins, he may have found a man's power does not lie in his actions, but rather his willingness to stand clear and let misguided power turn upon and destroy itself.

I cannot say she was a dutiful wife, and I cannot now say what her husband thought as he may have sat with her and listened to the pronouncement of charges and sentencing on a cold day in November, just six months before my own presentment.

Does not Corinthians teach us we, like Paul, believe in the simple truths of the Gospels, and this makes us but fools; we must question the Christian has words and deeds so powerful they make others weak and thus free of honor. We must then show we are none of this by showing our spiritual nakedness. We have nothing to hide, and thus none have reason to fear or subjugate us.

She is recorded as both a wife and a daughter, but nowhere does she appear in court proceedings as herself, a young woman with a name.

Did they perhaps try to hide her identity when the magistrates were so careless to reveal others like us? It would not be like them to choose to protect her when they seemed to relish in the satisfaction of finding and punishing Quakers, and those who would protect them. Rather this could be a sign and a warning to the good townsfolk, to her family who continued to be a menace to the community—to those who had not yet been revealed—a warning the days of tolerance, or their brand of it, were coming to an end. A woman with a name has also a face. A woman with a face has a voice. If the woman be a Quaker, and she is willing to speak aloud, then she is a danger to herself and her family.

I have no way of saying now, all these years later, whether I actually knew this woman, knew of her, or only prayed there were others like me out there somewhere thinking the same thoughts and asking the same questions, struggling with the same feelings. I have not a doubt her talk, and the gossip which would have followed, made its way with haste and embellishment to our village. With no one to deny it, I will take my liberty to at least give her credit for her courage and inspiration. We became forever sisters through the judgment of others who would question my sanity alongside of hers.

Her mother and brother were both summoned to appear at the same court for their attendance on the same day at the house of Nicolas Phelps. It was there many Friends were found, engaged in what the court called disorderly meeting, in the time of the public worship. Two men remained when the group was alerted, and were present when the authorities arrived. They readily professed themselves to be Quakers and were taken forthwith to the house of correction. Others made an escape, but were later apprehended. They, too, professed themselves as Quakers and were taken also to the house of correction. Others still, her mother and brother among them, managed to make their ways home without incident but were later summoned. Though her mother made her repentance to the court and was released, her brother owned himself a Quaker and was sent to the house of correction.

Two fortnight later, another of her brothers presented his statement with the same Lawrence Southwick from the house of bondage in Boston where they were then captives. Among them who signed the statement was Cassandra Southwick, goodwife of Lawrence, who would come to know the whip well and often for her crimes of faith.

And so, the stage was set for the young woman. Perhaps she, too, thought she had no choice, she was compelled by the treatment of the people around her, compelled by her faith, to speak up in a way which would garner attention, not for her action but for her spiritual courage.

> *The wife of Robert Wilson, for "her barbarous & unhuman goeing naked through the Towne, is sentenced to be tied at a Carts tayle with her body naked downward to her wast, & whipped from Mr. Gidneyes Gate till she come to her owne house, not exceeding 30 stripes, & her mother Buffum & her sister Smith, that were abetted to her &c. to be tyed on either side of her, at the carts taile naked to their shifts to ye wast, & accompany her.*

Upon the bench sitting in judgment of her were both Major William Hawthorne and the Worshipful Simon Bradstreet. Hawthorne was known to be harsh and vengeful, a trait which won him great favor in his campaigns against the savage Indians. But from the experience seems to have grown a bitterness and equally savage and judgmental nature against those peoples who might not favor his own views, even shall they be his oldest of friends. His laws and punishments were known to be of the most strict, especially as he applied them against Quakers.

It is no wonder he should pronounce her barbarous and unhuman for baring her innocence and faith through Salem Towne. He would look upon her as a savage, someone so far removed from the community—a kin in spirit to the Indians whose language was not his and whose customs were not his, but whose differences bred nothing but fear and mistrust. I would like to think he could no more look upon her from the bench, than he could have on the day for which she now stood in judgment; and she would stand there, straight and proud as I would. He could, after all, look upon her in no other way if he was to be seen as a pillar, a foundation of strength, and not a mere man.

Was he in the streets those weeks before and had he gazed unwitting upon her as many must have? Would he have recognized her from her previous business with the courts, or from the streets of the town? Would he have been shamed to admit he knew her, or worse yet, knew of her in a more personal way and he now allowed her take some measure of control from him by her very presence?

He could not. And so, it is my hope and my prayer Hawthorne should look upon her with the same disgust as he would have on the day for which she now stood in judgment; at least he would be constant and thus proud in his abhorrence though rigid and hard hearted as it may be.

And, what of the Worshipful Mr. Bradstreet? What would he recall as he sat facing this woman? Did he dare face her, or did he turn his eyes away? His own righteousness was stripped away, and the wounds not yet healed from his foray to London and his exchanges with George Fox. She was a daughter—he, too, had daughters. She was a wife—he, too, had a wife. She would be a mother one day, for it was the course of all young women. Mary Dyer had been a daughter, a wife and a mother. Yet his hand was upon her execution, even then.

Would he arrive home in the depths of the night, when his work was done, and cast his eyes down as his wife asked what he had done, again? Did he justify the whipping was for the governor an appropriate response to the King's demand for executions be not fitting to the men of the new colonies, and even so, a far cry better a punishment than death? Would he plead with her the matter was in making them obey, not in how the deed was done?

No. He likely spared her the gruesome details. He was not a man to beg and plead. She did hold her own failings and yearnings, for they plagued her often enough then, close to her heart in fear of her own self-betrayal.

The court could not reverse what had already taken place, nor could they wipe the memory from those who had witnessed it. But as they tied the young woman to the cart's tail and decreed she be compelled to walk once again naked and for their benefit, these men, strangers all, would put their hands upon her, turn her message of innocence and faith into a spectacle and exert their own control to spread it wide and far.

Her mother and sister were punished alongside her, for their influence upon her or perhaps only hers upon them. Poor Mr. Gidney was to be punished twice for the misfortune of having his house on the spot where this wayward young woman first chose to shed her burden, and then where the court chose to begin their parade.

And thus, *she was carried through all these inhuman cruelties quiet and cheerful, to the shame and confusion of these unreasonable men, whose names shall rot and their memories perish.*

Deborah was her name, but she stood by the other women of Salem. She was Anne Hutchinson—she was Mary Dyer—she was Anne Bradstreet.

And she was me. Sisters are bound by more than blood.

46

Three Vagabond Women

Mistress Deborah Wilson was the test of the new Cart and Whip Act. Her cause told them how much the community could withstand, how far the magistrates could go without risk of turning the majority of the community, the loyal and dutiful sheep of the villages, against them.

The winter was until then moderate as New England winters go. No frost appeared on the ground until the twentieth day of December. The sun blinded rather than brightened our days, and there was little heat but for the tempers and fear rising around us.

Word came of another disturbance, and I asked Eliakim to travel the twenty-one miles to Dover as a witness, more important, as a Friend. He would not argue for his own blood boiled at the decree. But he would not allow me to accompany him. He showed his apprehension by holding me more tightly through the night. I could not have asked for a man of more sincere or gentle a touch. I did not dismiss his concerns, not for the frigid winds, nor even for my young sons' discomfort in the long day of travel. Laying there, in the protection of my husband's warmth and strength and conviction of his own purpose, I could not explain the foreboding feeling holding firm to me, and staying with me until I could stand it no longer.

We may have known Mary Tompkins, Alice Ambrose and Anne

Coleman were lately come from Maine where they felt some little degree of safety. It took them not long to raise the ire of the Priest Raynor, who bore them still a grudge for their treatment of him just ten months before. This time, he excited Magistrate Richard Waldron of Dover, a man whose disposition fitted him to the Priest's purposes, to prosecute them. The law had allowed them free passage through Dover the first time; the Priest would not allow such generosity a second.

The new act allowed the magistrates to run Quakers, whether they be self-professed or only accused, out of town one way or another. And if banishment on the pain of death would not be tolerated, then they could drag the accursed out tied to the tail of a cart, naked and bleeding from the sting of the whip and conveyed from village to village until they were cast out of the jurisdiction. If once became twice, and still thrice so entertained them, a brand would be cast before they again would be turned out. Death under the old laws would be the only salvation for the unrepentant.

A hard snow came late the night of the twenty-first day of the tenth month. But this did not deter the constable. If anything, it inspired him all the more. The next morning, in the early hours of daylight, in the dead cold and upon the frozen hard ground, this equally cold and hard man made sure a mob of on-lookers gathered, more interested in the beating of three women than in their own health and the well-being of their families.

The words were harsh, and doubly so when I finally heard them through Eliakim's soft lips. *To the Constables of Dover, Hampton, Salisbury, Newbury, Rowley, Ipswich, Wenham, Linn, Boston, Roxbury until these vagabond Quakers are carried out of this jurisdiction...* declared Magistrate Waldron, his instruction thrust upon the ten men, elected for their loyal and just care to the colony, whose towns he meant to enlist in his cause to pass judgment for the women's sins by the twisted knotted thong thrice lethal as it would cut to their very bone. The end would come only after their last penance at Dedham.

The task was an impossible one, if it were meant to be carried out in the light of a single day.

Today, the towns follow a straight path, eighty miles due south as the crow flies from the starting point. But this was no migration for hunting or climate, nor even for survival. If the laws then forbade a punishment by death for treason of the Church, it did not forbid torture. And if the shortness of this torture for Mistress Wilson would not deter, then it would be made greater and greater still until, it would be believed, our folly would be ended by self-preservation. They could not have known, standing there in the frigid air, how much they underestimated our will.

These towns together spanned the north-south edges of the colony's jurisdiction, and the authority, from which Constable Waldron spoke. The towns are no longer much separated from one another; the selection of these constables no longer imply any relationship other than their place along this route.

The route today would still take a traveller along the banks of the bay, the wind made colder as it came off the calm waters between Dover and Hampton. From Salisbury to Newbury, the channel would have to be crossed. Today, a bridge crosses near the mouth, and though it is not the most narrow part, it is perhaps the shallowest, or even a place where the banks are such a bridge is made more solid. Perhaps, a bridge did then exist at this same spot. A bridge wide enough, and sturdy enough, for a cart, three women, and a raucous crowd. The channel upstream a short ways is cut by Ram Island and then again by Carr Island. Perhaps the brush and overgrowth on both made them unsafe and difficult to traverse. Or perhaps they served as a gathering place for more spectators.

The constable of Dover spoke these words from a pulpit of his own making. God had made him a man, as He has made us women, subjected to our own failings. We all must do what we each believe to be right. And it is the failing of a man's selfishness and arrogance which keeps him from permitting others a sense of right.

I imagine he glanced about to gauge the reactions of the crowd.

This was his moment, and he would cherish it, the bite at each word, and the passion of his responsibilities drowning out everything else. Vagabonds we were. Not fit to enjoy the comforts and rights of citizens. These men would have the community believe we had no place in any of towns of the colony. And, thus we must be run out, abandoned, an example for others who choose to forsake the time honored rules and Scriptures of man and God.

Waldron read on, his fists clutching at the paper, shaking perhaps and overcome with emotion. *You and every of you are required, in the King's Majesty's name...*

The constables of the other towns, having received their directive, were then positioning themselves at their village edges, or within nearby houses for the warmth, waiting with eagerness or apprehension, watching for the procession to arrive. Others at the more distant villages waited comfortable, or perhaps not so, in their own homes for messengers with news of the approaching party. Whether their hearts encouraged or protected them, they could not help but be drawn into this charade. They all would play their part. But surely, it would cross the minds of each there might be one who possessed the strength to stop it.

The only man not present, with a role in the day's events, was the King himself. How misplaced was his trust in his chosen emissaries across the water.

> *...take these vagabond Quakers, Anne Coleman, Mary Tomkins and Alice Ambrose, and make them fast to the cart's tail, and driving the cart through your several towns...*

Elakim described for me the scene under the gray dawn sky; the eerie quiet where even the falls of the nearby Cocheco river were frozen in the moment. A woman came forward and addressed the constable. "Put them in hand-cuffs," she shouted for all the crowd to hear.

Some in the crowd responded with shouts and jeers of their own. Others, Eliakim noted, stepped away, and shrank into the crowd. Waldron, with a smile upon his lips, did not raise his eyes from the page, but did a wave of his free hand to bade the constable of Dover, Thomas Roberts, to do as his wife required.

A deputy then tied the women to the tail of a cart which, for his convenience, was offered by a loyal man of the town. The leather straps were pulled tight, and Eliakim told me he could see the red skin of their freezing hands, strained, as they tried to move little from their stooped and unnatural positions. One of them he described as little and crooked.

A voice came from the crowd, meant to be hidden, but Eliakim knew the man to be James Heard, another of our Friends. "Are those the cords of your Covenant?" The little woman turned to the voice, but did not speak. The persecutors continued as if they did not hear the question.

After the three were bound tight to the cart, Waldron lifted his eyes and addressed the woman closest to him. "Who are you?" Having just read their names, he knew not which of the three women before him was which.

Said she, with her gaze engaging his, "My name is written in the Lamb's book of life."

With a barely noticed pause, he returned his eyes to the paper in his hand. "No-one here knows this book...and for this you shall suffer mightily."

The others uttered not a word; their eyes showed their satisfaction with their companions response. Another man, whose hands were idle, tore their blouses from their backs, with each a flourish and the cheering from the crowd rising with each rip of the cloth, the natural skin of their womanhood and their dignity thus exposed to the cold elements about them.

Eliakim confessed, though shamed, he could only watch, with intent and sadness, and think of me safe at home by the fire holding our two boys. The snow left on the ground by the nights storm whipped by the wind about his boots, the stinging cold catching his hair beneath his hat, his hands were deep within his pockets grasping at what little warmth his throbbing legs would provide.

Their attacker next kicked at the backs of the women's legs, their feet made unshod and left bare in the half-leg depth of snow. Their woolen skirts and petticoats were little protection against the biting cold. A man could be punished for treating his horse and his wife in this manner.

Magistrate Waldron raised his voice, leaving no question of the instruction he then gave, not to the constables readying themselves elsewhere but to the men and women of each of the towns.

Whip them on their backs, not exceeding ten stripes apiece on each of them in each town, and so to convey them from constable to constable, till they come out of this jurisdiction as you will answer it at your peril, and this shall be your warrant.

He seemed content to read the decree for all to hear. The constables of their various towns were to take up the reins of the cart at the edge of their town, drive slow and deliberate through their town, for their folk to see and cheer and meditate on the transgressions of these lonely women. At each town, another man was appointed to lay the straps against the women's backs.

Three women. Ten stripes each, in each town. Ten villages. A single man could not possibly have the strength to lay three hundred lashes. A woman could not possibly have the strength to bear one hundred lashes.

Standing nearby was Priest Raynor, a smile broad upon his face, his color high, and his eyes dancing with glee.

Years later, a man who was long retreated into the shadows would reinterpret St. Augustine of Hippo, *omne malum incipit a sacerdote, saith the proverb; that is, All evil begins from the priest, or, From the priest all evil hath its beginning.*

47

The Stocks

Eliakim turned, seeking the sounds of laughter and mirth of a man in the crowd; and he thought, even in their acceptance of this treatment, how can a man be so uncharitable as to laugh upon the cruelty on one inflicted by another? What he found was the priest, Reverend John Raynor.

The Reverend Raynor was at Dover since 1655. Of him, aside from this event, is written only good and kind words painting a diverse picture of a man who was thought to be meek and of humble spirit. A man who followed the Truth and was in every way unreprovable in word and deed—a true minister of old England.

Though his manner may not have merited censure, he did not hesitate then to reprove these women or those who might speak up within the crowd for them. His message could not be more clear. Priest Raynor considered not his intent for their deaths, wrought from the miles and the cold and the harshness of the thronged whip along the way, was on the same level of wickedness which was to be a Quaker and a believer in the Savior. He could not have thought otherwise than this was God's choice, and His alone, and therefore he, Priest Raynor, was merely showing His contentment in the matter.

I knew my husband well, and was not surprised to hear Eliakim describe how he acted out of his own fear and loathing for this man and those he represented, and without a thought to what his actions would wrought.

> *Eliakim Wardwell reproved the Rev. Mr. Raynor for his brutality in laughing at the cruel punishment of his friends, and as the narrative goes, "added one more piece of insolence to the list of Quaker outrages." For his offense, he was put in the stocks.*

Before he could stop himself, his voice rang out loud and strong even to his own ears. As he lay beside me under a starless, cloudless night, our hands clasped, our legs wound about each others, our eyes fixed on the wooden beams above our bed, his voice low and cracking with the remnants of anger still within him, he told me there was another voice rising above his own, also rebuking the priest.

"I turned to look upon the other man standing not more than two lengths from me; I did not know him either by sight or name." Eliakim went on with his story, his voice becoming distant. "Then I looked upon Priest Raynor who turned from his beatitude and, through contradicting eyes, recognized me."

Eliakim said all attention turned then to him and the other man. Constable Roberts stopped his reading, and a deafening quiet took hold of the crowd. Only the wind dared to howl. Raynor ordered the constable, *Take these men to the stocks for their insolence, and there they shall stay until this deed is done.*

Momentarily taken aback with the priest's tread on false authority, the constable must have thought better of his own rebuke, and decided to ride this run-away horse all the way to the barn.

"Roberts gestured to a deputy standing nearby. The deputy grasped the arm of the other man and then my own and led us, without force, to the town's stockade nearby and there left us, if not in silence, at least prevented from interfering further in the proceedings."

I continued to listen, still enthralled, but hearing how Eliakim's voice changed to one of dispassion. "Our knees were on the slick boards, our backs were bent and our heads and hands were secured between the worn grooves of two heavy planks. The sound of the iron lock clinking pierced my ear, and I instinctively tried to pull my hands back, but they were caught tight. At least the wood pressing against my throat was smooth," he said.

"I am William Fourbish," the other man said in a whisper. A man of Dover, he was not known before nor ever after.

"We were thus chained to the spot, nearly as exposed as the three poor women. We were made to watch, powerless. One lash, then two...three led to nine, then twenty-one...and finally, thirty lashes upon their backs. Tears fell from my eyes down upon the snow below my head, as the blood of these three women fell upon the snow beneath their feet, a stain upon the pure white.

"The deed was done in Dover, the constable then ordered the three to climb, naked and bleeding into the cart though their hands were still tied tight to the tail. *Time to move on to the village of Hampton if we are to make the most of a winter's day light*, the Dover constable chuckled."

Eliakim described how they did not move, their feet buried in red snow. They refused to do as the constable ordered, and this only served to enflame those about them in the crowd who could only fear the power of silence.

After some moments, one of the women with the barely perceptible movement of her blue lips, spoke soft and without emotion, and asked of the constable where was the copy of the warrant, as was their right by law to have.

By way of an answer, the constable ordered one of his men to once again lay his hands upon the naked flesh of the women, untie them from the cart, and place them one by one on the backs of horses standing nearby. When the first, the one who had spoken out, would not submit to this task, the confused man acquiesced under the watchful eye of his master to take her in his arms and push her from beneath up on to the back of the flitting horse. He placed her tied hands upon the pommel, but did not otherwise secure her. He wiped his arm across his sweating brow and turned to the next.

The rope knot holding the second woman to the cart was hard

tied, and the deputy concentrated on working his stiff fingers to loosen it. All eyes from the crowd were averted to the two women still tied to the cart. No one noticed as the one atop the horse slid off and fell to the ground. A dull thud. A few in the crowd took notice and gasped, and the Constable turned toward the sound, but none moved to her there, struggling to gain her footing on the slippery ground and raise herself up to stand once more, in silence, before the crowd. Her bare skin prickled with the raised bumps of a deep chill.

Frustrated by these diversions and the delay, Magistrate Waldron called upon the good men in the crowd for three volunteers who would yield themselves and their horses for the task, the intent being for each woman to be tied at the rider's back to prevent her from once again sliding off the horse. A man is a coward when he speaks in whispers for no one to hear, when he follows the actions of the crowd and lets everyone about him believe his convictions are their convictions. But when such a man is singled out, placed before the same crowd and asked to testify on his own behalf, he retreats and is left speechless. No other man, Waldron found, would thus risk the touch of a half naked woman and a heretic.

Lest the magistrate be forced to submit to his own request, and beginning to weary of this adventure, he withdrew a copy of the warrant, held fast within his heavy jerkin all the while, and placed it on the bed of the cart where the other two women were still tied fast.

Satisfied with the request honored, all three women climbed without quarrel into the cart without the hand of any man there standing.

Eliakim heard the clucking to signal the horses to start their walk toward Hampton village, though he could no longer see the cart as it rolled beyond the limited range of movement of his head. He heard the inaudible murmurs of the crowd as they dispersed, the excitement over and there no need to put off their own work any longer. And he heard the women singing, their voices loud and trenchant and full of their own bliss above all the other sounds around them.

48

A Noggin of Milk

Tuesday, the Twenty-Second Day of December, in 1662...

I heard no sounds, from either within or without. I felt suspended in a kind of nothing and as if Eliakim were moving away from me. I listened for his breath and a sign he had given over to his weariness and slept. Instead, I heard him sigh. He was not finished with his tale.

"The snow began to fall, light as it will, and a warning to the few who remained milling about the town square. They should make their way home to a blazing fire and a bowl of sweet milk to warm their insides. We were held there, our hands frozen against the iron cuffs, our necks stiffening, our heads immobile and unable to seek cover. I closed my eyes against the sting of the snowflakes and the crisp breeze," he said. "I listened to the whistle in the trees and heard the crunch of footsteps approaching. I took a rotting cold potato in the face," he said. "What use is a potato when it has no heat to warm the hands of a young boy who is made dauntless by the rantings of men."

Eliakim's voice was so low. I felt he was no longer talking to me, but to another presence in the room. His father entered my mind just then. I thought of the bruise I noticed rising above his left eye when he finally arrived home. He waved my hand away when

I tried to dress it, and he sat down by the fire, wrapped in a quilt, to gaze with love into the sleeping cherub-like faces of his sons.

"As the sun was setting," he said, "Waldron returned from Hampton and released us from the stocks without a word."

Eliakim took in a breath, held it as if he meant to go on but was contemplating his words carefully. He released the air from his chest, with slow and deliberate force. "I must go into town on the morrow."

I knew only courage in Eliakim, but this was something different. I lay there, very still, barely breathing myself.

Finally I heard the soft gurgle of his sleeping breath, and I hoped his dreams would not be as plagued by the sinister faces of these men as his day had been. As I drifted through the shrouds of sleep for the few remaining hours of night, my mind played over the events again and again. I could not let them go. I would not let him go alone.

Before first light, I rose and wrapped myself in a shawl to stoke the fire and warm the room before I would waken Eliakim and Joseph. William was well acquainted with my routine; he cooed softly, waiting ever so patient to come to my breast.

As my son and I sat upon a stool, he was warmed between the fire and my body, and I was more than usual aware of the chill against my back. I heard my husband stir in our bed above, the crackle of the fire alerting him of the new day. I resolved I would not be afraid. We each had our part in protecting each other and our boys, and it was time for me to stand with him.

We broke our fast in silence. I watched as he lifted each mouthful of porridge to his lips, his stare never left the uneven grain of the table, the only thing holding him up. When he was finished, he took his cloak from the peg—he did not argue when I also took mine—then picked up each of our sons and wrapped them in turn close in their blankets.

The snow stopped during the night, and there was only a light dusting on the path to the Hussey home. We arrived unexpected, yet they greeted us with warm milk fresh from the cow. I set the boys upon the floor near the fire and my sister's own children while she and her husband both stood silent awaiting our desire to explain. We told them quickly of the day past, pushing away the hot chicory Rebecka placed before us. She watched me, as I had watched Eliakim earlier, and I knew she needed no explanation. Rebecka wrapped me in her cloak, an extra layer against the cold, and kissed my cheek. We needed no words.

They bid us good tidings as the cart took us away, our boys safe with them as we meant to stand together with the three vagabond women. We determined to go first into our village to see if the women were passed on or still in the vicinity. There, we found a crowd, some come lately from Dover as Eliakim pointed out, but many others of our own town. We heard how Constable Fifield received the drivers of the cart the night before, and how he approached Magistrate Waldron and argued, with the light fading and the crowd dispersing, the effect of the punishment would not be so grand as it would by first light. Perhaps it would be better to wait until the morrow. The Magistrate succumbed easily, and bid Fifield enjoy his good night's rest in the warmth of his bed.

We found a place among the crowd, hidden but with a view clear enough. The women stood facing Constable Fifield in a stance at any other time would be considered right and respectful for a woman—their hands clasped before them, their eyes down upon their shoes.

Perhaps because of their show of respect, the constable of Hampton would have been content to risk ire if he failed the warrant and allow their cast-off rags to remain on, a thin shield against the raw throngs of the whip. But the women would not have it. They bade him set them free or commence with the punishment according to the warrant.

Fifield stiffened and spoke to the woman on the left. History did not record which of the women he addressed, and I no longer recall. I watched as resolve stole into his face, and I heard his words as if he spoke them to me. "Take off your garments."

Without a movement of her head or hands, she said in a quiet voice though all in the crowd could hear, "I will not do it for all the world." The other two joined their Friend in staring directly into Fifield's feverish eyes.

This was not the time for his courage to fail him. He turned to the crowd and roared, "I profess you must not think to make fools of men…I will do it myself."

But there his courage did end. His hand trembled as he tore the cloth from the bodies of the women, one by one. His hand trembled as he took the whip up. His hand trembled as he cracked it upon the women, one after the other. He was as condemned as were they.

A shout from above the chatter. "Whip them harder." Then another. "Make them feel it."

A man emerged. Fifield paused to take a breath, perhaps reflect on the chore at hand. But the man was eager to take the task from him and made to reach for the whip dangling from Fifield's hand. The Constable flinched, a wince spread across his face. He withdrew the whip from the approaching man, who stopped short with his disappointment.

I recognized this man and was not surprised he should attempt to interfere in this way. He was large and powerful and of long standing in our community. Anthony Stanyon. Fifield did his best to cover his intimidation, and he went about his task with more zeal until it was done. I did not know then what importance these two men would have to my own life. When next I would meet them, one would greet me with shame, the other with eagerness.

The whip tore through the air. A crack, the leather thongs breaking through the now still breath or of the delicate bones in Fifield's own hand through the violence of his thrash, I could not distinguish. The thongs were hardened by years of use, the sweat of many a man's skin, and the cold. They ribboned the women's dry and brittle flesh. The sound reminded me of heavy boots crashing down on dead leaves and twigs in an empty forest. It is with me even today. But the three women stood their ground, though their legs buckled and wobbled beneath them. Their tiny moans tore at my heart.

I looked at Eliakim, and he at me. Our tears were as one. His hand moved to block my slightest movement. He knew me well.

I heeded his warning and stood silent. But another, a young maid cried out, and the crowd only hushed her so they might not miss the count of the lashes. "No pity for wretches," they said.

I could not leave the maid to weather this crowd alone. I spied a milking can and a noggin nearby. I saw in Eliakim's eyes my own pallid face and my wild-eyed fear, yet I pulled away from him.

With her wooden noggin of milk drew near.
"Drink, poor hearts!" a rude hand smote
Her draught away from a parching throat.
"Take heed," one whispered, "they'll take your cow
for fines, as they took your horse and plow,
and the bed from under you." "Even so,"
She said. "They are cruel as death, I know."

Fifield's hand left a welt on my arm. He cast a long glance at me, but it was begging I saw in his eyes instead of rage. The women passed the noggin from one to another; the last dropped it to the ground by her feet. Through it all they watched me with equal measures of mercy and sympathy. They knew as well as I what price I might pay for my kindness. I dropped my head and turned away. I heard the whispers and thought of our pretty beast being led from our barn.

Eliakim and I quit the place, loaded ourselves back into our cart, and returned to our children. The vision of my morning was burned deep into my memory.

Later, we were told of how the Constable finished his task, and the women were again tied to the cart, naked and bleeding. He drove them out through the Seabrook woods, by the salt meadows and the barren sand hills, by the winter blue sea, until they came under the waning grey sun to the shouts and sneers of Salisbury.

As Eliakim and I returned to Rebecka and John, and told them of what transpired while we wrapped our boys for the journey home, I knew this was not the last of those poor women we would see.

49

Walter Barefoot

When the procession came to the boundaries of the town of Salisbury, the scene changed.

Constable Fifield made little ceremony of handing over the whip to the next man who was to carry out tyrant Waldron's order. The next man duly executed his instruction to the letter, bearing down on the three women who, by this point, had received twenty stripes apiece. This man dispensed with the trouble of removing their clothes, and so their skirts were well stained by blood, the tatters of their shifts could no longer be distinguished as white muslin cloth, their waistcoats little more than rags. The women's shoes were in the cart, an idle reminder of the brutality the constables were compelled to wrought upon them. Their stockings fell away in tatters after miles of walking over rocks and brush and any other impediments in their path. Their hair long since fallen from the pins and bindings meant to hold it away from their faces, matted with dirt and twigs and ice so the three women were nothing more than the savage vagabonds these men had earlier branded them.

When the constable of Salisbury was done, worn and dripping with the sweat of his labors, he handed the whip to a townsman nearby, Walter Barefoot, and asked if he would take the charge, as the constable's deputy, to convey the women through the town of Salisbury and on to Newbury.

It took Goodman Barefoot no time to realize, in choosing him, the Lord offered a way to end this madness. Moved by compassion and a deep-held conviction of their innocence, he did not even pause to consider the hazard in breaking the law if he failed to deliver the cart, with the women bedraggled behind it, to the constable of Newbury, let alone if he set them at their liberty.

In the crowd at Salisbury was Edward Wharton, again come into the colony though he would at once be recognized. The presence of the three women, whom he knew well, slashed at his heart. Before he could speak out and give testimony for them, Thomas Broadbury, who was then the clerk of the courts for Hampton and Salisbury, spied him and called out, "What are *you* here about?"

Wharton turned to his accuser and with every bit of courtesy he could muster, replied, "I am here to see your wickedness and cruelty, that so, if you kill them, I may be able to declare how you murdered them."

Barefoot did take the cart with the three women, but with them laying upon a bed of straw instead of dragging their wounded and bloodied feet and backs. Major Robert Pike walked beside him every step. Pike was a leading man in the lower valleys of the Merrimack river, known to be an advocate for freedom when it came to religious belief and against the ecclesiastical authorities taking hold outside his region.

Priest Wheelwright, now old and tired and perhaps not a little forgotten, lately returned from England and installed at Salisbury as the town's pastor, urged the men to drive on through the village and into the hands of the Newbury constable as the warrant required, this being their safest and most righteous way to deliver the women out of evil's hands.

The crowd of instigators from Dover and Hampton turned back as they grew bored of the proceedings, shivering in the bitter winds, and guilty of laying chores aside for this growing folly. Perhaps they were not a little afraid of the changing attitudes of the people as they moved further south. The people of Salisbury began to gather, but instead of the jeers and cheers and moans of support for the magistrate's order, they prayed in silence as they surrounded the little cart and the three men whom they looked on only as praiseworthy.

Clear of the boundaries of Salisbury, Barefoot and Pike stopped to dress the women's wounds as best they could, and cover them against the growing wintry cold. They turned the cart not toward Newbury, but onto a lesser used road back to Hampton village, determined to bring the women into the colony of Maine where they could receive the assistance of Major Nicholas Shapleigh, the constable of Kittery and a known supporter.

With the day waning and the temperature dropping rapidly, Barefoot and Pike spotted the light of our candles, and knowing our house and the welcome they would receive, they stopped for warmth and sustenance and a soft pillow for the night before continuing their journey out of the colony.

We welcomed the travelers as we would welcome any Friend. Eliakim quickly aided the two men in carrying the women into the house and laying them with care upon a bed of straw I set before the fire, all of our quilts pooled for their comfort and warmth.

None of the women spoke, and the little crooked one seemed to drift in and out of sleep, her breathing barely detectable. The other two simply stared into the fire, their eyes not blinking or moving. Their fingers and toes were as blue as their lips, and their skin was pale but shone with a layer of sweat despite their coolness to the touch. They each took a sip or two of tepid ale, but nothing more.

The men went to the barn, leaving me to strip them of their tattered and grime-filled threads and stop the bleeding as best as I could. I bathed their arms and legs, and left them clinging to one another, covered naked to let the heat once again build around them, while I prepared a tea made of flowers I knew to be soothing and suited to rapid healing, and poultices of dried yarrow. The stripes on their backs continued to seep, and their blood soon enough soaked the quilts and straw upon which they lay.

My first task was to keep each of the women from fading into stupor. None of them could stomach the tea, their weak retching making me cringe. So I used a softened cloth dipped in the tea to wash the delicate skin around their ears, their necks and finally the bony surface protecting their hearts. At first their breathing became more rapid, and I feared they could not last long. But the tea worked its magic as I hoped it would, and each of the women in turn relaxed despite the soaked and stiffening blankets. They fell into a shallow sleep, their breathing slowed, and their limbs lost all rigidness.

I turned them one by one onto their bellies and applied the dried yarrow poultices to staunch the bleeding. I recently found this remedy to be much in demand in my house, and was pleased to see it worked with surprising quickness on these poor suffering creatures.

When the men returned, they sat at the table and talked in low voices while I stayed near our sleeping guests. Barefoot praised my courage to Eliakim at taking the milk to the three women, but was quick to condemn the same act as foolhardy. A twinkle in his eye let us know the irony of his own actions was lost on no one in the room. We did not need him to warn either of us of the price for our boldness. I recognized the knowing look in Eliakim's eyes of the man who would stand by me no matter the consequences.

In the shadows of my memory, and for our part in rescuing the three women, I watch as Eliakim took the whip a few days later. The court records say nothing of this, and so I now can not truthfully attest to it, but I can say Major Pike would not face Eliakim with such gratitude when next they would meet.

Neither is there any record of consequence to Goodman Barefoot for his defiance of the warrant, but more than a score of years later, he would be appointed Governor of New Hampshire.

50

A Sturdy Herdsman

January, in 1663...

Wenlock Christison again visited with his thanks for the care and concern of his natural sister Alice Ambrose, who with her companion vagabonds remained in our home until they were well enough to move on to Kittery, in the Maine colony. We graciously entertained him for several days. On this visit, it was his turn to listen as we described for him the growing tensions in the territory and the sacrifices we had already made.

He settled easily into our routine, helping Eliakim with the chores in the barn and fields and me about the house, tending to our boys. I found him to be surprisingly useful about the cauldron.

One morning, before the men gathered their cloaks to attend to the milking, a knock came at our door. We were not startled by visitors at unseemly hours for we frequently received wayward Friends with kindness and refuge. Eliakim opened the door with a smile, but it quickly turned on the man standing there. Reverend Seaborn Cotton. The three of us were dumbfounded to see him at our door. Christison rose from his stool and joined Eliakim at the door.

Cotton was visibly startled to see our Friend, whom he clearly did not expect to so casually rise from our table and come to greet him. After a brief pause during which the men all looked with suspicion upon one another, Cotton looked beyond the two men and said to me, "Mistress, I beg of you, return to your home and your family. Join us at the next meeting."

When no response came from my lips, Christison spoke. "What do you do with a club in your hand?"

I had not before noticed in Priest Cotton's hand was a large truncheon, and I thought this a very strange tool for a man to bring if he meant to appeal for my return to his fold. Like the Apostle Paul as he faced the people of Corinth, our pastor spoke with a voice of meekness and gentleness, as would Christ Himself, but he delivered his warning most effectively. "See what your actions have wrought. I will be bold if I must come again."

I rose and took a few steps, to make sure the Priest saw I held my infant son within my arms.

The Priest then turned his gaze back to Eliakim and Christison. *For though we walk in the flesh, we do not war after the flesh.* Cotton clicked his tongue in disgust at what he perceived standing before him: a weak and craven and intrusive meddler.

Cotton did not move from the threshold of our home, a sturdy herdsman with the fiercest of his swine gathering closer behind him. The movement drew my attention, and I saw Constable Fifield there, near to Cotton but not with him perhaps. The presence of these chattel would likely have brought comfort to the Priest, and perhaps he thought for his protection, but most likely with the hope I might be compelled for fear of both God and man. He turned to face Eliakim—and did not further acknowledge the presence of our guest—puffed his chest and, abandoning his first ruse, said in his booming preacher's voice, "I have come to keep the wolves from my sheep."

Eliakim turned to me, and as always with softness in his voice, reminded me of chores requiring my attention.

As soon as I departed from the Priest's view, but not the sound of his voice, Cotton continued. "I have come to understand, Goodman

Wardell, you here entertain a deviant whose name I know to be Wenlock Christison. Neither his words and tone, nor the manner in which he beat the truncheon against his leg, could bely the antagonism brewing within him. He went on with his slippery speech, "This gentleman is not known in these parts, and we fear his purpose here is to bring mischievous intent upon your family. We have come to set straight the matter." Here he lifted the corner of his mouth in a half-hearted smile; he was anything but meek and gentle.

Our invitation to this Quaker preacher into our home, not once, but several times, presented Cotton with a challenge to his authority. Speaking out as we did in the presence of the people of Dover and Hampton was to undermine the effects of his own words and the submissiveness of his flock. We could now expose him, remove his cloak of spiritual power; we could be a force against him and his selfish purposes.

Eliakim spoke with calm and patience, but with strength. "I have no doubt who I entertain may be of interest to you, but I equally have no doubt what transpires behind the door of my home is of no concern to you."

From where I stood, I could hear the loud, ringing song of the wrens hiding in the briers trying to chase away these interlopers. It made a curious serenade. After a moment, Eliakim bade him a kind farewell and made to close the door. It was then I saw the white knuckles of the Priest's hand grasp the door and prevent Eliakim from moving it.

"May we enter?" Cotton's pretense at a smooth manner now gone.

"No sir, you may not." Eliakim's voice was steady and he made no move to indicate the Priest would be welcomed into our home. The insult was clear to all. Even so, to deny entrance to the town's clergy could be taken as a sign to deny God, but Cotton made no move to push the matter.

He removed his hand from the door, and remained on the threshold. As Cotton stood a full head taller than Eliakim, he was able to lean in and look about the room without difficulty. He stopped his gaze upon me as I had stopped my work at sweeping in the corner. He smiled again, before withdrawing and returning his attention to Eliakim who did not waver in his stance to block the Priest's entrance.

"I remind you. You are rated for my hire." The threat was most evident in his tone.

When Cotton received nothing in the way of a response from Eliakim, he turned to one of the men waiting behind him and directed him to the barn to see what might be pillaged. "Mind," he said, "this man's debt is great."

We had lost much already, and I feared these men would leave us little to survive the winter. But before the men could move out to do their Reverend's bidding, Christison stepped forward and said, "Spare this good man and his young family, it is me you want."

At this, Cotton raised his arm in a signal to stop the man in his tracks. He said only, "I will have my fee," then he swung his arm forward and pointed a bony quivering finger at Christison.

Two of the men verily lept toward our guest, our Friend, and grabbed him one by each arm. They haled him away, dragging his feet in the dirt, which slowed their pace. Christison did not struggle, neither did he serve in their endeavor, but he maintained his dignified countenance. I heard him call out to Cotton who was at the head of the procession, the valiant champion, "Are these your sheep?"

Constable Fifield held back and whispered to Eliakim they would carry Christison to town. Later we were told the drove instead stopped at a house just a quarter mile away, perplexed to carry the uncooperative man further and too weary to continue the near two miles to town. There Cotton left him, and charged two men to retrieve their horses and carry the vagabond on to Salisbury where they were to turn him over to the constable there. When the party arrived, they found the constable gone, and so, without further instruction from the priest, were left to release Christison to his liberty.

51

Nathaniel Boulter

...and the priest (old John Cotton's son) to obtain his end and to cover himself, sold his rate to a man almost as bad as himself... of coming in the pretense of borrowing a little corn for himself, which the harmless honest man willingly lent him; and he finding thereby that he had corn, which was his design, Judas-like, he went...and measured it away as he pleased.

Just two days later, Eliakim found a man he knew only by sight standing outside of the barn. He immediately tensed as he greeted the man. Nathaniel Boulter was a brash man, one who was known to accuse his neighbors, and be accused, of a variety of transgressions. We had heard once a man, offended by this Boulter, dared to call him out in front of twenty of the town's folk and brand him with the title of rogue. Boulter, as was his want for attention more than justice, sued the man for defamation.

Now, here was Boulter, surveying our barn and the pen with the last of the remaining livestock. To Eliakim's surprise, Boulter respectfully asked if he might borrow some corn as his last crop had not been rich, and with the harsh winter his cattle were little fed.

"We, too, sir, have suffered the same harsh winter." Eliakim was cautious, though it was not in his nature to turn a neighbor away, and no word or deed had ever passed between the two men against which he could be judged. Though we could no better afford to lessen our own stores, Eliakim was a harmless and honest man, and always willing to help those who might suffer more than we.

Together, the two, man to man and neighbor to neighbor, walked into the barn. Just minutes later I heard Eliakim take his leave of Boulter, and bade him repay the debt upon his own good harvest. Eliakim returned to the house and told me only he had given the man a sack of corn, assuring me we had plenty for ourselves. He stood before me, took my face in his hands and looked as loving as always into my green eyes, and he laughed. Greed is not their color.

Later in the evening, Goodman Marston came to us and asked after the man he had spied walking from our farm with a sack full of our corn. As Eliakim relayed the story, Marston's face fell nearly to the ground.

"But what troubles you, my friend?" asked Eliakim as he reached out to clasp the man's arm. I stepped forward, concerned for the old man and saw plain the furrow of my husband's brow as it began to knit.

Marston waved Eliakim's hand away, a signal of only concern toward us and not an affliction of his own frail body. "I heard it said in town this Boulter took the bag of corn straight away from your barn to Cotton, where it was then meted out to the loyal. Boulter described the inside of your barn, right down to the number of corn sacks. He has bought your rate. Do you know this man, and of his reputation?"

There was nothing untoward in the priest selling a townsman's rate at his own desire, for a share, as an accepted means of disbursing the riches of one among others not so fortunate—while still lining his own pocket.

"Aye, but it is God's will we should help those in need."

"Eliakim, you are a good man, too good, and it blinds you. Boulter is prey to Cotton's will, and besides, he is in need of nothing but what another has, and to bolster his own profits."

"Then you call this man a Judas." Eliakim continued on, talking to none but reasoning to the answer to his question out loud. "Boulter came to me, being under the will and desire of Cotton, and he lied so he may measure out my purse. As Jesus took the ointment and used it upon Mary's feet, Judas would claim the value of it for the poor. So Boulter would feign to share what corn others might take for excess. If Cotton then sells my rate to Boulter, he is the holder of the moneybag, and can take what he will, a share to Cotton, and the people know none of it for having seen his public generosity. Then they, both Cotton and Boulter, should be rich at the expense of one and the esteem of the many.

Eliakim looked to me, then again upon our Friend. Marston completed the thought. "Cotton wishes to distance himself from you as he claims you have distanced yourself from God. He perhaps has some devious thought and must provide cover against the misgivings of the congregation."

Eliakim bade our Friend a blessed night and good fortune on the coming of the next day, then closed the door gently. He turned to me, his face a mantle surrendering the soul of one who has departed. "It is a sad time we have been forced upon. Though we cannot choose our neighbors, we must choose our friends more wisely." With these words, he walked away to light the lamps against the setting sun.

The very next day, Nathaniel Boulter came to our house once more. He stopped before the door, but did not knock. I happened to see him through the window and I called to Eliakim who was then stoking a fire so I might cook our evening meal. My husband went to the door, and opened it to find Boulter, smiling, then, without a word, turn toward our barn. Minutes later he carried two sacks of corn, one upon each shoulder, to the wagon waiting near by. He returned to the barn for another two sacks, and again for a third time.

Eliakim stood still, by the door, watching but not moving, not speaking. He would not raise his hand to any man. But we knew now how this would go for us. We knew now we had no friend in the law or the church. We knew to complain would be to lose more.

Boulter set himself comfortable upon the seat of his wagon, smiled and tipped his hat before turning the horses toward town.

52

The Priest's Rate

February, in 1663...

No one would argue a priest worked not for himself or even for his family, but for the whole of the community, and so the community is called upon to bear the burden of his and his family's maintenance to free the priest of distraction so he may serve the community to their most extreme potential.

A man may have chosen not to take the freeman's oath, and thus removed himself from the responsibility of government or membership in the church, or he may have fallen on hard times leaving him without the coin to offer. But as long as a man was in the community, and he had the will and the means to contribute, he did have the responsibility of the community. The priest's rate, in coin or deed, was meant to be his contribution to ensuring the good grace of his fellow townsmen. But like fines for breaking the laws, the rate could also be used to exact punishment for breaking the covenants.

I could not blame the season wholly for the icy winds swirling around us. We felt no break, and could not distinguish December from January, January from February. The days became one like another, the months one long day and an even longer night. Try as we might we could not leave our minds and our senses to those few errands which were needed to sustain us through this time.

The said Eliakim being rated at another time to the said priest, Seaborn Cotton, and the said Seaborn having a mind to a pied heifer Eliakim had, as Ahab had to Naboth's vineyard, he sent his servant nigh two miles to fetch her; who, having robbed Eliakim of her, brought her to his master, for which his servant not long after was condemned in himself.

It may have been in town, at the commons, or it may have been when Cotton ventured to our house on the occasional visit to cajole again for my return to the meeting—Eliakim was not, apparently, worthy of his cajoling. However it came to be, Seaborn Cotton, the good Reverend, the shepard of a wayward flock set his eye upon our livestock.

"You have a lovely pied heifer. Let me have her as I have no stock of my own." With a narrowing of his eyes, and a twitch to his lips, he added, "You have not attended worship for many months, and my rate is due."

He knew asking for such a gift would leave Eliakim with a dilemma, how to answer without showing either disrespect or pride. But he was not asking for a gift, he was not even asking for the payment of his rate.

"In exchange, I will see your slate of absences from worship is wiped clean, and you will no doubt be blessed by God as you have not for some time. This, Wardell, must be well worth the price of the heifer, do you not think?"

As humble as he could be, Eliakim answered, "If payment of my rate is your desire, I will be glad to trade my time and labor toward whatever project you have want."

Silence.

"She is our only heifer, and even should you offer money with which to pay for the beast, I could not replace what she is worth to my family. We are fortunate but unfortunate people, and we live, or die by the little we have and what we can do by our own hand."

Again, silence. Cotton knew well by what means fortunes are made—and lost.

"Would you take some of our corn or grain store, or perhaps eggs from our fat chickens? We might spare even some milk from the dairy cow. She is our only heifer," repeated Eliakim.

It is not in me to have a hateful heart, but I could think of nothing which would harden me more than to watch as Cotton brought my Eliakim nearly to begging for mercy.

Still Cotton did not speak a word. He merely smiled with half of his mouth, allowed a whisper of a grunt from the pit of his belly and turned to walk away.

Were this bovine the ugliest of creatures set upon this earth, Eliakim and I could not have cherished her more. She was raised from the first heifer we received in kindness from old Goodman Mingay, now five years gone. We thanked God for his peaceful rest. This, our prized heifer, was calved in her fifteenth month, at the same time we forsook the priest's worship. There should be no connection between these two events, I merely recall one with the other perhaps because I always seemed to feel a sadness for the heifers. A first-time mother has a glow about her, she has energy like at no other time in her life. Her first is the wonder and the future. Perhaps it is the same with a heifer. A cow giving birth is only the nature of procreation, but there can only be once for a heifer. We looked forward to the new calf by summer.

From afar, you might believe her pristine white sides became the canvas of some malicious mud-throwing. How we laughed as we told stories of errant children stumbling upon her alone, defenseless, meekly chewing upon a clump of grass and minding the business of no one but herself. Thinking to get her attention, or disrupt her as boys will want to do when they are not the center of the universe, and cause her to bellow out a long and sorrowful *mmmoooooooo,* they would gather some wet mud and take careful aim. Once thrown, they might exclaim how their paint took on the shape of this or that—now let us try another and see if we can change the picture.

The poor heifer was left to her business, with splotches, large and small, marking her forever to stand apart from the other cows in their suits of white or brown or black. On closer inspection, her eyes would capture your attention and would engage you. She was no ordinary heifer, with ordinary intelligence. She may do little with her time except chew cud, but she was methodical about it. We watched her often planning her route or choose a path, then stop to consider whether this was her best course, and then change.

She had a personality, which is what made her beautiful. And perhaps that was why Cotton wanted her. A prize.

Many of our friends told us of the tales about Eliakim passing throughout the village. These tales told of how we were flourishing with brimful grain stores and abundant with livestock. It was Nathaniel Boulter we could thank for these lies, and for the accusations which implied our wanton hiding of these riches so we would not be compelled to share or give unto our neighbor in need.

One day, I was returning from the coop, a basket of eggs swinging from my arm. A man appeared before me, and startled me for I had not heard him approach; Eliakim was nowhere to be seen. He kept a respectful distance, but he would not look at me, keeping his eyes always on the ground or twisting and pulling at the cap in his hands. His voice was of a child imploring me not to harm him, or blame him for his misdeed.

I knew him, and perhaps I should have been fearful. There was, during this time, a young man who lived in Hampton who was frequently called to court for stealing. What his family circumstances were, I cannot say. What his beliefs were towards the spiritual community, I also cannot say. He appears only in the court records for his repeated thefts. But I will not begrudge his situation or his beliefs, for God requires me to see his light shine on all equally.

I hesitated. "The pleasure of your visit, kind sir, is mine."

Still he did not lift his eyes to mine but he spoke softly. "There is no pleasure in my visit."

He chose few words to explain the Reverend Cotton had sent him nigh these two miles on foot—he not having a horse to carry him—to take the pied heifer. He spoke this with the knowledge of an awful kinship.

Eliakim then came upon us. He must have heard the man's words, or perhaps he was anticipating such a visit and had already given much thought to why this man would approach our house without business or horse in the midst of a day. Though he reached out a hand to the young man to touch him upon his shoulder as his gesture of kinship, his words were tainted.

"And will I be called to a feast where I will be betrayed to the whole of the town, and then led away to be stoned to death as had Naboth when he refused Ahab his family's vineyard."

The man could only shift his feet nervously, his eyes never hinting at understanding of what Eliakim said or meant, nor seeking or denying Eliakim's approval in the matter. My husband, like me, blamed him not for being the messenger and the punishment he might face should he be disobedient to Cotton's wishes.

We could do naught but watch in silence as he led our only heifer away. A heifer moves slow. It would take the rest of the day for the young man to walk her the two miles to town.

We heard from our friends, the man, was piteously placed in the middle of Cotton's quarrel with us, was arrested soon after presenting our heifer to his master. His crime: stealing.

Our heifer was not returned to us.

As if to compound our distress and uneasiness, John Hussey came to us not long after. Usually a carefree and jovial man, there was no mistaking the fear blanketing his face. His hands shook. When I asked if there was something amiss with Rebecka or the girls, his face softened little, and he replied he had taken them to the safety of our father's house, then come here. "Something must be done," he said.

As Cotton had sent his servants to pilfer our stores and livestock, so had he sent two of his churchmen to the Hussey house. He and Rebecka watched, immobile, as these betrayers led all of Hussey's fat kine, and a fat calf away and tied them to their cart's tail. Then they returned to take twelve bushel of wheat, which they loaded onto the cart. Finally, they pushed their way into the house and took what provisions the young couple had there and filled their pockets.

Our own experiences taught us of the futility in the situation. I bent over in pain for my sister and her children.

John could not be still, he kept turning in circles and raising and lowering his arms, but he continued with his rambling. "They left only a flitch of bacon. 'This is all you will have of those fat kines,' they said. They threw the plates and cups against the wall. There was such contempt on the men's faces, I hardly recognized them. Why would they strip the bedstead? The baby mewled so loudly in Rebecka's arms, I covered my ears. Oh, but I reached out to her, shielded her. Imagine trading or selling our children's blankets. Theodate was cowering wrapped about the hem of her skirt."

Becoming more composed, and then able to look Eliakim in the eye, John said, "They looked at Rebecka, then the babe and the child. 'Give us ten pound or your children,' they demanded, 'the choice be yours.'"

Spent, John became restful and lowered himself into a chair. Several moments went by before he could finish his story. I cried and said a silent prayer.

"I do not have ten pound, and when I said I would give my own life to keep my children safe, the turncoat let out a great bellow of a laugh as he turned toward the wagon and made a slow roll out of the yard."

Word was swift to reach us of Elizabeth Hooten's imprisonment in Hampton for speeches against our Reverend Cotton for these deeds he had wrought, and of a fine feast the men made of our spoils.

53

Isaacke Perkins

March, in 1663...

A quiet man requires a quiet mind. Isaacke Perkins loved his family, but could not often bear the lack of quiet in his home. He would sometimes, more often of late, walk away without a word and trudge the paths about the village with never a destination set in his mind.

Not a fortnight passed since Cotton's sheep assaulted my sister and her children when Isaacke chanced upon their house during one of his walks. Knowing she with her husband and children were not at home because he had just left them with his own wife, his concern grew for he found the door standing open. Coming to the house he called out before he entered, unsure of what he might find but knowing he should above all be cautious.

> *Your officers came, and finding nether John Hussey nor his wife at home, they got into the house, like impudent thieves, and made search therein, and finding some flitches of bacon, they took a flitch or two; but, not finding a way to go forth below, because they could not make fast the door after them and there were none in the house, they attempted, like felons, to get out at the hole of the window above. Before they had quite finished, John Hussey's wife's father, Isaac Perkins, came forth, who, espying*

them, although one of your people, he rated them soundly, and made them leave one of the flitches behind them.

Inside Isaacke found the stools had been knocked about, cups and knives and pots littered the room. A pool of cold stew jelled on the wooden floor boards. As he wandered about the house he found his granddaughter's beds torn apart, the fire wood usually stacked neat by the fireplace was scattered. The sight was just as John had described the last attack.

When he heard noises above, first the scuffling of feet, then something falling to the floor, and finally loud and frantic whispers, he made for the stairwell. He eased his way up and when he reached the landing, he found two drunken men trying to push one another out of a window which would barely allow for their heads to pass, let alone the bulk of their shoulders and middle girth.

"Impudent thieves," Perkins called out. Both men stopped and turned with the same looks upon their faces as his own boys when he caught them in an act of disobedience. "What say you?" he said finally.

The men lowered their heads, what could they say for themselves. "It is Priest Cotton," said one of the men finally. Both moved to cover their pockets, which bulged, with their hands.

Isaacke need not have questioned them further, but instead rated them for their cowardice and held out his hand. Ignoring him, the men made to walk out, past the older man, down the stairs and out the door as if their congenial visit was at an end. Isaacke stopped them, grabbed one by the arm and pushed the other back for he was still a man with some life in him.

"Let us pass old man," one of them spat out in a garbled tongue. But Isaacke still had the better of them as they tried to totter away.

"I will have what you hide in your pockets," said Isaacke, as he reached into the pocket of the man whose arm he still held.

The second man slipped away and down the stairs, and Perkins heard his feet hit the threshold of the door while he still stared into the eyes of the other. With nowhere to go, the caught man emptied his pockets of the flitches, the bacon falling to the floor.

Isaacke released him to fall down the stairs in his haste to be gone and out the door.

"Tell Cotton he has the kine, he has the calf, and he has the bushels of wheat. The least he can offer in the way of charity is to leave the bacon," Isaac called out after them.

Isaacke tidied the main room as best he could, and placed the flitch of bacon on the table. Then he made for home to report the crime, and spare a warning for his daughter and her family.

54

Hireling

Monday, the Twenty-Third Day of March, in 1663...

Gone was our pretty beast. Gone was our prized heifer and much of our other livestock. Gone was our wheat and our corn. Gone was any means by which we could trade goods for coin. With the winter not yet finished, we were left in penury.

Without the means to plant and farm all of our property in the coming spring, Eliakim went to Salisbury, to another of our Friends, Goodman Edward Gove, with a bargain to sell him thirty acres of land bounded by Salisbury common, in the part of the town they now call Seabrook. Gove knew of our circumstances, and was saddened, but he agreed to the offer. He, in turn, made a bargain with two other men for their lands including a dwelling house, cow house and cow-common share in Salisbury, and upland in Hampton. For all of this property, Eliakim and the other two men agreed to eighty-five pound; Eliakim's share being the smallest since our contribution consisted only of farmland.

The good folk of Hampton who still looked upon us with kindness offered to help in other ways, but we were not want to draw undesired attention to them, nor were we in need of charity. Eliakim said to me one night as we looked upon the last garden stores, "As long as my back is straight, and my legs are strong, and my hands are mighty, I will work." He returned to those early years, before we were wed, when he worked the Reverend Wheelwright's farm as a hireling. When he was not doing what he could for our farm, he was doing what he could for others in exchange for supplies and provisions to sustain us.

55

Still More Lashes

I could bear the judgement, the shame, the sacrifice for myself. Eliakim and I had often of late talked about the punishment meted out to us, of our fears for our own small boys. And we were agreed it was God who had set us upon this course, and we must see it through.

But I could not bear the threat upon my sister and her young girls. Her adventurous spirit set her on this path; I followed, willing, and we always greeted life's tasks and mysteries together. But when she held her first child she changed. No more did she let risk guide her; no more did she fight for the sake of the fight.

I watched her change from restive to reserved, more like the women in the village who kept their tongues and followed their husbands. And as her eyes and her sight lowered itself to the ground, I in turn raised my own eyes to meet hers. I squared my shoulders, I stood by my husband instead of behind him. I raised my sight to the sky, to the birds, to the clouds. To the heavens.

Nor could I bear Eliakim's remorse at having failed me and our children. Though he did not speak his thoughts aloud to me, I knew by the sorrow in this eyes he was questioning himself and his faith. Was he led astray and into the desert where he weakened in the face of every of his tests? Did he ask a silent God why his bread was turned to stone? Was his footing unsure as he climbed to an unsound pinnacle? Had he bargained away his family and his home for false beliefs? Nay! I would not watch as he crumbled and withered and blew like the sands in the desert away to nothingness. Whatever our trials, we would bear them.

The next lash pulled me into an abyss without end. I heard the flutter of wings above my head. I heard Eliakim calling out to me. I heard my babies cry.

I lost count, and I lost feeling throughout my body. There was little left of the strength in my legs to hold me up. My feet were twisted, my knees buckled, my face scraping against the rough wood. My breasts felt as torn and bleeding as my back. The bindings and the pole were the only things keeping me from crumpling to the ground. My shoulders were pulled out of their sockets from the weight of my body, small as it might have been. My wrists were raw from the pull of the rope holding me to the pole.

I could no longer see through the fog before my eyes. I could no longer hear any sound but a humming consuming me and leading me through a dimness like none I have ever or since felt. I remember a numbing cold devouring my body as if I walked naked and burning with fever into frozen spring waters. I shook with a violence I could not stop. I watched myself sinking into the deep water, my legs gone, the stripes on my back gone, my breasts and the milk within them, gone. My face was empty of any features which might distinguish me. My red hair gone ash. I thought to release myself to this fate, let go of everything holding me back.

I asked, nay, I begged God to relieve me of this pain, of the suffering. My penance to be paid freely with my life.

Through my swoon, His voice came to me; He answered me with His kind words and His gracious warmth. *Child, thee must seek out the ones thou hast most love. Thou work here is not yet done. Open thine eyes.* His hands lifted me. *Stand.* His command. *Live. I am the protector.*

56

A Voice

Saturday, the Twenty-Eighth Day of March, in 1663...

"My husband," I called out as we lay, side by side, sated with our love, the moon starting to fall toward a new day.

"My wife," he responded, his hand reaching out to caress the soft fur between my legs. He rolled over to explore the perfect skin of my belly, once again flat and tight, and awaiting the seed of another son to take root, unmarred by the stretching of the first two. He reached over to bury his face in the cleft of my bosom, and he breathed in the musk he had left there. Then he kissed each nipple, tasting the sweetness of the milk rising with the sun and his touch.

I let him play once again, responding as I always did, but when he was done he repeated, "My wife, what troubles you?"

This time I turned to him and I placed my lips gentle against his, my hands into his, my body merged with his. "I cannot stand by another day and suffer the priest and his punishments."

He pulled me closer, tried to pull me into him, protect me. But he knew he could not stop me.

"He sent for me yet again," I went on, "the priest. He begs me again to come thither on the morrow, to return to the flock, to turn my back to weakness, *leave the grasp of the devil*, he says. He asks for a reason for my separation."

"They are in a miserable condition," said Eliakim into my ear. "They are blinded with ignorance and their persecution sustains them. They have nothing else."

I did not respond, but went on with my thoughts aloud. If I did not put them to the air, then I feared my own lack of courage would bury them forever. "I can delay no longer, I cannot turn my back one more time. I cannot watch quiet as he inflicts his sufferance."

Eliakim was quiet. He knew my intent was not to turn back on a path made nocuous and merciless, but to march forward. He often showed me the changes in my own nature since we were wed, and I often thanked him for his guidance and patience.

I did not know if I should go on, and tell him further of my plan, or if I should wait until he asked. I reminded myself once upon a time I would not speak or act until another had driven me into a corner. But it was another life, and I another person. And so, I decided to lead him this time.

"I mean to show them the Light I have seen," I said. "To beg for their understanding. Men, in their wretchedness and inhumanity, have stripped the cloth from the backs of good women, laid bare their souls and their spirits. Tried to whip them into submission, quiet their voices, shun their beliefs, control them. But they have not succeeded. They have not succeeded because it is they who are naked. It is they who stand before God, exposed and shivering in the cold with no coat to protect them, no heat to warm them. It is they who cannot see what lies beneath the surface. It is they who take the whip every time they enter the meeting house. They beg to receive the Spirit but they are unable to welcome when knocking upon their door It comes.

I said this all with one single breath, and I stopped then to replenish it. I was anxious to gauge my husband's thoughts. Though my mind was made up, he and God only could influence how I meant to continue my quest.

His silence lent his permission for me to continue, his support for what I had in mind. "I am here, and I too have a voice, and it is time I spoke aloud."

His next words struck me as a hammer striking an iron anvil. "They will not hear, they will not listen." This was not his lack of faith or belief in the cause we had taken up. It was his fear for my safety and my life. It was his fear I might meet with the same fate which had taken Mistress Hutchinson and Mistress Dyer.

"They will not hear, and they will not have the chance to listen, if I do not speak aloud in a voice they can understand."

"And where will you make this speech?" he asked.

"The three women were to have gone to Newbury had not Goodman Barefoot diverted them, and saved them. It is there I shall go, and carry on their task."

"And do you mean also to go to Rowley, Ipswich, Wenham, Linn, Boston and Roxbury, each in their turn to speak to the good people there?"

I laughed and kissed his cheek. "No, good husband, I think my speech shall only need Newbury to hear my words."

So, it was done. We lay there in the quiet, our hands clasped, our breathing soundless, and listened to the first of the birds awaking and chirping for their meal.

57

Newbury Meeting House

Sunday, the Twenty-Ninth Day of March, in 1663…

Once again we turned our old mare and our little cart toward the house of John and Rebecka. William nestled upon my lap, wrapped within my cloak; Joseph sat quiet on the bed behind us buried in the warmth of the straw. Eliakim clicked his tongue and we set off, both of us in quiet contemplation. It was lecture day, but we would not be going to the Hampton meeting house.

When we arrived at the Hussey house, our brother and sister greeted our unexpected visit as always with smiles and warm bread and milk. Rebecka sat quiet as I told her of my plan; the look in her eye spoke loud of concern, and also of misgivings. Although she and John no longer attended worship either, they were more cautious and now muted of their disdain. They accepted their fines and prayed they could fade into the shadows, and continue to live peaceful under the protection of his father.

I kissed each of the boys upon their heads, told them I would love them always. I turned quick to the cart, again fearful my courage would not hold up if I looked any longer into my children's innocent faces. Eliakim helped me up and then settled himself beside me. We set off again in silence. This time towards Newbury.

We arrived to the booming voice of the Reverend Thomas Parker who had been at Newbury for nigh on thirty years. It would have been this same Reverend Parker who baptized the child born on the fourteenth day of March in the Year 1638 in Newbury, and recorded as the unnamed Perkins daughter.

Eliakim stepped down from the cart and came around to hold his hand up, and help me down. I threw back my hood to reveal my face and my head still covered by my cap, a fresh new white linen one I had made for the occasion. I thought briefly whether I should leave the cap, and thus leave my hair wound tight to my head, or whether I should bare all. Having settled in my mind to bare only a part of my physical presence would be to bare only part of my spirit, I removed my cap and the pins from my hair and released the red flowing locks to fall down upon my shoulders. Eliakim reached up silent, has he had the night before, and ran his fingers through the cascade of burning curls.

Next, I unfastened the clasp at my neck holding the cloak about me and I removed the heavy warmth of the cloth. I folded it, careful to set it upon the cart bed. A shiver rushed through my body, carrying away any last vestige of fear. I then pulled the kerchief from my neck, the tantalizing skin peeked through my hair. This would be enough to taunt any man to sin, but I meant to expose all of my innocence and all of my spiritual embrace to them. Eliakim took the thin cloth from my hand and dropped it on top of the folded cloak.

He came to me and gently took my hands from my breast where I had started to unfastened the buttons of my waistcoat. He did this for me, his hands feeling the way down from the first to the last button, while his eyes never left mine. The waistcoat off, and folded atop the cloak and kerchief, he loosened the ties of my skirt, then began to pull away the laces of my bodice. With each pull, the pressure of the bone stays lessened and I caught myself taking in deep breaths of the cool air, and feeling a sense of freedom. When he was done, he removed the listless garment and threw it to the pile of straw. I made to speak and chastise him for his carelessness, but thought instead to laugh at the gesture.

There I stood, my skirt loose about my hips, my shift hanging about my shoulders, my nipples made large and erect by the rustling of the fabric and the instant change in temperature, my hair hanging about my face, and I thought were it not for the sun rising behind me, and the cold winds coming off the seas to the east, I could be standing in my home, my boys asleep and breathing softly by the raging fire; Eliakim standing before me.

He said, "This is enough. They will see you no different clothed thus as they would see you clothed not at all."

"Good husband, I think you have more fear than I."

"Good wife, I have more love."

I smiled for the gifts I received from Him, and from my good husband. But this did not deter me. I set my path and I intended to complete my journey. I put my hands to my skirt and I loosened the ties and let it fall to the ground to pool about my shoe-clad feet. Eliakim bent down, caressed my legs through the thin layer of my petticoat, lifted them one by one, and picked up my skirt. This he folded with clumsy hands, and set it with the other garments.

My shift and petticoat were next as bumps rose on my arms and back, and an image of a Winchester goose came to mind. Then Cotton's voice whispered in my head, *The outcast dead.* I shook my head to rid it of the voice and the image. I would not let either steer me afar.

History has been delicate with my memory and has portrayed me only half unclothed, and truth be told I have no recollection. Eliakim would not speak of this day for the remainder of our lives together. So I am left with only the knowledge of who I was then and who I was to become, and I place myself there where I would have been. Which is to say, I stood there fully naked, in God's glory, with nothing to cover me except my shoes and stockings. I recalled the three vagabond women whose feet were made torn ragged and bleeding from the miles of walking, and their screams when I made to clean and dress them; as agonizing or worse than the pain from the lashes on their backs. I left the stockings and shoes on for no other reason than to protect my feet from the sharp stones of the path to the meeting house door, and the splintering wood of the steps and floor inside.

There I stood, wrapped in Eliakim's arms, his hands stroking the unblemished skin of my arms, my shoulders, my back, and my buttocks. I listened to the cadence of the Reverend's voice coming from inside the walls I meant to disturb. Eliakim clung to me, too long, until I felt his manhood, and his tears upon my cheek.

"It will be well," I said. Then I pushed his arms away, and I turned toward the little building, and I walked with my head held high, a smile upon my lips and God's warmth and Light to guide me.

58

Ipswich

Tuesday, the Fifth Day of May, in 1663...

A crack against my ear. A whistle through the air. A puff of smoke by my nose. The wind. A bird calling—*chickadee-dee-dee-dee*—the last of its call fading away. I tried to listen for its mate to answer, but nothing came.

A fire crackling in the distance. The smell of chicory and fresh bread. A baby cooing, and my milk letting down. William would soon reach his first year anniversary. My back ached from the weight and the burden, and the twisting of my spine. A mattress of fresh straw and a pillow of new down to ease my stiff and cramped joints.

The fresh musk of Eliakim just come in from the fields, the sweat still upon his body. His hands cupping my breasts. The sweet scent of my sex sliding down my legs.

My mind struggled to hold on to images, to smells, to sounds but they were all muddled, disconnected from a body no longer able to feel anything but pain and agony. Let go, I thought. Find what is in your head and hold it close to you, I thought.

Pain is what reminds you of life, I thought.

59

Newbury

Sunday, the Twenty-Ninth Day of March, in 1663...

I pushed open the door, and the Reverend's voice struck me as a blast of freezing rain. The meeting house was newly built just two years earlier to accommodate the growing community. Ahead of me was a gallery with three substantial rows of seats, to my left another of the same construct. Just ahead of the alcove in which I stood there was a third. The room was full of people, and full of heat, and full of scripture. All eyes were locked on the priest before them. So consumed was the priest in his own words, though he looked straight at me, he did not see me. In his grip were the people sitting there, their backs straight though the benches had no backs to hold them thus, they did not hear the creak of the hinges or the clop of my boots against the wood floors as I took two steps into the room. I left the door ajar behind me.

I stood there, a young and tender chaste woman, and I looked upon Reverend Parker's wickedness, the wickedness of all the Puritan priests, the rulers of our community, the elders of our family, of my husband. I was not at all offended by the truth hidden in the corners of this room, the truth men would not speak, the truth women such as me no longer feared. I stood there—*a sign, indeed, significant enough to them and suitable to their state, who, under the mask of religion, were thus blinded into cruel persecution.*

I was not at all offended.

Some would say it was a hard task, me standing there modest and shamefaced, and others would say some mental aberration took hold of me. The only thing taking hold of me there was truth.

It was a woman who finally saw me. I heard her scream, but I did not see her. All eyes turned to me, but I kept my gaze on the priest. I watched every movement of his face from his jaw dropping open to reveal the dulled and bruised gums where teeth had once been. His right eye twitched and fluttered like a baby bird learning to fly. The loose and wrinkled skin covering his jowls melted further from his jagged cheek bones. Beads of sweat appeared on his brow. His hand held suspended, his thumb and forefinger pressed together, forgotten along with the declaration he was in the midst of making. Lost was the beauty and the holiness, the charity and humbleness which would forever characterize his life. And left standing there was the shell of man, confused and confined by his own words then slowing to a drip from his open mouth. This, at least, is the image I have kept of the man whose face is faded into history.

I felt a hand clench upon my shoulder. I had not noticed, through my attention to the priest, a crush of men were then descending on me. Through the swell, I saw women shrinking away into the walls, their hands raised to their mouths, quelling their gasps; their arms covered their eyes, blinded them to the scene playing out before them. These women were blinded to very nature of their men.

The men were in such a rage they clawed at my arms, grappled with each other, beat each other away for the privilege of being the one to take hold of me. They tore at my breasts. They grabbed at my hair. One slapped me across the face. Another pinched at my buttocks. Still another thrust his fist into my belly. In the melee some fell to the floor, but this did not dissuade them. They merely swung at my legs, tried to pull me down with them. The riot grew to a feverish pitch, and the uproar deafened me.

Through it all I heard God speaking to me in calm whispers. *Hold your ground. These are the actions of desperate men. This is the discipline of their church, their religion.*

I stood fast with the cross both heavy and light as a feather upon my shoulder, and I prayed for each and every one of these men made sightless and unquestioning by their loyalty to cruel persecution.

They picked me up from the floor of the meeting house, as many men as could squeeze through and place a hand upon my body. Every part of my body was covered by the rough and pitiless hands of men. Every crevice of my body was invaded.

I gave myself over to whatever might come because it was not me alone these men meant to defile. My body was only the symbol, the chalice from which all women before and after me would drink in spiritual communion.

Out the door they piled, slamming and scraping against the wood of the door frame. They tore the door free of its hinges and I saw it hanging there as we passed into the yard. Here they threw me onto the ground with such force I rolled once, twice, thrice before I came to a stop in a crumpled mass. The shouting was nothing but a cacophony. There were no words, only harsh and discordant sound clashing over me.

A boot landed against my back. I felt drops of rain and then realized the sun shone down instead upon the spittle clinging to my face.

60

Ipswich

The Fifth Day of May, in 1663...

The thud of boots approaching. Eyes stuck closed by sweat and dirt and blood. Stinging from every nerve. Fever rising.

I rested upon one leg lying in a pool of acid mud, my skirt beginning to dry and crust in the heat and sun. My arms were still held high above my head, the leather bindings caught on the stump of a branch. The skin of my arms was tearing from my body.

Would they leave me there to hang, a symbol to the community? The thought was a mist in my weary brain.

"I am truly sorry, Mistress." The words sounded very distant, from a voice I felt I should know, but could not place. I cannot know to this day if they were real or only my hope speaking aloud to me.

Suddenly I was released from the ties binding my hands, released from the rigid pole holding me, and one dislocated shoulder came down hard against the ground. My head followed. My neck twisted, and lolled before it came to rest. I heard the sound of boots stomping and kicking, rising and fading all around me. From my position they were all the same, I could not tell one from another, could not distinguish friend from foe.

The jeers and the hisses, hoots and gibes, their tones harsh and callous and loud while the pity so soft I could but feel it through the open wounds. But this was their shame, their confusion. This was the admonition of their elders.

I heard the black birds come. Some clothed in their robes, guarding their secrets, demanding my devotion, enticing me with their words. Beside them the innocent call of the shrike, who would instead come to butcher and impale their prey so they may tear the flesh from my bones. And the hawks circling above them, waiting, patient, for the moment when they would swoop and catch me in their claws and carry me helpless away.

The voice in my head urged me, *Do not waver now. Do not give them your strength. Now is the time for you to reach for the Light.*

Kill-dee, kill-dee—at first soft, a warning. I watched it approach, its wing bent and broken. Its call reached a fevered pitch as it came closer. Then the flutey whistle of the oriole. I wished to warn them both away, shoo, do not fear for me, protect yourselves from these predators. But I saw the sun rising behind these wondrous creatures. The Light shone down upon us.

When these men found their words alone could not control me, they turned to their brutish methods. They sought to diminish me, body and heart and soul. They turned to cruel whips and torture, for they had nothing else. And yet they could not reach the spirit still.

Eliakim came to me. I heard him pushing men aside, growling as a mother bear would growl at any threat to her cub. He picked me up in his arms as if I weighed nothing more than a newborn babe, carried me to the cart, and eased me upon a blanket he had spread over the straw. He covered me with another. These simple gestures were enough to call my tears forward, softening the crust in my eyes. I could open them only a slit and I did not know where I was.

All I saw before me was a single mockingbird clothed in a brown coat to cover his pale belly and hide his white wings. It watched me, its eyes intent and knowing. It stood upon the branches of a hawthorn, tiny feet planted firm between the small sharp-tipped thorns. A sentinel. I watched as it turned its head to peer at the few men left lingering about. The intruders, the threats it recognized. My mind cleared for just an instant, and I realized it was this one bird, this one small creature who had called them all out, shown them for what they were. And then called in the defenders, the guardians.

I heard voices. Eliakim for sure. Then John, and I thought of Rebecka. Mistresses Hutchinson and Dyer. Deborah Wilson. Ann Coleman and AliceAmbrose and Mary Tomkins. Elizabeth Hooten. I heard them singing. Then, perhaps, I heard the voices of Goodman Barefoot and old Marston, and surely there was our good Friend Wenlock Christison. Priest Cotton. And then I remembered.

The cart started to move, slow and as gentle as the old mare could manage. At first the jostling caused a rage against every bone, every muscle, every nerve of my body. Eliakim walked the entire way, one hand upon the mare to sooth her, one hand upon the cart to gauge its rocking. Steady. Steady. They have murdered my sleep, was my last thought before I succumbed to the loss of my innocence and purity, my peace of mind; before I succumbed to a dreamless, disturbed sleep.

The next thing I remember Eliakim again held me in his arms, my body limp, the barest of whispered mews escaping my throat.

"Hush," he purred into my ear. "You are safe."

He carried me into our lovely home. A blazing fire warmed the chill wracking through my body despite the heat of the day. He lay me down before it on a fresh bed of straw and my prettiest blanket just as he had each time I was near birthing. Rebecka pressed a cup to my lips, but I could only cough and choke and raise my hand ever so slightly to push it away.

Three days passed. I learned Rebecka had been there the whole of the time, dressing my wounds, nursing and caring for my boys as she cared for her two girls. I recall none of it. Not even the pain.

She told me how I talked much throughout my fevers, how I described every one of the twenty-four ticks of a clock, and every thought kept my mind working. She cried with me, and comforted me. She could not have suffered more if she had been there as witness. But, she would not let me repeat a single word to anyone else. I must be thankful, and I must turn my gaze to the future. I must think not of myself, but of my children and my good husband.

As the fire died away, and I listened in the quiet of the night to Eliakim's soft snores, to Joseph and William giggling in their sleep, and I lay there alert to every lash eased by the cooling compresses and yarrow poultices, every scar beginning the process of mending my torn body, I remembered everything. My mind was not at rest, and I knew this was not to be the end of us.

61

Puritan Worship

Old Willi. Marston, being presented by the grand jury at Hampton court for absenting himself from the ordinances on the Lord's days, and the presentment proved, was fined for six Sabbath days' absence. Eliakim Wardall and his wife for twenty days' absence and Jno. Hussey and his wife for twenty days' absence, were fined, one half the number of Sabbaths being abated.

Tuesday, the Fourteenth Day of April, in 1663...

The five of us stood together, facing the jurymen. While Marston and Eliakim and John looked to the foreman of the grand jury, Anthony Stanyon, Rebecka and I looked to the foreman of the jury of trials, our uncle, Abraham Perkins, who would pass the sentences.

As I stood there, in my most humble presence, I had no doubt each and every one of the men sitting before us knew of my exploit a fortnight before. Their minds were surely drawn back to Newbury meeting house, back to the riot which my actions caused, and the grand jury might well call for my indictment for it on this very day. But I saw no expression on any of their faces, just as I hoped they saw none on my own. The deed was done, and I held no regret for it. Absenting ourselves from the Puritan worship and my act of innocence were separate and distinct from one another, though they were born of the same questioning of faith and search for truth. I was so caught up in my thoughts, my consideration of whether our call to present ourselves to this particular court was nothing more than a matter of timing and coincidence or whether the magistrates wished to make a closer connection between my actions, I did not hear Perkins call out the fines for our twenty days' absences.

"... what say you Wardell?" Perkins concluded. Eliakim would speak for me just as John would be called on to speak for Rebecka.

Eliakim knew from the summons the dates of our absences and was prepared with his reply. "Sir," he started for he could not do otherwise but show respect not only for the court but for my kinsman, "my wife did give birth to our second child. I could not leave her during this time to tend alone to our infant. For this reason, we both absented ourselves from worship on the Lord's day."

At this explanation, I raised my head slightly to acknowledge the correctness of my husband's words.

Perkins turned to John and asked also for his testimony, to which John replied the same—Rebecka gave birth just two months before my own. Perkins nodded his acceptance of both, as he knew well this had been the case.

"Half the number of Sabbath's abated, half the fine waived."

As we all five turned and walked out, I whispered to Rebecka we should tell Father of our uncle's kindness to us all. When we cleared the doorway, away from the curious glares around us, she turned to me and smiled her assent.

62

Healing

May and June, in 1663...

I spent many weeks, days and nights, upon my elbows and knees atop the straw pallet before the fire because I could not suffer the agony of any other part of my body touching anything even so soft as my own bed. The delicate skin became dried and hard and cracked. But my arms grew strong, and my back grew strong, and my heart grew strong. The kindness shown to me by family and friends during this time sustained me. When Rebecka or our mother was not about, Eliakim would dress my wounds with warm water and cool compresses. At night he lay with me there on the hard floor boards rather than be apart from me. Even during those nights, he would stay close enough so our bodies' heat would warm each other.

As my physical wounds healed with time and distance, I remained true to my sister and my husband in their refusal to speak of that day. Though their words and their concern stayed with me, it was not enough to keep the images and the thoughts from my mind.

I did not venture beyond the walls of our house and our barn, but rather distracted myself with my gardening and my chores, and the pleasures of watching my boys grow strong and healthy. As Joseph approached his twenty-ninth month, he fancied nothing more than running about the yard, calling to all the animals in his wake. I gave him a small basket and taught him to carefully pluck the eggs from the nest boxes, choosing the clean and whole ones, but honoring the broken ones by cleaning out the mess and removing the wet and soiled straw. He learned quickly and soon I encouraged him to go alone to gather more eggs as the sun began to set. While he showed his excitement at learning this task, and being found worthy to perform it without me standing close by, he preferred to dirty his hands while he cleaned the nest boxes, and lay new shavings or straw to line them. Eliakim built him a small milking stool, and I would watch as he tried to teach Joseph the finer points of milking our dairy cow, that is, being gentle with the poor girl's teats.

Our tiny William reached his one year anniversary a chubby and happy babe. He still nursed at my breast, but he was a curious child and would often trace his fingers along the tiny red raised lines of the remnant of the splinters decorating my skin. He grew bored quickly, and when he was full he would toss himself to the floor, steady his hands in front of him and push himself up onto this wobbling legs. Reaching his arms out to steady himself, he would raise his gaze up to me and laugh, thus losing his balance and falling back to the floor with a thump. This was, for those next weeks, our favorite game.

When I was able to once again climb the ladder to our loft space, and once again able to stretch my body out and receive the soft tick and blanket upon it, I would lay my head on Eliakim's thick, strong legs as he sat on our bed with his back propped against the wall. The back of my head rested against his belly, his hand upon it stroking my hair away, rubbing the taut skin above my eyes. When the tension there was released, he moved to my shoulders, kneading gently between the bones. He pushed away my shift to unearth the skin of my arms, my breast, and finally my back.

At first, I pulled away. Not from pain, though there was enough of it still to the touch. Nay, it was the shame—and then the fear. How could he want to touch me? How could he not see the straps coming down on me every time he traced the lines with his rough but gentle fingers? I saw the leather thongs reaching out to my body, searching for an unmarred space. I heard the snap, and the whistle as they travelled through dead air to seek me out.

How could he ever look at me again?

But he was insistent. He would not let me move from the protection of his body. He would often just lay his hand upon me, not moving, just breathing. When I no longer made to stir, he would touch the parts of me left unchanged. The skin of my forehead, the curve of my arm, the crevices between my fingers. The notch behind my ear was still a welcome spot for his lips.

When he felt my body slacken, when my breathing became shallow, when my eyes closed without despair, he knew I had returned to the old sense of comfort, to the safety of his touch. The hardness which tried to take hold of my heart and my body melted away, and we were as we once had been.

As the heat rose, he peeled away my damp and cold covering and he explored my body as he had once done every night, searching not for the smooth landscape like cream and honey, but finding a new web of ridges and ravines, where we could escape together, just he and I. Many was the night I would reach out my own hand to his beautiful face and find it wet with tears. In the morning, I rushed to recover myself before the cries of my sons woke the dead. Eliakim stood and took me in his arms, skin upon skin, lips upon lips, and his hands made me a promise for the next nightfall.

63

With Child

August, in 1663...

I was soon happy to announce I was again with child, this time eager to share this news as I was eager to share each day, more precious than the one before, with my husband. A happier man I have never seen. Perhaps this would be the daughter he longed for. Perhaps this would be the atonement I sought.

As I grew stronger, I could see Rebecka struggled more and more against the strains and hardships brought on by the increasing attention to our family. These burdens took their toll on her. I carried my third child without her support and companionship.

We received the news of the birth of Cotton's fourth daughter in much the same way we received the news of our three Friends hung pendant from the gallows-ropes in the Boston square. We spoke not of these things aloud, but we each knew the beat of the heart and the beat of the drums was not so very different. The whispers lingered in our heads—*Quaker, Sabbath-breaker, witches-hereticks.*

64

Magistrate Bradstreet

Tuesday, the Twenty-Ninth Day of September, in 1663...

The General Court summoned Eliakim again to answer for our continued absences from the meeting house. My absence from court could easily be justified by my injuries which were still in want of mending and by the added difficulties of my latest condition, but the truth of it was I had no love for the village of Ipswich, and I cared not to make trip along the cart path through Newbury. Rebecka remained with me. With John by his side, Eliakim rose to face Simon Bradstreet, who sat as judge upon the bench. It was not enough for Bradstreet to pronounce Eliakim's crime. With smug indifference, and surely because I did not appear before the court myself, the Magistrate took the opportunity to upbraid me before the assembly. At this, Eliakim pitched forward and charged the Magistrate in as loud and angry a voice as any gentle man can muster, not caring for the consequences or who might be attending the proceedings.

John described Bradstreet as being stunned by Eliakim's outburst, but he sat there with his face taut and his lips tight and his hands straining against each other in a clasped fist. He listened as Eliakim accused him of malicious acts toward his four Friends whose deaths Bradstreet still carried with him, and then lay other disgraceful acts before him. Bradstreet's face twisted and his eyes became large and cloudy white, two tiny dots of menacing black, a wolf about to lunge. Yet, he allowed Eliakim to continue.

His seething rage liberated by Bradstreet's restraint, Eliakim continued taxing the Magistrate. "You, sir, upbraided my wife, you reproached my wife, and she but an honest woman." He charged Bradstreet with making me suffer through sentencing at Ipswich, without law, and for being lashed so cruelly. Eliakim knew well enough Bradstreet had skillfully avoided any direct hand in any of these causes, but it was of no matter; it was Bradstreet who sat in judgement then and there, and it would be on Bradstreet my husband would thrust the full weight of blame.

Were Eliakim to have ended his censure there, I believe the Worshipful Mr. Bradstreet would have completed his sentence to Eliakim and John, recorded their fine, and moved to the next cause.

If only we could have remained so innocent. If only we had not, all of us, reached a boiling point. If only Eliakim had known who sat in the room behind him.

Priest Cotton listened, quiet and respecting the court's procedures, and watched as Magistrate Bradstreet still did not speak, rather he looked down upon Eliakim with savage scorn. Eliakim, spent and angry, his eyes full of fire, threw back on Bradstreet a railing even I thought too harsh when John told me of it.

"Your daughter has surely deceived you with her dishonesty," he spit at Bradstreet. Bradstreet's daughter was the wife of Seaborn Cotton.

Bradstreet would take no more of this impudence. What was only a moment before a look of contempt, then became a violent wrath. He jumped from his seat, knocked the papers from the table before him, and reached for the first object he could lay his hands upon. He raised a pewter tankard over his head, the contents dousing himself and several men sitting nearby with tepid ale, and he shouted to the men sitting on the court, "If such a fellow should be suffered to speak so in this Court, I will sit here no more."

Robert Pike, yea the same man who before walked with Goodman

Barefoot to save the three women, rose and reached out to Bradstreet's waving arm, pushing it down and taking the wet tankard from his hand. He picked up the stool laying on the floor behind Bradstreet's feet and eased the Magistrate back onto it. He had no choice but to turn to the other men of the court and say, "Charge this man" as he waved to the deputies to take both Eliakim and John out.

As Eliakim and John were dragged from the hall, Priest Cotton stood by, his arms before him, his hands stiff as he curled the brim of his hat with twisting fingers. When they were near upon him, Cotton said in a low and simpering voice, "I am sorry you chose not to return to the fold and hear the words of the Lord." Outside, the deputies threw the two men down upon the ground.

65

Hampton

Tuesday, the Thirteenth Day of October, in 1663...

Eliakim and John presented themselves as summoned to the quarterly court. Even while the proceedings took place in our own town, Rebecka and I again chose not to appear with our husbands. Neither the men carried coin in their pockets, for what little we had we meant to spare for our survival through the winter. It had been a hard year.

Since the charges were made at the last General Court session, only the jury of trials appeared to hear any testimony and pronounce the sentence. Judge Bradstreet did not attend, but Abraham Perkins sat again upon the jury, though this time he was not the foreman, and thus would not speak for the proceedings.

Eliakim and John waited and listened through twenty-one causes. The Reverend John Wheelwright was there with a property claim, withdrawn. Goodman Christopher Hussey was there, sitting next to his son, to sue a neighbor for trespassing, verdict for Hussey but appealed by the defendant and bound for a future court session. Constable Fifield was there with a separate suit for trespassing but against the same defendant, verdict for Fifield and appealed. Nathaniel Boulter was there, as defendant with a verdict in his favor in a claim by the Town of Hampton and as plaintiff for a debt owed to him, withdrawn.

The court records show Eliakim answered the charge for his not coming to the ordinances on the Lord's day was the result of his being a hireling, and it was false worship. Every man or woman from Hampton in the room knew well the level of want to which we were diminished; many of them were in receipt of Eliakim's labor and benevolence and glad for it. But each of them cringed at his lack of reverence. The foreman feigned no notice of Eliakim's retort.

Several causes followed before the foreman called on Eliakim again. This time for his charging the Worshipful Mr. Bradstreet the previous month at Ipswich. For this violation, the foreman sentenced Eliakim to fifteen stripes at the common whipping place this present afternoon. In Hampton, the court met in the meeting house, and the whippings were done tied to an old but solid oak tree just outside its doors, but set a respectable distance away.

"John Hussey," the foreman next called out. "Come stand with your brother." Neither father nor son dared a look to the other. The foreman waited until John took his place beside Eliakim, then continued. "For your absences from the public ordinance, and the absences of your wives, I fine you each five pound for twenty absences, the rest I will allow"—here, the foreman hesitated, looked with sharpness at the men sitting on the jury and the clerk who paused his furious transcribing and looked up, and finished—"for those circumstances for which you were necessarily detained at your homes."

There would be no explanation nor any more for the record of the abatement of the fine; the foreman dared to remind us he was not an unkind man.

Before either Eliakim or John could speak with respect to their ability to pay, the foreman said, "There is marsh and meadow to be had in place of coin, at your choosing." And so the town took what was left of us. The skin from Eliakim's back; few animals to work the field and give us milk, and no marsh or meadow grass to feed them; whatever we had of our dignity.

The foreman called on old William Marston and fined him for

ten days' absence, then bade the jurymen feast hearty, for the afternoon would be a long one. He turned to Constable Fifield and directed he ensure Eliakim present himself for his lashes when the court came to the house again; this foreman would want the whole of the court to be a witness. This would be Fifield's last act as constable for Hampton; John Cass was be sworn constable when the court returned. I wonder did Eliakim and Fifield both feel some measure of relief such as they might enjoy a peaceable respite in the warmth of the high noon sun?

When Eliakim, John, and Fifield saw the men of the jury of trials tramping back to the house in which the court sat in Hampton, Abraham Perkins among them, they rose from their comfortable places on the ground to greet the men, for how else should they present themselves if not in good cheer. The foreman, not to be daunted by their discordant countenances looked past Eliakim and John and went straight to Fifield. "Let's be done with this, there is other work which requires our attention and the days grow shorter. Strip him to his waist and bind him to the tree."

Eliakim could not but think of me and recall how he watched helpless as Fifield tied my hands. I did not struggle, nor would he. And just as he watched, anticipating, as Priest Seaborn Cotton approached me through the crowd, he spied the priest now approaching him. But this time, Cotton held back. So, Eliakim called out, "Come and see the work done."

Pleased with the invitation, Priest Cotton edged his way close by the oak tree where Eliakim was held tight. John stepped back, allowing the crowd of jurymen to consume and then flow past him. Fifield took Eliakim's shirt in his hand at the neck and pulled away hard; lessons he learned throughout the year as he was made to yield the whip over and over again made this time quicker and easier.

Close behind Cotton, old Thomas Wiggin trotted into the fray as much to protect his friend, the Reverend, as to exert his own authority as magistrate. "I pity these for thy father's sake."

Eliakim grasped the irony of this barb immediately, for Wiggin had never known Eliakim's father nor could he have known of the relationship Eliakim's father held with Cotton's own father.

Wiggin turned to Constable Fifield who stood silent, his whip hanging limp from his right hand, and attempted to turn an expression of pity to one of violent scorn. He called out, "Whip him good and hard!"

Cotton stood there, his arms crossed upon his breast, at the front of the crowd, near upon the scene. The whip was the same cat-o'-nine tails Fifield used on me, the community whip. Eliakim later described his thoughts as he waited for the deed to be done. The cords were nearly as big around as his fingers for the sharper cracking sound to train the animals without actually striking them. *Spare the animal, but not the sinner.*

The lashes came one upon another, without pause. This was Fifield's mercy, as he had tied my hands loose in mercy to me. When the fifteen stripes were satisfied, and the jurymen trod back to the meeting house to resume their causes, Fifield loosed Eliakim from his bindings. Eliakim let his hands fall from the tree trunk and rest on his thighs where he stood, his body swaying in slight motion until he could call his strength forward and recover his equilibrium. Taking in a sharp breath, Eliakim raised his head and his eyes greeted Priest Cotton still standing by the tree. Though the jurymen were well inside the meeting house, a few dispirited souls languished in the shade of the event just finished and seemed to be watching for Cotton's reaction.

Eliakim's gaze bore into Cotton and he let loose the thinnest of smiles, "Seaborn, hath my pied heifer calved yet?" knowing full well she had.

The tale of Cotton's thievery wrought on Wardell was the topic of many a gossip well into the spring and summer months, so it bolstered Eliakim's spirits when a few of the townsfolk howled with laughter and took up his question to a chant.

Hath my pied heifer calved yet. Hath my pied heifer calved yet. Over and over, Eliakim heard the song. He felt none of the sting of the fresh lashes as he watched the Priest try to slink away with his head down and his eyes shielded, his purloined vengeance at his feet.

And so it was my time to tend to Eliakim's wounds of the body, the mind, and the soul just as he had tended to me. Together we worked to push the events of the last two years from our minds, but in the process we cut all ties. We could not quit the place without also quitting the people. All of them. It was plain to us both we would stay in Hampton until the child was born, but no longer.

Afterword

Lashes and Rose Petals

As troops of robbers wait for a man, so the company of priests murder in the way by consent; for they commit lewdness.

So it was then in New England how those who would escape the tyranny of old have now come unto themselves, the priests and leaders of men, to destroy and undo those they sought to save. They became what they most feared, what they most reviled.

They took our coin, they took our property, they took our livelihood, and for what? For shallow minds and bully wants, for desires of the flesh when hearts could not be spared.

But for a few who stood and received the threats, the curses, the shame, the lashes as if by rose petals. Women, who like I, would stand quiet no longer, no matter the cost.

They did not break us.

On the 23rd day of May, in the Year of our Lord, in 1664, in the early hours of the blossoming spring, Eliakim and I welcomed our first daughter.

I lay with her, there before the fire, and I told her everything. "Lay your head, little one, upon my bare breast. The splinters are long removed, their marks are faded and the scars long forgotten."

"Just one year. It was just one year. I hold thee now with the same arms which held me fast to the post surely meant to bind the horse but not the rider. *Escape not while thy master sits and judges his strength and good fortune.*"

"But now I feel softness and love return to me in answer to the anguish I offered up for the thee to share the Light shining on us. While one year has gone, the blood of my life leaked from this very breast, the red blood of my pain, the sticky blood of my courage against they who could understand nothing but fear. From this breast now leaks the sustenance which brings you life, the warmth in my heart, the comfort I feel with thee in my arms."

"Come, Eliakim," I said looking up into his tearing eyes, "she is healthy. Hear her cry with the joy of life we have given her. God has blessed us, and our shame is no more."

We named her Margritt for she was our pearl, a symbol of the precious value of truth we held forth through all the deception, through all the suffering.

Like dogs and swine, these men who would be corrupt and profane and sensual, who would not know the value of the Gospel they preached, might try to trample us down. But we would not put our pearl before them, we would not give them cause to tread on her. We would not let them tear us further apart. For this, we would sell everything we had left and we made our way to the colony of Rhode Island.

We found nothing to our liking in Rhode Island, and so we moved on to Shrewsbury, in New Jersey where we heard of their Concessions and Agreement promising full toleration of non-conformists like us. There we found, along side our Friend Edward Wharton, the village of Gravesend upon the Long Island of the Sachems, and the promise of one hundred twenty acres with equal allowances for myself and our children from the Sandy Point along the bay West North West until it did come to the mouth of the Raritan River.

There we found a place where Friends could gather at our home without fear or reprisal. There, we were the pillars of our community.

And there I gave birth to six more daughters and a son. Could there have been any more clear of a sign from God?

The year we left Hampton, Rebecka gave birth to another daughter, her third. She and John remained in Hampton and settled back into a quiet routine. They were there blessed with another fourteen children until her last, who they aptly called Content, was born in October 1685. Our father died, at his home in Seabrook, a month later. John's father, Christopher, died the following March in 1686, in a shipwreck off the coast of Florida. Mother saw her last child married in 1689, then removed from Hampton with John and Rebecka and their children to a Quaker community in Brandywine, in the county of New Castle, in Delaware where they lived out the remainder of their lives. Those of my brothers and sisters remaining scattered to the winds.

There is little left in the annals of history with respect to Eliakim's mother, Elizabeth, after she removed with her four children to Hampton in 1647. She, along with her only daughter, Martha, may have found their way to Brookline, near Boston, at some point; and there they are reported to have died just three weeks apart in February of 1697. Eliakim's brother, Benjamin, married and lived out his life in York, Maine, a sympathetic destination for many. He served in King Phillip's war. Finally, Samuel, Eliakim's youngest brother, left a legacy of his own. On the twenty-second day of September, in 1692, Samuel along with seven women were hanged, having been found guilty of witchcraft. This was the last such execution before the public could no longer stomach such trials.

We never saw any of them again.

Author's Note

An internet search of Lidia Wardell, or one of its variant spellings, will call up any number of sources where you'll find any number of tellings of her walking naked through the Newbury meeting house, and being whipped for the crime. These stories all originated with one source—George Bishop's *New England Judged by the Spirit of the Lord, In Two Parts*—which was reportedly based on first and second-hand accounts given directly to Bishop himself. Bishop was a staunch advocate for the Quaker movement, publishing some thirty works on behalf of those people, in addition to letters to the King of England, the British Parliament, and His Highness Oliver Cromwell, before his death in 1668.

When I started digging into this woman and her story, I found this single event was just the tip of the iceberg. The *Records and Files of the Quarterly Court for Essex County* provided not only more detail, but context and a chronological accounting of many of the events leading up to, and then following, Lidia's historical act, all culminating in a picture of systematic persecution of Lidia and her husband, and the people closest to them. I uncovered more events documented in the New Hampshire legislative documents for the years of 1623-1686 as well as the state papers and provincial documents for this same period. I even found dramatic commentary in the poetical works of John Greenleaf Whittier, himself a Quaker with ties to that era and region. Finally, I can't praise enough the evolution of genealogical research and the availability of information via a multitude of internet sources. From these sources, I was able to piece together Lidia's life, as well as all the people around her, which allowed me to layout a complete timeline from the beginning of the Winnicunnet Plantation until Lidia and her family were forced out of their Hampton home.

I had to tell this story using the real people in their real environments, experiencing real events, because I felt like it all might be too unbelievable if I relied solely on fiction. Obviously, most of these people are completely, or relatively, unknown; there are few diaries or biographies or even pictures to help us to know and understand who these people were. What's left of the lives of people like Lidia, her husband, and her other family members is limited to court or other official documents, and that means only the aspects of their lives that garnered sufficient attention, most of which was negative, of the town's leaders and/or clergy.

What I found remarkable, as I built my massive timeline spreadsheet, with I kid you not over 250 columns and nearly 1300 blocks of information, was how the characters of these people seemed to form before my eyes as I laid out their lives, month by month, year by year, and event by event. I'm fully aware many of my sources were slanted in favor of the Quakers, and thus, rightfully or wrongfully, painted a sinister portrait of the court and clergy who played a part in this story; but, I did try to be fair to everyone, and rely on multiple corroborating sources where I could. I was careful to leave events where and when they occurred, when I could reasonably ascertain that information, and I was equally careful to fit other events in logically with respect to where and when they might have occurred. At the end of the day, my intent was to create a plausible connection within a series of events not before presented as associated or interrelated, and provide sensible insight into the possible motives of the people involved for their actions—the people are real, the events are real, the connective tissue, so to speak, is all fiction.

I want to note here two important take-aways: first, while this story has more than its share of tragedy, I meant it to be a story of strength and courage. The more I learned about Lidia, the more these two characteristics stood out in my mind. I believe these are not born in a person, rather they are developed over time and space in response to the actions occurring in people's lives, and that's the way I tried to portray Lidia. Each of the events of her adult life, placed end to end bear this out.

The second thing I want to point out relates to the Reverend Seaborn Cotton. I have portrayed him as a cruel and vindictive man because, like with Lidia, the events in which he played a part led me to that conclusion. However, I want to be clear in saying no documentary evidence supports this. To the contrary, one of the few, if only, remaining documents created by his own hand shows him to be sensitive, if a love of poetry and literature and music can be associated with that trait. His journal, more or less, ignores the subject of Quakers, mentioning it only twice and then with respect to forbidding the attendance at their meetings. Quakers were viewed, then, in ways we would describe as fringe or radical; they were defiant, but in a passive aggressive way. However we want to look at it, their behavior generated fear—fear of the unknown and superficially not understandable. A common response to fear is self-preservation in whatever form that may take. One of the points I try to make in telling this story is the Quakers were behaving not unlike the Puritans behaved in England prior to their escape to the colonies, but a generation had passed and much can be forgotten or overlooked in that time. The fact that Cotton's journal doesn't dwell on the Quakers or their behavior indicates to me that he either did not trouble himself with them anymore than he would trouble himself with anyone else in the community; or, he was generally oblivious to how his own behavior would manifest and be perceived. He could not have been oblivious to growing tension created by the Quakers and the courts reaction to them because the prosecution of Quakers, overtly or covertly, became a routine occurrence for a period of time. We can never know whether it was a level of arrogance and self-absorption which led Cotton to do the things he did to Lidia and her family, or a level of ignorance and fear that overcame so many during that time.

Finally, a comment on the language. Authors must make a decision whether to speak in a voice representative of the time and place of their characters, or speak with a contemporary voice that might be more comfortable for the reader. Using a representative voice in historical fiction, and especially when the story is set centuries in the past, can be challenging and can put off many readers. My thought was to use Lidia's voice, as much as I could in contemporary times, because it is she who is telling the story and I felt it required as much authenticity as I could reasonably garner from reading available texts from the times. By the same token, reading those texts is difficult at best, so I tried to balance the two. All I ask is that you give Lidia's voice a chance.

Acknowledgements

I can't thank Mike Parker and WordCrafts Press enough for taking a chance on my book, and, especially on me. Without him, I'd still be looking for an adventure instead of living one. Thanks to all the people who showed me the courage and a way ahead. And finally, thanks to the team of people who have been there to launch me on this adventure, and keep me going (and sane) in the process.

Ancel, Cathy, Joanne, Betisa, Chris, Eric, Sierra, Jon, Joi, Sarah, Tom, Jess, Andrea, Emma and so many others—you know who you are, but you may not be aware of what your support means to me.

Bibliography

Aenesidemus. "Omne bonum a Deo, omne malum ab homine." *Latin Discussion.* 27 August 2015. http://latindiscussion.com/forum/latin/omne-bonum-a-deo-omne-malum-ab-homine.24333/ : 2019.

Besse, Joseph. *A Collection of the Sufferings of the People Called Quakers, for the Testimony of a Good Conscience ... Volume II.* London, England: Luke Hinde, 1753. Image copy. *The Hathi Trust Digital Library.* https://babel.hathitrust.org/cgi/pt?id=uc1.31175034931157;view=1up;seq=7 : 2019.

Bishop, George. *New England Judged by the Spirit of the Lord, In Two Parts.* London, England: T. Sowle, 1703. Image copy. *Internet Archive.* https://archive.org/details/newenglandjudged00bishuoft/page/2 : 2006.

Bowden, James. *The History of the Society of Friends in America.* London, England: Charles Gilpin, 1850. Image copy. *Google Books.* https://play.google.com/books/reader?id=n11CAAAAIAAJ&hl=en&pg=GBS.PR1 : 2018.

Bradford, William. "Journal." Database with transcriptions. Pilgrim Hall Museum. *The Pilgrims decide to emigrate to America despite the perils and dangers* (www.pilgrimhallmuseum.org/pdf/ Bradford_Passage_Emigrate.pdf : 9 December 2018).

Cushing, Abel. *Historical Letters on the First Charter of Massachusetts Government.* Boston: J.N. Bang, 1839. Image copy. *Internet Archive.* https://archive.org/details/historicalletter00cush/page/n5 : 2019.

Ellis, George Edward. *The Puritan Age and Rule in the Colony of the Massachusetts Bay, 1629-1685.* Boston: Houghton, Mifflin and Company, 1888. Image copy. *Internet Archive.* https://archive.org/ details/cu31924080782000/page/n513 : 2019.

Emerson, Ralph Waldo, *History.* Chicago: Alden Book Co., 1886. Image copy. *Google Books.* https://books.google.com/books : 2020.

Harrison, Samuel A., M.D. "Wenlock Christison, and the Early Friends in Talbot County, Maryland: A Paper read before the Maryland Historical Society, March 9th, 1874" Baltimore, 1878. Image copy. *Internet Archive.* https://archive.org/details/wenlockchristiso00harrrich/page/n3 : 2019.

King James Bible

Massachusetts. "Records and Files of the Quarterly Court for Essex County." Database. *Salem Witch Trials Documentary Archive and Transcription Project* http://salem.lib.virginia.edu/home.html : 2018.

Morison, Samuel Eliot. "The Reverend Seaborn Cotton's Commonplace Book." Colonial Society of Massachusetts: April Meeting, 1935. Cambridge Massachusetts. https://www.colonialsociety.org/ node/486 : 2019.

New Hampshire. Legislature. *Documents and Records Relating to the Province of New-Hampshire, From the Earliest Period of Its Settlement: 1623-1686,* 40 vols. Concord, MA: State Printer, 1867. Image copy, *New Hampshire Provincial and State Papers.* https://archive.org/details/newhampshireprov01none/page/n5 : 2019.

Plimpton, Ruth. *Mary Dyer, Biography of a Rebel Quaker.* Boston: Branden Publishing Co., 1994. Image copy. *Internet Archive* (https://archive.org/details/marydyerbiograph00plim : 2019.

Robinson, Enders A. *Salem Witchcraft and Hawthorne's House of Seven Gables.* Maryland: Heritage Books, Inc., 1992.

Sanborn, George Freeman Jr. and Melinde Lutz Sanborn, *Vital records of Hampton, New Hampshire : to the end of the year 1900,* Boston, Massachusetts, New England Historic Genealogical Society, 1992.

Sewel, William. *The History of The Rise, Increase and Progress of The Christian People Called Quakers, Intermixed With Several Remarkable Occurrences.* Two Volumes. Baker & Crane, New York. 1844. Image copy. *The Hathi Trust Digital Library.* https://babel.hathitrust.org/cgi/pt?id=hvd.32044081811796;view=1up;seq=430 : 2019.

Whittier, John Greenleaf. *The Complete Poetical Works of John Greenleaf Whittier.* Boston: Houghton Mifflin and Company, 1892. Image copy. *Google Books.* https://books.google.com/books : 2019.

Wikipedia. https://en.wikipedia.org : 2015-2019.

"William Leddra's Last Letter." *The Friends' Journal*, Eighth Month 28, 1886. Image copy. Pennsylvania, *Friends' Intelligencer and Journal* https://books.google.com : 2019.

Wise, Jennings Cropper. *Col. John Wise of England and Virginia*

(1617 - 1695), His Ancestors and Descendants. Richmond: The Bell book and stationery co., 1918. Image copy. *Hathi Trust Digital Library* (https://catalog.hathitrust.org/Record/005785113 : 2019.

About Jae Hodges

Everyone has a history and a story. Jae uses the most alluring stories from the chronicles of her own ancestry and others around her to create timeless tales of everyday people making history. On her quest to capture the essence of walking in their footsteps, she travels and uses her pencil and camera lens to imagine them in their own surroundings.

Jae lives on the Tennessee River in Alabama with her husband and companion pooch.

Also available from

WordCrafts Press

Grace Extended
by Paula K. Parker

Angela's Treasures
by Marian Rizzo

In Times Like These
by Gail Kittleson

The Pruning
by Jan Cline

Katie's Plain Regret
by Sara Harris

www.WordCrafts.net